The Counsellor

By

Gillian Jackson

RB
Rossendale Books

Published by Rossendale Books

11 Mowgrain View, Bacup,
Rossendale, Lancashire
OL13 8EJ
England

Published in paperback 2012

ISBN 978-1-906801-75-5

Dedication

To my husband and family
with thanks for their help and support
and being there for me.

Prologue

1996

Maggie Sayer smoothed the soft green fabric of the rather expensive dress over her hips, turning to check the effect in the shop's ornate cheval mirror. It was perfect, well apart from the figures on the price ticket but everyone deserves a little spoiling sometimes it's good for the soul. The reflection presented not only a stylish, well cut dress but a happy, confident woman who at twenty nine, slim with shining auburn curls an olive skin and hazel eyes, was convinced that life could not be more perfect. Chris, her husband of three years had booked a two night break at a fabulous country house hotel in celebration of their wedding anniversary at the weekend, the anticipation of which buoyed Maggie's present good mood, bringing a light flush to her cheeks. She was a woman in love who knew that her love was reciprocated.

Turning her attention to the young sales assistant hovering close by and obviously anxious for a sale, Maggie smiled, telling her she would take the dress.

Stepping out of the comfort of the warm shop, the bitterly cold late September wind tugged roughly at her coat as she quickened her step to avoid being late. Hugging the collar closer to her throat she laughed into the biting wind, even the wild, murky weather couldn't dampen the high spirits of the day.

But what Maggie Sayer did not know that afternoon, was that before her anniversary weekend was over, she would become a widow.

The pale autumn sun struggled to break through the gray clouds as with barely a minute to spare and taking the stairs two at a time, she pushed at the heavy office door, completely unaware of the impending news waiting to shatter everything she held dear. As the door reluctantly creaked open Maggie almost collided with May, the office supervisor, a thin wiry woman of indeterminate years, generally thought to be well past retiring age and who appeared to be unusually agitated, shifting her weight from one leg to the other. Something was wrong. The tension in the atmosphere was almost tangible as Maggie became aware of the eyes of colleagues' focussed in her direction. May began to speak, the words stilted, distant, unreal. All Maggie heard was 'Chris…hospital.'

Shaking her head, a thin nervous smile flickered briefly across her lips, this couldn't be happening; it must be a mistake or some sort of sick joke. May, normally a morose character, spoke kindly but with a demeanour which gave away how serious the situation was.

'I'll take you.' May's voice was barely a whisper as she gently took Maggie's arm to steer her out of the office, with sympathetic glances following their every step, confirming the worst possible scenario imaginable.

The Friday afternoon traffic was heavy and the usually short journey to the hospital took what seemed to be an age. Maggie thought she ought to be asking questions, 'When? Who? Why?' but her mouth was dry and the words refused to come, as if her brain was trying to function through a thick fog. Later she would remember getting out of the car to be ushered down an endless hospital corridor, with the smell of cleaning fluid and over-cooked cabbage lingering in the air. Lifts hummed and pinged, travelling ceaselessly up and down with a disembodied voice announcing each floor number. Maggie stood in a doorway, an observer, watching as nursing staff worked frantically around a high hospital bed, shouting indistinguishable words to each other. The man on the bed was bare-chested with monitors clinging to his body. Broad shoulders and soft blonde hair did resemble her husband, but it couldn't be him. Chris stood tall and strong, with blue eyes that crinkled at the corners when he laughed, and he laughed a lot. This man's hands were still. Chris's hands were large, busy, and capable. Hands which could tackle repairs with ease, hands that effortlessly opened jars which she had wrestled with, hands that could hold and comfort her when she was sad and hands that gently cupped a spider to release it outside rather than killing it. It couldn't be Chris. He was the strong one, the one to make all the plans, like their anniversary weekend. He was the organizer, the practical joker, the life and soul of the party. He was her husband, her best friend, and her protector.

For two days the man lay on the bed whilst doctors performed endless tests and monitored him. Maggie felt utterly useless, all she could do was stay as close and as long as they would let her. A massive brain haemorrhage they said, there was nothing they could do, he would never recover. Holding his hand, willing him to get better, she could not face the reality that he had already gone and it was only the machinery keeping his heart beating and his lungs working. They left her alone with him, telling her she must say her goodbyes. Chris's parents had already gone, his mother led by her solemn husband, looking pale and on the point of collapse.

Maggie thought of all their plans, the weekend away, the family home they would one day exchange their little flat for, the children that now would never be born, the places they wanted to visit but never would. Life without her husband unfolded before her like the mouth of a cavernous tunnel reaching out to engulf her into its inky darkness. Chris was the only man she had ever loved, three years was not enough, not nearly enough…

Chris was dead and a huge part of her died with him. Spiralling into a deep, dark depression, she could no longer function, didn't want to function. He was dead. Maggie felt as if she was dead too.

Chapter 1

2011

'I just love daffodils,' Maggie announced chirpily as she walked briskly through the reception area of the doctors' surgery.

'Remind me to put some on your coffin,' came the quick reply from the receptionist.

Maggie leaned on the counter, laughing,

'You know Sue; you have a completely negative attitude to Monday mornings. Would you like to talk about it?'

Sue answered with an exaggerated smile, moving away to pick up the telephone. Carrying the daffodils to her room, Maggie buried her face in their bright yellow trumpets, savouring the evocative scent of spring and new beginnings. She took off her coat and hung it on the little hook in the corner. At forty-three, she was still an attractive woman, five foot six with a slim build and naturally curly rich brown hair, as yet showing no gray and cut short to frame her heart shaped face. Expressive hazel eyes enhanced her appearance, not a classical beauty but certainly an attractive woman. Scanning her diary for the coming week she noted that there were two new clients to see, although the first, Julie Chambers, had been due to start a couple of weeks ago… and a month before that too.

'Could be a 'no show',' Maggie thought, although she hoped not. Julie was a GP referral and Dr Williams must be keen for her to come as he usually didn't give second chances, and any 'no shows' were put back on the waiting list. Julie was the first appointment that morning, booked in for 9.30am, after which there was a client who was coming to the end of her sessions, and in the afternoon a private client followed by a meeting with her supervisor.

Maggie Sayer was an excellent counsellor having developed an interest in therapeutic counselling after firsthand experience of its benefits fourteen years previously when her husband had died quite suddenly. Naturally she'd been devastated, only getting through the funeral and its associated bureaucracy with the help of her own, and Chris's family. People tried to be kind and she received the usual platitudes, but also some insensitive and unhelpful comments.

'You were married such a short time, life will soon return to how it was before.'

'How callous,' she screamed inwardly, as if Chris had never existed. Three years of marriage may not be long but she couldn't begin to imagine life without him, it seemed as if they had been part of each other forever, his death made her feel like her heart and soul had been physically ripped out of her body.

'Why not get yourself a puppy?' A well-meaning neighbour had suggested. Could a puppy replace a soul mate? Worse still were the friends who began to avoid her simply because they didn't know what to say. Words weren't always necessary but a hug, or someone to listen, who wasn't embarrassed at the mention of Chris's name would have been welcome.

As the weeks passed Maggie had sunk deeper into herself, living an unreal existence, craving, whilst at the same time hating the solitude and wanting only the impossible, Chris.

She had returned to work but functioned only in the physical, her heart and mind rarely in attendance with her body. Mistakes appeared in her work; sometimes she would sit in front of the computer screen in an apparent trance. Colleagues tried their best to help but it became obvious that she needed more time to grieve.

Prescribing anti-depressants and a month off work, her GP tentatively suggested that Maggie should consider staying with her parents or a friend for a while, a proposal which brought a vehement refusal; she would have none of it. Staying in her own flat was important to her, it was Chris's home too and the place where she could sense his presence, remembering the times they had shared and imagining that he could still walk through the door at any time. Their home was the place where she felt closest to him, still able to sense his masculine presence. During the first few weeks, Maggie had stood for long periods of time beside his open wardrobe door with her face pressed into his clothes, breathing in his scent, pretending he was still alive. Although that had passed and his clothes were long since donated to local charity shops, she still took comfort from the home they had shared and couldn't bear to leave. Maybe some time in the future but not so soon. So she had left the surgery with a prescription and a telephone number for a local counselling service.

That was the start of Maggie's interest in therapeutic counselling. It was a long hard struggle and there were times when she had to force herself to go to the appointments and times when she was unable to speak when she got there, yet eventually Maggie began to see these sessions as her life-line and with the support she received from the counsellor and later from group sessions, she came through the other side of her depression and life once again took on some semblance of normality. The experience however had changed her whole outlook on life prompting a re-evaluation of where she was going. Her clerical job no longer seemed worthwhile and a strong desire was growing within her to help others who found life hard to cope with. In doing this she hoped to find the fulfilment she was looking for and some degree of peace in her life.

Fourteen years later, having worked as a counsellor for the last ten of those years, Maggie was a forty-three year old widow, without children; not what she had anticipated for herself, yet she had found the contentment she longed for. Her work brought some measure of fulfilment, her own life experience having given an understanding and empathy with others which equipped her well in acting as a catalyst for many clients who, like herself, had become overwhelmed by what life had thrown their way.

And yes, she had also found herself a puppy. The neighbour had been premature with such a suggestion so soon after losing Chris, but as time went by Maggie did feel the need for companionship, so five years ago she'd adopted a mongrel pup from the local animal sanctuary. His mother had been a Labrador and his father of dubious pedigree but he seemed to favour his mother and Maggie had fallen in love with his golden silky coat and huge ears. An oversized tongue, which hung almost permanently from the side of his mouth, gave him quite a comical appearance and Ben had proved to be an excellent pet. True she had never cured his taste for wallpaper, but gradually, as he stripped the walls of each room, Maggie had re-decorated using paint which was thankfully not to his taste.

Chapter 2

Julie Chambers did arrive for her appointment and was sitting in the waiting area at 9.30am promptly where Maggie met her and invited her to come through to her room. Julie was in her late twenties, twenty-eight according to the medical notes. Generally, Maggie made a point of not reading Dr Williams' lengthy notes on his patients, except for any basic details that may be relevant. This gave her an open mind with no pre-conceived ideas; a blank canvas allowing her to form opinions directly from the client and enabling a relationship to be built on mutual trust.

Julie's gray eyes darted around the room, not so much appraising the surroundings, but more as if searching out potential threats. For such a young woman she appeared weary, not just physically but what would have once been described as 'world weary'. A slightly built woman Julie was what Maggie might enviously call petite, but there was little else to envy about her appearance. She had the makings of an attractive girl, but obviously didn't take much care of her looks for one reason or another, with long straight hair sitting flatly on her scalp and pushed carelessly behind her ears. Julie wore no make-up and her skin was sallow, with premature lines already visible around the eyes and mouth. Her clothes too had a washed out, worn look, a gray tracksuit with a thin jacket, quite inadequate for the present spell of cold weather. Old trainers completed her appearance; to her credit everything was very clean, but certainly not fashionable or even practical.

Maggie dismissed first appearances, smiling warmly whilst inviting the younger woman to sit down. The room they were in was shared with a colleague in the same large health centre. It had been arranged with as much care as Julie's appearance seemed to lack, Maggie having been the influence in the décor, with her male counterpart being content to leave that side of things to her. It was a square room with a high window and cream blinds to keep out the sun, unnecessary today with slate gray skies above, and a cold wind blowing. The walls were painted in a neutral shade of cream with a couple of tasteful landscapes to break the monotony. The only furniture was a large desk underneath the window, a small bookcase with glass-fronted doors and two comfortable chairs beneath an inexpensive Ikea standard lamp with a small coffee table to the side of one of the chairs. The fresh daffodils were on the corner of Maggie's desk, completing a very simple but warm, comfortable and welcoming room.

Julie took a seat as Maggie closed the door then settled herself in the other chair. The first meeting was usually the most difficult for the client and often for the counsellor too. Julie had no idea what would transpire during this first visit. She was half expecting to be bombarded with questions and was unsure if she had been right to come at all. Maggie's first task was to outline what was known as 'the triple harm clause', which incorporated the three exceptions to confidentiality.

'Thank you for coming and being so prompt Julie.' She began,

'My name's Maggie and before we start today there are one or two things I need to mention. We have up to an hour for this first session, and everything you tell me is confidential, but there are some exceptions to this, for example, if I feel that what you're telling me indicates that you may harm yourself, someone else or particularly a child. Is that okay with you?'

'Yes......... but I think I'm probably wasting your time.' Julie began.

'Now why would that be?'

'Well, I really don't know why I've come. Dr Williams kept saying he thought I would benefit from counselling, but I don't exactly know what counselling is, so how can it help?'

'That's very honest of you. Perhaps you'd like to tell me why you went to see Dr Williams in the first place and then we can chat about how we can help you and if you have any specific questions then I'll try my best to answer them for you.'

'I suppose…well, I'm rather accident prone and I've seen Dr Williams two or three times for little things since the New Year, and I have two children so I often see him with their complaints too.'

'What do you mean by 'accident prone'' Maggie asked gently.

Julie lowered her head.

'Here we go' she thought, 'the questions are starting.' She looked up at the woman sitting opposite her, trying to read her expression, feeling suddenly like a little girl in front of the headmistress when she was usually so strong. God knew how she'd had to be strong for her children, but it was hard, so hard, and she was getting tired. Tears began to prick the back of her eyes; she swallowed hard and sniffed in an effort not to cry.

Maggie spoke softly, 'If I ask any questions that you don't want to answer, that's fine. My only reason in asking is to make sure I understand what you're telling me. If I misunderstand, I won't be of much use to you.' she smiled, willing her client to open up.

Julie looked down again, fiddling with her hands. Maggie noticed how bitten down her fingernails were, some of them appearing to be quite sore. There were a few seconds of silence but she was comfortable with this, never feeling the need to rush her clients. They needed time to think and to decide whether she could be trusted, after all, this relationship was all of ten minutes old.

'I fell down the stairs a few weeks ago and my ankle was swollen. Dr Williams checked it out for me, and then I cut my arm in the kitchen about a week or so later. I strapped it up myself, but it became infected so I had to come to the surgery again.' Julie's short account seemed a little rehearsed; however Maggie accepted her story as true, asking next,

'Is that when Dr Williams suggested you might benefit from seeing me?'

Julie reddened slightly and Maggie realized she was asking too many questions and decided to take it a little more slowly.

'I haven't read any of your medical notes. That's how I prefer to work. My job as a counsellor is to listen to you, without forming any opinions or judging you in any way. I hope that by our meeting together you'll feel confident enough to share any concerns you might have, no matter how trivial you think they are. We all need someone to talk to at some point in our lives.'

'Even you?' Julie asked. Maggie laughed softly.

'Especially me,' she said light heartedly, yet truthfully. 'But this hour is all for your benefit Julie. You can talk about whatever you want to and if I ask anything you're not happy with, you don't have to answer, you can tell me to butt out if you like. It's all about making you a little stronger and helping you to focus on what's right for you.'

A very slight smile flickered across Julie's face. Maggie looked into her watery gray eyes, trying to see into the soul of her client. They were dull eyes with no spark of the life which should be evident in such a young woman, but there was a measure of intelligence behind those eyes and a wistfulness which gave her the feeling that Julie had never quite reached her potential and could have such a different life to the one she was apparently living. Maggie could feel a connection, an empathy and already felt concerned for this new client and a desire to help her find whatever it was that she was looking for. Julie paused for a few moments then began again,

'I did tell the doctor that I had been feeling a bit weepy lately and finding the children hard to cope with.'

'Would you like to tell me about that too?'

'Yes…I think I would.'

****

Maggie tidied her desk, grabbed her coat and scarf and hurried towards the door. The session with her latest client had proved to be a promising start. Julie hadn't opened up completely, but had talked about feeling tired and generally unhappy with life, only becoming animated when talking about her children, obviously the joy of her life, yet reluctant to talk about her husband, Jim. She had gleaned from the session that Julie had a boy of eleven, Simon and a three-year-old girl, Chloe. Simon was due to start secondary school in the next school year and his mother was anxious that he may be bullied or fall in with the wrong crowd. Nothing had actually given foundation to these worries, but they still presented a problem to Julie which Maggie took seriously. Yet looking back on their hour together she sensed that there were other more difficult issues troubling this new client and her hope was that she would be able to reach out to her to offer the kind of help which was needed.

The next client of the day had come bustling in wreathed in smiles. Things had been working out well for this lady and they had previously agreed to make this their last appointment. It was always satisfying to see a client gain in self-confidence and begin to make their own decisions, and this lady was a classic example, ending her sessions with a new sense of empowerment and Maggie was genuinely pleased for her.

****

Home and lunch were next on Maggie's agenda. Opening the front door, Ben bounded up to greet her, expecting his usual fuss before she'd even shrugged off her coat.

'Come on then, garden for now and walk after lunch.'

Ben knew the routine and ran through the kitchen to the back door. Letting him out, Maggie quickly closed the door to keep out the chill wind that was getting up, smiling as she watched him sniffing around from the kitchen window. The move from her little flat in the town centre to this terraced house in the suburbs had been partly for her dog. The flat had served its purpose for nine years after Chris died. The familiar things they had bought and memories of their life together there consoled her to some degree, and had felt at times like a warm, comforting blanket which she could wrap around herself whenever the need arose. Maggie would always be grateful for the financial security which Chris's practical thinking had provided. There was sufficient provision to enable her to give up her job and train as a counsellor when the time was right. Also in time, it felt right to move on to what would be a more permanent home, a comfortable little house only a few minutes' drive from town and the surgery it was perfect, situated in a pleasant area close to open fields, which Ben had come to regard as his own personal space. The house was manageable, with two good-sized bedrooms, a lounge, kitchen-diner and a small garden for Ben with a patio for Maggie.

Whilst she stabbed at a potato with a fork, preparing it for the microwave, there was a whining at the back door. Letting Ben in he brushed up against her legs making her think how good it was to be missed. Opening a tin of tuna to complete her meal, Maggie looked down at her ever hopeful pet.

'It's no good looking at me like that, there's only enough for one here. You can have your biscuits.'

Ben sat with his head on one side, his ears cocked and his long tongue lolling from the side of his mouth. All he needed to do was to look at Maggie and give a pathetic little whine, it worked every time.

'Okay, okay, but just a little taste. I can't resist those big brown eyes and warm doggie breath on my legs.'

It was all part of the routine. She treated Ben as her best friend and he thought that was quite the right thing to do. After lunch there was just sufficient time to take him for a run in the fields before leaving once more to visit her next client.

Private clients were usually seen in their own homes or occasionally, if that was inconvenient, the practice manager let her use a vacant room at the surgery. Advertising wasn't necessary, as most clients knew of her by word of mouth or from the surgery. Financially these clients provided Maggie with the little luxuries in life. She could manage well on her basic salary, but the work wasn't full time and she liked to keep busy. The afternoon's visit was to a long-standing client who lived a couple of miles from town, after which there was a session with her supervisor, a requirement for all counsellors for their own well being, then her day would end with another walk for Ben, and hopefully a glass of wine with a good book in front of the fire.

Chapter 3

Maggie's evening went as planned with the exception of a phone call from her friend Sue, the practice receptionist.

'Just thought I'd let you know about the fireworks you missed this afternoon,' she began. Maggie sat down with the phone, tucking her feet up and anticipating one of Sue's stories, which could be quite amusing if taken with a pinch of salt.

'This rather rough sort of guy came in at about two o'clock. Very wound up he was, and obviously a bit worse for drink. Don't you just love these new licensing hours? Anyway, he kept demanding to know if 'his' Julie had been in today and what she'd come for. One nasty piece of work there all right, mind, I have to give him credit for his extensive vocabulary, he used some words even I hadn't heard before. Well the upshot was that Laura called the police. We couldn't calm him down. He kept demanding to see the appointment book, old fashioned too eh? He left quickly enough when the police arrived and of course he hadn't found out anything, but I did check the computer and noticed that you had a Mrs. J. Chambers in this morning?'

Although Sue's last phrase had obviously been a question, she didn't expect an answer any more than Maggie intended to give her one.

'Wow. Don't I just miss all the fun?' Maggie replied lightly, but warning bells were beginning to jangle inside her head, she knew this could present problems. Going to bed that night her thoughts were still with Julie Chambers, hoping the young woman would return to give Maggie the chance to help her through her difficulties, whatever they may be.

As Maggie walked Ben over the field the next morning, the beauty of the scene ahead struck her. They'd taken this path a hundred times before but never in weather quite like this. The frost was unbelievably beautiful, so thick it looked like snow, but a dry, crisp frost, unlike the damp foggy sort usual for this time of year in England. It was perhaps colder than usual too, well below zero but exhilarating for both of them. The trees, which only yesterday had looked so dark and bare without their leaves, took on a silvery brightness, which with the thick frost on the grass, lightened the whole landscape, giving an ethereal feel to a familiar landscape. Ben raced ahead, keeping his nose close to the ground, following one curious scent after another. They were both reluctant to turn back and spoil the magic of the early morning walk, but Maggie had a client at 9.00am, another first appointment, and she felt the need to be in the surgery early in the light of what Sue had told her the night before.

****

The large airy reception area was almost full of early morning patients for the doctors and the practice nurses. Maggie was grateful that her earliest appointments were never before 9.00am. With everyone already busy, she went straight to her room, where a memo from Dr. Williams asked her to call him before beginning work. Buzzing through to his extension and listening to his soft Scottish burr asking if he could pop in to see her, Maggie was glad to be early and, anticipating the reason for his request, pulled out the brief notes she'd made after Julie Chambers' visit yesterday.

Note taking was always kept to a minimum and only the bare bones necessary to keep her in touch with each client were recorded. This was partly for confidentiality but also as a reminder of each case's details. If a client had briefly mentioned something or someone whom Maggie felt was pivotal to the situation, she noted it after the session, to keep her thoughts fresh and to remind herself of things the client may have trivialized but which could be of greater significance. These were usually intuitive. With experience, many counsellors develop a heightened sense of intuition, rather like a detective trusted his 'hunches' and acted upon them. Facts such as the number and ages of clients' children, whether they had parents who were living and other such details were noted purely for her own reference. Memory is fallible and Maggie liked to have a reminder of things which were important to each individual and which could be revised before their next visit. All such notes were kept securely locked away in her desk drawer.

Dr. Tom Williams tapped on her door a few minutes later. He was a perpetually cheerful man with a fatherly, reassuring air, never seen at work without his jacket and a tie, even in the hottest summer weather, a fact that his patients and colleagues thought suggested constancy and a permanence which was a comfort to all. The senior doctor in the practice, he was well liked by the staff and thought to be the personification of the ideal GP amongst his patients. His hair was snow white and he had rather prominent matching eyebrows and a round pleasant face, a rather bulbous nose and a ruddy complexion. Maggie had often thought he would make an excellent Father Christmas. His demeanour today however was rather more solemn.

'We had an incident after you left yesterday,' he began

'Yes, I did hear. Was it Julie Chambers' husband?'

'It certainly was. He's one of my patients too, although I haven't seen him very often in the surgery. I want you to be careful Maggie, I know you won't want my opinions at this stage and I'm not going to stick my nose in where it isn't wanted but just to let you know that we could have a tricky situation developing here. This Chambers fellow strikes me as a volatile type. Anyway, I'm here for you if you need me.'

'Thank you Tom, that's always good to know. My immediate concern is whether or not Julie will return for more counselling, we didn't get too far yesterday and I feel she could really do with opening up a little. If it's causing a problem for her at home it may prove too difficult to keep coming and the easy option would be to give up.'

'Then we'll just have to hope she perseveres. Now remember, if I can help at all…'

'Yes, thanks I know.'

Maggie locked her notes away and checked her diary. Peter Lloyd, one of Dr. James' patients was due in soon. Dr. James didn't write such copious notes as Tom Williams so all she had to go on was his date of birth; he was fifty-two years old, his problem written up as depression. Could be anything; a clean sheet for her to form her own conclusions.

Peter Lloyd was in the waiting area and stood to follow Maggie when she quietly called his name. He was a little less than six foot tall, medium build with thick, straight gray hair, cut conservatively short and, Maggie noticed, rather piercing blue eyes. He was quite smartly dressed, presumably for work and he smiled pleasantly, giving the appearance of a confident personality. After introducing herself and giving her usual verbal contracting, she smiled at Peter and began,

'Would you like to tell me why you're here Peter?'

'Well, I suppose I've been finding life quite difficult lately… I went to Dr. James to see if he could give me something to help me sleep. He says I'm clinically depressed, but it's just that I'm going through a difficult time at the moment. I don't know if counselling will really help. I thought maybe he was passing the buck, not that I would blame him, I know doctors are overworked these days and it probably isn't his job to listen to me rambling on about my problems.'

'He wouldn't be passing the buck, I'm sure. You must have told him a little about how you were feeling for him to diagnose depression. Dr James would have felt that the appropriate course of action would be for you to see one of the practice counsellors to try to help you get over this. Perhaps you'd like to share something about how you're feeling now and we can take it from there?'

Peter readily took the lead and began to tell Maggie about his present circumstances. He had been divorced for about a year and the breakdown of his marriage had come as a complete shock. Peter had assumed his marriage was fine, no better or worse than the next man, although he was aware that his wife was missing having their children at home. Their two adult daughters were both living independently, one married and the other at university and his wife, Angela, had found the changes difficult. He had put it down to classic 'empty nest' syndrome but with hindsight Peter felt he should have perhaps given more time to her but things at work were exceptionally busy. He was an architect and a partner in a small firm which was just beginning to make a name for itself.

'I suppose you've heard it all before, neglected wife feeling unappreciated, time on her hands, finds a younger man who makes her feel like a woman again.'

This last sentence was spoken with more than a little sarcasm.

'No I haven't heard it all before. No two people's lives are the same,' Maggie said softly, 'How did you feel about your wife finding another man?'

'How do you think I felt? Bloody angry!' Peter paused, looking away from her as he thought.

'I'm sorry; I didn't mean to sound angry with you.'

'But you did feel angry?'

'Yes, of course. But not just at Angela, at myself most of all. How could I have not seen it coming? I felt such a bloody fool.'

'And how do you feel about it now?'

'Still rather foolish I suppose. At first I kept hoping she'd come back. I tried to see her a few times, after a bit of Dutch courage, but needless to say it didn't work out. I reckon I've just got to accept that it's over. She's started divorce proceedings and is living with this guy now, and they're talking of getting married. She refuses to see me, I only find out how she is through the girls and I don't see them very often.'

Peter continued to talk quite freely. Maggie was both pleased and surprised at how open he was for a first visit. Men so often found it difficult to share their feelings, it was generally women who were more in touch with their emotions, the male psyche was wired differently. They often found it hard to admit to any kind of emotional trauma, thinking it wasn't 'macho', but that issue didn't seem to be present with Peter. He talked about the demands of his work, his recent problems with sleeping and his regrets about not giving more time to his wife and daughters. All too soon the hour was over and she had to draw the session to a close. Satisfied with the way things had gone, she asked Peter if he would like to return to continue next week. He readily agreed to the suggestion, thanked her for her time, and went to make another appointment at the reception desk on his way out.

Making herself a cup of coffee she mulled over the session with this latest client, uncertain how this would work out, but then was she ever? He had been remarkably candid about his situation, and seemed to be an intelligent man with a good understanding of his problems. Perhaps he just needed a sounding board to organise his thoughts and emotions and he would move off after two or three sessions to kick-start his life. Or perhaps there was something more? Peter Lloyd occupied much of Maggie's thinking for the rest of the day.

Chapter 4

Julie and Jim Chambers lived in a small rented terraced house, close to the town centre. It was a quiet street with the houses opening straight onto the pavement, no garden and just a small yard at the rear. Julie was grateful that their landlord owned several other properties in the area and was reasonably good about maintenance issues. She also appreciated that the bills were small as money was scarce to pay them and her husband expected her to be able to manage on very little.

Jim was unemployed, having never held down a job for more than a matter of months throughout their marriage, usually due to a falling out with his employers over time keeping, bad attitude and disrespect for almost everyone he came into contact with. However, he was never short of money for himself and she suspected he had some sort of sideline going on with a couple of his dubious friends, but she would never dare to question him about it. Money for his beer, cigarettes and a flutter on the horses was never in short supply, but when Julie had bills to pay or the children needed shoes, she had to practically grovel to get enough and yet Jim expected his meals to be tasty and ready for him on demand. Necessity had made her adept at cooking nutritious meals on a very tight budget. Her efforts unfortunately were taken very much for granted but for her there was the satisfaction of knowing that her family ate well, albeit cheaply.

When as a teenager she first met Jim he had seemed mysterious and exciting. He was older than the rest of her friends, darkly handsome in a brooding sort of way with deep brown eyes and straight black hair. Julie had been captivated by his wild and undisciplined attitude to life and authority. He was just the sort of boy her parents would disapprove of, which only added to the attraction. At first she could hardly believe that he was interested in her, a shy quiet girl, not in the least worldly wise or mature. Flattered by his attentions and suddenly gaining a new status in the eyes of her friends was a heady experience for Julie. It was obvious that he wasn't the sort of boyfriend she could invite home for tea on Sundays, so Julie went along with his suggestion to keep their meetings secret from her parents. It made her feel grown-up, as if she was now an adult making her own decisions, when in fact Jim was the one calling all the shots. He didn't even have to coax her into doing what he asked, she readily agreed with all his ideas, adopting them as her own and convincing herself that she was at last taking responsibility for her own life. Her infatuation completely clouded her judgment but by the time Julie began to see another side of Jim it was too late, she was pregnant.

He was of course the first one Julie shared the news with, hoping in her young romantic heart that he would be pleased and they would live happily ever after. The reality was a cold hard shock. In her naivety, she hadn't considered that Jim would be angry. He had always been temperamental but Julie usually felt it was somehow her fault and resorted to begging and pleading until the mood was broken. But this time he was furious, shouting that he wanted nothing more to do with her and that the baby probably wasn't even his! Julie was devastated, the reality of her predicament shattered all her girlish hopes and dreams leaving her feeling that she had nowhere to go and no one to turn to. For weeks she kept her secret to herself, growing more fearful with each day. Her concentration at the sixth form she attended slipped dramatically and inevitably questions were asked. Her parents were concerned thinking that perhaps she was struggling with the pressure of her studies, but Sarah was more perceptive. She was the elder by two years and until recently they had been close, but when Jim came on the scene she had found her little sister was distant, even secretive and having a steady boyfriend herself meant that they no longer spent much time together. Now Sarah had her suspicions and confronted her sister, a sweet relief to Julie, and the warmth of their relationship returned.

Sarah promised to support her in any way she could which was called upon almost immediately for the task of telling their parents. It was so much easier to face them with her sister as an advocate and Julie was surprised when her parents expressed disappointment rather than the anger she had expected, causing her to regret ever deceiving them.

But this was all history now. Jim had married her, more because of pressure from both sets of parents than a desire to do the right thing. Julie had clung to her romantic idea of married life, an ideal that had been chipped away over the years. She had hoped that Jim would settle down to providing for his family and enjoy being a parent, but it didn't take long to realise that those hopes were in vain. He rarely showed an interest in his son and Julie fell into the role of peacemaker during Simon's babyhood and throughout the various stages of childhood, when his father seemed to find him nothing but a nuisance.

Jim had wanted no more babies, much to Julie's distress, but he took no responsibility in the matter and when she fell pregnant with Chloe, seven years after Simon was born, he was incensed, blaming her all over again.

That was the first time he had hit her. It had almost happened before, but Julie had learned to read his moods over the years and managed to diffuse situations as they arose. Her first fear had been for the baby. Jim's hand had swiped across her face with such a force that she had fallen backwards onto the sofa. If it hadn't been for a soft-landing perhaps she would have lost the baby. Maybe that had been Jim's intention? She would never know. He didn't strike her again during the pregnancy, but shortly after Chloe's birth, three years ago his violence became a regular occurrence. With her usual resignation, Julie made excuses for his actions, again blaming herself for having somehow annoyed him, and being grateful that the children never witnessed their father's outbursts. The thought of leaving him had only fleetingly crossed her mind. The truth was she had nowhere to go and no one to turn to for help. Jim had made it clear in the early days of their marriage that her family was not welcome in their home. Her parents had tried to keep in touch until it became obvious that it only caused their daughter more problems so they fell into the routine of only sending birthday cards for her and the children. Julie managed to make the occasional phone call to them when Jim was out, maintaining the pretence of everything being just fine. It was easier for her parents to believe this story and so probing questions were never asked. With her sister it was a little different. She had never wanted Julie to marry Jim having been aware of his reputation, but couldn't persuade her to leave him. Sarah had tried to maintain a relationship with her sister but eventually also left her alone, with strong words exchanged between the two. Sarah had washed her hands of the whole situation and the last time they had any contact, she told Julie that she wanted nothing more to do with her until she came to her senses and left Jim.

Since Chloe was born Julie had felt quite alone and would have loved to renew contact with her family again but the truth was she was afraid of Jim's reaction. In her own mind she had convinced herself that he would change and that when the children were older he would be able to relate to them better. After all, men weren't very good with young children were they? She had also persuaded herself that the children would miss their father if they left and that they needed him for their emotional security. Always the optimist, Julie had accepted her lot, counted her blessings and brought up her children in the best possible way.

But now the pressure was beginning to tell on her. The strain of living in fear of her husband and his moods was becoming too much to bear and the quiet strength that had always helped her to keep going was deserting her. She was constantly tired and felt weepy over the most trivial of incidents. Fear of her volatile husband seemed to be growing, weakening her resolve to be strong for the children, and there were many nights when she crawled into bed wishing she would never wake up. It was only Simon and Chloe who gave her the motivation to get out of bed each day and the desire to keep them occupied so that Jim wouldn't be disturbed from his lie in.

Julie's head was full of conflicting emotions. At times her fear was so real and consuming that she didn't think she could carry on any longer. Even when alone in the house or playing with Chloe while Simon was at school, tears seemed to well up from nowhere, triggered by nothing more than a fleeting thought, and an overwhelming sadness seemed to be resting heavily in her chest, like a physical growth that threatened to take over her whole body.

Tom Williams had been Julie's GP since her childhood; perhaps that's why he had sensed there was more troubling her than a swollen ankle. His perception hadn't been intrusive; in fact she was pretty sure that Dr. Williams knew more about her situation than he had been told, or than he let on. No wonder he was such a popular doctor and yet he never rushed her, always making her feel valued even when she was trivializing her own injuries. When he suggested that a counsellor might be of help, she'd at first queried the idea, but his gentle manner brought her round and although having to answer personal questions troubled her, on the other side of the coin the thought of having someone to talk to appealed to her.

The first session hadn't been as difficult as expected. She liked Maggie from the outset, there were no airs and graces about her, she seemed an ordinary woman who genuinely wanted to help. It wasn't like some kind of interview as Julie had initially expected, with lots of embarrassing questions. Maggie had made it clear that she could talk about anything and any questions that were asked didn't seem prying or too personal. It had made Julie feel in some way in charge of the session, that it was her time, and although she hadn't been totally honest and up front, perhaps, given time she could be. What a relief that would be, yes Julie certainly wanted to see her again.

The front door slammed and Julie knew instinctively that her husband was in the house even though it was unusual for him to come home much before six in an evening. She was in the little yard at the back of the house playing with Chloe on her tricycle, both enjoying the late afternoon sunshine but wrapped up warmly against the bitter cold.

Jim looked at his wife through the kitchen window, his dark expression telling her all she needed to know. She went inside, leaving Chloe alone in the enclosed yard.

'Hello, have you eaten? Chloe and I have had some soup; I could soon warm some up for you?' She kept her tone light, wondering what had brought him home at this hour and fearing the mood that was so obviously brewing within him.

He didn't answer for a few minutes and silently watched her as she tidied around in the kitchen.

'Well?' he sneered. Julie turned to look at him, her legs beginning to shake and a knot tightening in her stomach.

'Well what Jim?' She tried to sound casual, keeping her voice light and hoping it didn't sound confrontational.

'Don't come clever with me. You've had two days to tell me what you're up to, that's long enough, spit it out!'

'I…I don't know what you're talking about.' She was beginning to panic now. The smell of alcohol was on his breath and her worries were for Chloe as well as herself.

Jim grabbed her by the arm and pushed her ahead of him into the living room. His fingers bruised the soft skin on her upper arms but she was more afraid of the dark, angry look in his eyes. He pushed her down on the sofa, demanding,

'Tell me!'

'Jim, please, I really don't know what this is all about.' He leaned over her, so close she felt sick from the smell of his breath.

'You're not as clever as you think, are you? You were seen on Monday, going into the surgery. I want to know what the hell this is all about.' Jim's voice was rising. Julie was herself panicking; Chloe was alone in the yard and would be able to hear her father shouting.

'You know I've been seeing Dr. Williams for an infection, I needed some more tablets, that's all.' She desperately hoped he would believe her.

'Lying bitch!' he snarled as he punched her full on in the stomach. Julie doubled back into the sofa, bent with the pain. He caught hold of her hair and dragged her upwards, landing an open handed slap across her face. Her head was spinning and she felt sick but tried to think. The tirade went on.

'It wasn't any doctor you were seeing but that bloody do-gooder counsellor. Did you think I wouldn't find out? Are you stupid or what? No wife of mine is going to go snivelling to those busy bodies down at the surgery, d'you hear?' A second slap enforced his words. Julie thought she was going to pass out.

'Chloe,' she thought, 'Please God let him stop.' Closing her eyes she waited for the next blow but as if in answer to her prayer it didn't come. Instead, the front door slammed even louder than before and when she opened her eyes he was gone.

Struggling to stand, nausea washed over her and her head was spinning but she forced her legs to move. Chloe was still alone in the yard and she could hear crying. Opening the back door she could see her daughter, still sitting on her little tricycle, quietly sobbing. Her small face was streaked with tears and her eyes large and frightened. Julie gathered the child into her arms and went inside; the pain of her heart tantamount to the pain in her body, as she rocked Chloe gently back and forth.

Chapter 5

'Damn the bloody thing!' Janet Rea shouted as the shards of glass spun around the tiles on her kitchen floor. Her reaction was totally incongruous to such a minor incident; she didn't even like the glasses which had just become a set of five. A year ago Janet would have thought nothing of a breakage like this but then a year ago she would never have spoken aloud such words; swearing, even mildly, had been alien to her, having been brought up to believe that bad language, especially from women, displayed a lack of vocabulary and was an unfeminine thing to do. This belief had been passed on to her own, now grown up children, which was why it was a relief to be alone in the house during this latest little outburst.

Sweeping up the broken glass she muttered one or two other choice words under her breath, feeling justified at their use because it made her feel so much better and released some of the tension and inexplicable anger which seemed to be two of her constant companions these days.

Making herself a cup of tea, Janet moved to the lounge, curling her legs up on her favourite seat, cupping her hands around the warm mug and consciously trying to relax. Her body was tense, the muscles knotted in her shoulders and upper arms. Even her face was set in a frown and her teeth clenched, which after a while was hard work to maintain and brought on a headache. Rolling her shoulders and screwing up the muscles in her face in an attempt to ease the stiffness, she reached for the leather bound notebook which these days was never far from her side. She had stuffed a pen down the spine of the book which was beginning to crack the binding of the pages. Somehow this seemed to mirror how Janet was feeling about herself; her binding had been unravelling for almost a year now and she was only just beginning to repair her life which some days seemed such a mammoth task. Today was one of those days, the broken glass just the final straw and it was still not yet noon. Opening the notebook was an effort; even though it contained words she herself had written it was still something of a shock to see them set down in black and white. Her counsellor, Maggie, had suggested keeping this notebook, a kind of hybrid, part diary, and part memoirs. At first the idea didn't appeal but she had been so low that anything was worth a try, anything that is which didn't require too much energy; Janet was lethargic to say the least, her get up and go had truly gone in the last twelve months.

As always, she began by reading what she had already written. The first sentence expressed her ambiguity about what Maggie termed her 'healing process'.

Today I decided to be proactive about my future although I have no idea whether this will help me to overcome my demons or just remind me of times I would rather forget. My counsellor, Maggie, suggested writing down my thoughts and feelings, the idea being to chart my progress (that is if I make any,) and to help me face issues I may have previously buried in some deep dark place in my subconscious.

So this is it, my journal, my best friend or my worst enemy, I have yet to decide, but Maggie seems okay, I think I can trust her and no one needs to read this, thank goodness. There'll be no red pen marks or corrections to make, in fact I can shred it or burn it if I want, which will probably, (according to Maggie), give me a new sense of freedom. I'm not a hundred per cent sure if I believe all this psychobabble or not, but when you get desperate you'll try anything, and I've been pretty desperate lately.

So, where to begin? Oh yes, (as if I could really forget), when I was a little girl, from four or five years old, my wicked uncle did despicable things to me and I've lived my life pretending they never happened… until I reached that milestone of the big 50, and I haven't stopped crying since.

As Janet read her own writing, for the umpteenth time, she could pick out the bitterness and sarcasm in her words. Staring transfixed at the pages before her, it was as if she was suspended in another world, all reality having deserted her. The ink on the notebook began to smudge and she realised the tears were falling again. She didn't want to be that bitter and twisted person who had written those words but her heart and mind seemed to be filled with contempt for others and even herself. Perhaps she was apportioning blame, on herself, her abuser, her family, who knew? Faced with such anger and bitterness set out in her own handwriting was a shock. What was she becoming? How she wished at times to just curl up into a little space and cease to exist. The world would be better off, her family would be better off. Goodness knows she must have been a pain to live with this last year, unpredictable to the extreme, morose, sullen and moody to say the least, it was amazing they hadn't all disowned her.

Turning the pages of her journal, Janet read the account of the last meeting with Maggie. She had told her counsellor of the kaleidoscope of emotions that raced around her mind, so many different feelings pounding in her head simultaneously. Maggie seemed to understand and they discussed how to channel these emotions appropriately, and Janet remembered expressing a desire to actually do something positive rather than just talk. Talking to Maggie, to her husband, her GP, her sister, even her children, the journal was full of 'talk'. She had admitted that she was no longer coping with life and was facing up to the fact that it was all brought about by those formative early years when she had been sexually abused by her 'uncle'. For over forty years she had blanked those images from her mind for various reasons, shame, embarrassment and guilt, whatever. But then the nightmares had started again and the panic attacks and depression and everything came tumbling out, first to her poor unsuspecting husband who had begun to wonder where his wife had gone and who this harridan was in her place, then to her GP and eventually to the rest of the family and Maggie.

Janet put the journal back on the coffee table. A year of feeling like this was enough and she was heartily sick of it. Through her anger she could draw strength, there were no dirty secrets left lurking in her subconscious, they were out now and it was time for them to be ousted. Four sessions with Maggie had helped more than she had expected, and with this kind of support from someone who knew and understood what she was going through, Janet was determined to get her life back again and give her family back the wife and mother they had lost.

****

It was nearly the end of another busy week and Maggie had the afternoon to herself. After a quick tidy round and an ear tickling session with her dog, it was time to leave for lunch in town with Sue, a treat anticipated with relish and one which would almost certainly lighten her mood. Friday afternoon was Sue's half day off work and they took advantage whenever they were both free to meet up for a couple of hours 'girlie' time. Today they were trying out the new bistro on the high street, a bit expensive, but they had been assured it was well worth every penny.

Sue had been Maggie's closest friend since they met at the surgery several years ago. Their friendship seemed an unlikely alliance; Sue was quite the extrovert, rarely showing any kind of serious side to her personality and always ready with a witty remark or comment whatever the situation. She was ten years younger than Maggie and as opposite in looks as in character, with long blonde hair, usually knotted and pinned to the top of her head, baby blue eyes and a ready smile. They were similar in height with Sue slightly heavier, or curvier as she would describe it and she dressed quite outrageously at times. With a penchant for shoes and handbags, Sue could appear to be high maintenance and possibly shallow but Maggie knew there was another side to her friend, one rarely seen but certainly worth seeking out. There was a great compassion for people underneath the bubbly exterior. True she didn't suffer fools readily, but she was the sort of friend you could rely upon in a time of need; one you would most certainly want on your side, the very best sort of friend to have.

Seated beside the window, the two women opened the menus to choose their meal.

'Goodness me,' exclaimed Maggie, 'Who was it recommended this place to you? They must be millionaires.'

'Don't be such a cheap-skate. You get what you pay for in these places, besides, it's my treat and I'm starving so hurry up and choose.'

They decided to skip the starters in favour of deserts and both of them ordered the lamb cutlets in rosemary and redcurrant jus, served with creamed sweet potato and seasonal vegetables.

'Okay then, what's the latest gossip?' Sue eagerly asked.

'Just the usual exciting stuff. Had to take Ben to the vets last week for his annual jabs, you should have seen the look on his face, the big softie. And the highlight of my social life at the moment is planning a trip to Scotland to see my parents. Thought I'd go in a couple of weeks to coincide with Mother's day.'

'That's it?' Sue looked disappointed. 'No budding romance or hot dates you want to tell Auntie Sue about? I had hoped for a dishy waiter or two here, but they're all on youth training schemes by the look of them, zits and all.'

Maggie laughed, 'How about you, anything you want to tell me? Do I need to buy a new hat or anything?'

'Oh don't, you sound just like my mother. It wouldn't be fair to tie myself down to just one man now would it? The rest of the male population would be devastated and you'd have more work on your hands than you could cope with.'

'That reminds me Sue, how is your mother, you haven't mentioned her for ages?'

'Ahh, you haven't recognized the symptoms then? I'm in denial, trying to pretend the old witch doesn't exist. I can't think what came over me letting her move so close to my flat after Dad died. She thinks we should be joined at the hip. Much more of it and I'm going to hide the old bat's broomstick, that'll fettle her.'

Maggie chuckled 'Is she still smoking?'

'Oh yes, but I'm not supposed to know about that, she tries to hide it, but it's so obvious.'

'Are you sure it's just tobacco?' Maggie asked mischievously.

'Now there's a thought, maybe it's some illegal substance she's on, and that's why she signed up for the night class in lap-dancing. And here I was thinking it was plain old dementia. Hey, you're not going to charge me forty pounds an hour for this are you? If so you can buy the lunch.'

'No way.' Maggie answered, 'I'm strictly off duty for the rest of the day so how about a bit of retail therapy after this?'

Chapter 6

It was virtually impossible for Maggie to prepare for new clients. If they were coming to the surgery then they were almost always referrals from one of the practice GPs and she would have a few brief notes consisting of a name, age and a reason for the referral, which was often less than a sentence. In the case of Karen Jenkins it was only one word, depression. Maggie's friend Sue had once likened counselling to a blind date in that it had the possibility of becoming a good, even great, relationship, but it could also fail miserably if that spark of trust which bonded the relationship couldn't be found. A pretty fair description she had thought at the time.

Karen was thirty years old, a petite honey blond with a pretty, oval face and well proportioned features. Wide blue eyes gave a startled bambi like appearance, and her smooth pale skin needed no make-up, although she wore a little blusher and lipstick. Maggie was older, taller and although still quite slim, was larger boned than her client and felt somewhat matronly in comparison, which could be an advantage if the younger woman saw her as a mother figure.

The allotted hour began with a brief outline of the confidentiality of their sessions and the exceptions to it, which Karen seemed to understand and appreciate, and then she gave this new client the opportunity to ask any questions.

'I don't have to lie on a couch or anything do I?' was the first question.

'Not unless you really want to.' She smiled.

The smile was returned and the ice was broken. The younger woman was obviously nervous but it was a good sign that there was a spark of humour in her reactions. Putting a client at ease and laying the foundation for a relationship was always the priority for the first session.

'Perhaps you'd like to tell me why you're here today? All I know is that you've been depressed lately, do you think you could tell me about it?'

Karen took a deep breath as though facing an ordeal which couldn't be avoided.

'Doctor James prescribed some anti-depressants for me, but I'm not really happy about taking them. My mother used to take them years ago and eventually became addicted. I know they're much improved these days, but I've always had a thing about pumping my body full of chemicals, I'd rather face my problems head on, so he suggested that counselling might help.'

'You're right about anti-depressants having improved since your mother's time, and yes, counselling is an alternative way to deal with depression. Does your mother still take them?'

'No, Mum died twelve years ago, that's really the reason I'm here... she was murdered.'

'Oh Karen, I'm so sorry.' Maggie felt an immediate empathy with her client; she was so close to her own mother and couldn't imagine losing her, but to lose a loved one through murder was unthinkable.

'Thank you, but it's rather complicated to tell really.'

'Just take your time; you only have to tell me what you want to share. The hope is that as you verbalise your thoughts and problems, you'll find the solutions through your own processing. My role is to listen, perhaps reflect with you on what you're saying to try to clarify how you feel about things and I hope I'll be able to support you in getting well again.'

'I think I could have done with you twelve years ago.' Karen smiled rather sadly.

'Did you not have counselling or any other kind of help at the time?'

'No. I was only just turned eighteen and I really didn't know what help was available. My GP at the time gave me a prescription for sleeping tablets but nothing was mentioned about counselling.'

Maggie nodded; looking into Karen's face she could see the pain this young woman had been carrying for so long. How she had slipped through the system and been left to cope without support was appalling. Her client continued.

'I've always thought I'd managed quite well at the time, there was such a lot to do and I have a younger brother, I suppose he kept me going, I wanted to be strong for him. When Mum was killed my grandmother moved in with us to help, but she was in bits herself and in many ways I felt I had to care for her too. We muddled through day by day really, but it was hard. I remember having to identify Mum's body, I think that was the worst bit, and then we couldn't have the funeral for months. It was awful thinking of Mum being kept at the morgue, but they couldn't release her body in case they needed more samples for DNA. It was six months before the police managed to make their case and we could finally arrange the funeral. I think we were all like zombies during that time, these things move so slowly. I got to the point where I could have screamed at the police liaison officer if he mentioned 'procedures' one more time.' Karen paused, lowering her eyes to focus on her hands which were clasped so tightly in her lap that her knuckles were white. Maggie remained silently attentive, giving the time and space for her client to collect her thoughts and continue when ready.

'And now the police have been in touch to inform us that her murderer's been moved to an open prison and will be released, in stages they assure me, into the community on bail.' There was a note of anger in her voice. This man had taken the life of her mother and ruined her own life and those of her immediate family. Anger was an understandable emotion and so, thought Maggie, was the depression, but she needed to know a little more about Karen Jenkins in order to appreciate exactly what she was going through.

'What about your brother and grandmother now?' She asked, 'Are you still close?'

'Gran's in a home now and she's rarely lucid. Alzheimer's. It's just as well really; losing her daughter like that really aged her. She did the best she could for us and I suppose now she won't have it all dragged up again, I'm not going to tell her he's being released, I don't think she'd understand anyway. Mike and I are still close. He's married now with a little boy and another baby on the way. I'm still single so I suppose they're my closest family and we see each other quite often.'

'Have the two of you discussed the release?' Maggie was keen to know how much family support Karen had.

'Yes, he knows. He rarely talks about that time and I usually go along with that, but since he found out about the release he's been furious. I've tried to talk rationally with him but I honestly feel that he might do something silly. He lost his mother when he was only fifteen and he had to grow up far too quickly. The publicity at the time affected Mike too, it was horrendous with the press almost camped on our doorstep for the first few weeks. None of us could go out without being asked stupid questions like 'how do you feel?' Mike took it all rather badly; I just hope he'll manage to come to terms with this release.'

Karen was looking pale and tired. Maggie was amazed at how well she had managed to tell her story, but as their time was coming to an end there was just one more thing she was puzzled about.

'You've mentioned your gran and your brother, but not your father. Was he not with your family at the time?'

'Oh. I'm so sorry,' she sat upright and took a deep breath, 'I assumed you knew, but of course how could you? My father was the man who murdered her.'

****

No two days were the same for Maggie which was one of the things she loved most about her work. Her clients were from every walk of life and their needs and problems were as diverse as they were themselves. It was satisfying to see a client move on, taking back control of their lives which for one reason or another they had lost, but not everyone made progress quickly or easily. Making her way to the surgery the following morning, her thoughts were on one in particular. Janet Rea had attended four times over the last four weeks, which at an hour a session was not a long time and Maggie was conscious of being constrained to work within an allotted time frame which in this case, eight sessions, was already half way through, yet she still felt a long way from helping this woman to resolve her issues which went way back into her childhood and had scarred her life in so many ways.

The surgery was buzzing with activity as it always was by 9.30am each morning. The waiting room was full and the receptionists occupied with patients, either on the telephone or seeking elusive prescriptions, which, like socks in the washing machine, had a habit of disappearing. Maggie made her way to her room, an oasis of calm in the busyness around her. Janet was due in at 9.15am so she had just enough time to make a couple of phone calls. Almost as soon as Maggie had passed through the surgery waiting room, Janet arrived and found herself a seat tucked behind a pillar, burying her head in a magazine she had pulled from a shelf, not with any desire to read it, but to use it to avoid eye contact with any other patients, particularly anyone she might know. The title of the magazine hadn't even registered in her mind and could have been upside down for all the attention she was giving to it. She hadn't meant to be early but had been awake since 5.30am, her brain working overtime anticipating this meeting with a mix of longing and dread at the same time. A hand on her shoulder broke into her thoughts and she lifted her head to find Maggie smiling down at her.

'Come through Janet, please.'

Janet was happy to follow and find sanctuary from the many pairs of watchful eyes in the waiting room.

'Sit down and make yourself comfortable. Are you warm enough? I can turn the heating up a little?'

'No, I'm fine thanks; it's actually quite mild today.'

Maggie continued the pleasantries by reminding her client of their confidentiality agreement and the exceptions to it, then looking directly at Janet, tilted her head to one side and gently asked if it had been a good week and how she was feeling at present.

'Pretty much the same really, the mood swings still catch me unawares but I suppose I'm learning to cope with them. I had thought the Fluoxetine would have helped with that but it doesn't seem to make any difference.'

'It might be a good idea to see your GP about that, you've been on them quite a while now and they should have kicked in. He may want to consider changing the dose.' Maggie suggested. 'Now, if I remember correctly, at our last meeting you seemed to feel as if you wanted to do more than talk, do you still feel that way?'

'Yes. To be honest, I'm sick of talking. It has helped I know that, and I needed to talk things through to get them out into the open, but I feel it's time to move on. I don't have a lot of energy or motivation at the moment but I think I need to be doing more. Keeping the journal helps and I can see things more objectively through it but what next? I don't want to stand still, I'm afraid I might slip back, I want to move on, it's been more than a year now and I want to feel better.'

'Good.' Maggie grinned. 'If you really want to move on that's a great sign, so how about we try a more practical approach to our sessions?'

'I'm ready to try anything.'

Maggie walked over to her desk and picked up a small pile of blank postcards and a pen. She set them out on the coffee table so they were visible to herself and her client.

'We'll start with a list shall we?'

Janet moved to the edge of her seat, putting on her reading glasses to see what Maggie was doing.

'I've got dozens of these,' she spread them out, 'So, you can use as many as you like. What I thought we could try was to write down the things you want to deal with in your life at present, one issue per card.' She was smiling as if she was teaching a conjuring trick; Janet smiled with her, her interest piqued. She picked up a card, took the proffered pen and then wrote at the top of the first card, *Anger*. Showing it to Maggie she asked,

'How about that? Is that what you mean?'

'Great. I had a feeling that would be your first.' Maggie took the card and placed it to one side of the table, giving Janet another blank one.

Hatred, she wrote and reached for another. *Tearfulness,* came next, then *Nightmares, Panic attacks, Lethargy, Self blame, Guilt, Self loathing.* Janet didn't stop until she had used more than a dozen cards. For some reason, writing her emotions and problems down seemed cathartic and she didn't even know what they were going to do with them yet.

'Now, let's prioritize them.' Maggie shuffled the cards together then spread them out again on the table in a different order. 'Pick out the one you are struggling with the most at the moment.'

Even though Janet had written *Anger* first, anger wasn't her primary emotion at that moment in time. Perhaps it was being with her counsellor, a woman she was beginning to trust, in a safe place where she didn't have to pretend to be okay, but the card she picked up after a moment's deliberation was *Guilt.*

'That's a good one to start with. Why 'guilt' Janet, do you know what you feel guilty about?'

Janet wrinkled her brow and sucking thoughtfully on her bottom lip quietly replied,

'I feel that I'm causing a lot of pain and trouble to a great many people and yet I can't seem to pull myself together. I'm moaning on about things that happened over forty years ago, things I should never have let happen and that I should forget about and move on with my life.'

'Wow, that's a whole lot of guilt to be carrying. Let me just sum up what you said, you feel guilty about causing pain and trouble to others; you feel guilty about not being able to pull yourself together; you feel guilty about moaning about historic events; you feel guilty about 'letting' them ever happen at all; and you feel guilty because you can't forget and move on with your life. That's a pretty big list there Janet. Let's look at it more closely. Has anyone ever complained about the 'trouble' you think you're giving them?' Maggie asked.

'Well, no…not really, but they must be sick of me by now, I'm even sick of me.'

'Who must be sick of you Janet?'

'Paul my husband, and the children, although I do keep certain things from them; a few close friends too, but I try to avoid them, I'm not very good company at the moment. Then there's Dr. James and you, I'm taking up your time too when there must be people out there with far worse problems than I have.' Janet paused, looking weary and incredibly sad.

'So really what you're telling me is that no one has complained about you but your whole family, your friends, your GP and even me, are all fed up with you and want you to pull yourself together. And you also believe that a little girl of five years old should have had the wisdom, vocabulary and strength to stop a determined adult predator from abusing her?'

'Maggie no! That's not what I meant; it sounds so awful putting it like that.'

'Well, while we're on this subject of guilt; let's dig a bit deeper shall we?' Maggie moved the box of tissues closer to her client as large teardrops began to fall, then she continued, her words blunt, but her delivery and manner gentle.

'You've shared memories of your childhood experiences with me and I'm honoured that you've felt able to do this, it shows a trust for which I'm grateful, but it also shows considerable strength on your part, a strength which you haven't yet fully realised. What happened to you when you were a little girl was appalling, but it's a fact we can never change and one we're trying to get you over. You said a few minutes ago that what happened all that time ago you should never have let happen. Janet, you were five, six, seven years old. He was an adult, he should have been the one to protect you, but instead for his own gratification he took away your childhood. You did not have a voice in this matter, the blame lies squarely with him, not you. When you go home today I'd like you to find a photograph of yourself as a child. Have a good look at it and try to remember what it was like to be a child of that age. If the memories are too painful, try a more objective approach. Think of your own children at that age, or any child you may know now and about what kind of life they lead. You need to try to love the child that was you. It sounds a strange concept I know, but this guilt is bound up with what you wrote on another card, 'self-loathing'. We're working on what is called the 'inner child' and an understanding of what happened in your childhood and how it affected your development will enhance your recovery. You're on a journey Janet, but there's no timetable for it. Everyone processes things differently and with differing timescales. You've done a lot of the hard work with all the talking over the last four weeks and I hope that's helped you to face the facts of what happened. It's a difficult thing to bring out into the open and you've shown a great deal of courage in doing so. What I'd like us to do now, if it's okay with you, is to begin a learning experience. Understanding why we feel how we do is the cornerstone for rebuilding our lives. We've looked at guilt feelings today and what I want you to take away with you is the fact that you should feel no guilt whatsoever about your abuse. It was solely his fault, you were a little girl and you have no culpability in what happened, whatever. Find that photograph and begin to love the child that was you. As for guilt in the present day, I certainly don't feel that you're causing me any trouble, that's my job and I love the opportunity to help people. And as for your husband and children, perhaps you should ask them if you're causing the pain you think you are. From what you've told me about your family, I think you may be surprised. Should you really assume what they are thinking without asking them?' Maggie paused, looking at Janet and feeling her pain and confusion, then she continued, 'I'm sorry, that's been quite a lecture hasn't it? I hope as we work through these cards it will be a learning curve for you and a positive aid to your recovery. If it's not working for you or it's too emotional, we can slow down or go back to other therapeutic tools. This is your time and you can decide how to use it.'

Janet was surprisingly upbeat as she made her way home from the surgery. Today's session had been significantly different from the first few and so much more positive. Maggie had taken more of a lead which was certainly appreciated, she understood that it was her time but honestly, to talk for nearly the full hour was so tiring and she felt today's approach suited her better. Janet felt she had learned something about herself too and, yes, even about her abuser. Perhaps learning and understanding what had happened in her childhood was the key to her recovery and she couldn't wait to get home and write all her thoughts down in her journal. It had been a terrible year; could there possibly be some light at the end of this seemingly endless tunnel?

Maggie too reflected on this latest session with Janet as her client left the surgery. She was always amazed at the resilience of human nature and pointed these strengths out to her clients whenever she could. When depression takes its vice like hold on someone's life, the 'Janet's' of this world very often lose sight of previous good times. The negative thoughts and emotions obscure many of the more positive aspects and achievements in their lives, and Maggie took every opportunity to remind her clients of how much they had accomplished, in their past and in the present. Seeking help was, for many, a bold move which took courage and determination. Maggie admired this irrepressible trait of human nature and believed that each person had hidden depths which enabled them to cope with the brickbats life threw at them. She viewed her role as facilitating her clients in rediscovering their strength and moving on with their lives in their chosen direction. Her part in helping others somehow gave Maggie strength and purpose and the resilience to carry on with her own life.

Chapter 7

Roberts Brown & Lloyd, trading as R.B.L. Architects, was the up and coming new firm in the town and surrounding area. This was mainly due to the innovative, contemporary designs of its three partners. Peter Lloyd was the eldest partner though not the senior. The three men had decided to set up practice on completely level terms, giving them all an equal say in the business. They each brought their own strengths into the partnership, Peter's particular flair being on the financial side and costing. He had left his old firm after realizing that he was in a rut and becoming bored. It had seemed to him that it was time to take some risks before he was too old to change. Had he foreseen the cost of these risks, in family terms, Peter might have thought twice. But he threw himself into the new venture with enthusiasm; it was just what he needed to stir him from the complacency and monotony of his old job, which held no prospects for change or advancement. The two younger partners, Stephen Roberts and Charles Brown, were true rising stars. They took on clients individually, but really shone when they worked as a team, some of their designs having been highly commended in professional journals. They were really making a name for themselves and teamed with Peter's experience and level headedness, it seemed to be the perfect partnership.

In the first few months Peter became caught up in the excitement and challenges that each day presented. Not only were his colleagues talented architects, they were two of the most agreeable men he had ever met. Work was a pleasure, something it hadn't been for a long time. It also became absorbing and time consuming, but he thrived on it. Yes there were problems; demanding clients, projects that seemed fated to overrun in cost and time, but this added to the challenge and he loved it. His focus had been so work orientated that he had been genuinely unaware of the worsening situation at home.

Peter and Angela had been married for twenty-four years when he changed his job. Their silver wedding coincided with the first anniversary of R.B.L's launch, an extremely busy time with new commissions coming in and their reputation taking off in a phenomenal way. The latter of these events was the one that occupied most of Peter's time and energy. He was working a six day week, usually quite late into the evening and his thoughts were business centered even when he was at home. Angela said very little about the new firm. She had always been a supportive wife but saw architecture as more of a job than a career. Although pleased for her husband, she was never enthusiastic and preferred other topics of conversation when they were together. Peter was perhaps a little disappointed that she didn't share his enthusiasm but then he couldn't get excited about choosing new curtains for the lounge. It was just the way things were, the way it probably was for hundreds of married couples all over the country. Their children, both girls, were grown up and living independently. Jane, the elder, was married to a policeman and lived in a neighbouring town, accessible enough for frequent visits. She was expecting their first baby and that really did enthuse Angela. Rachel, their youngest was in her final year of teacher training and she considered herself entirely independent, except perhaps where finance was concerned.

Peter enjoyed his life, he provided well for his family and they too were happy, or so it seemed. With hindsight, he should have sensed things were not right in his relationship with his wife. He did notice that she was quieter than usual, absorbed in her own thoughts, but he put it down to her possibly going through the menopause, coupled with the girls both having left home and he was confident that it would sort itself out and life would settle back into some kind of routine. He was comfortable with routine.

Angela too had tried telling herself that her restlessness was just the result of circumstances, a combination of missing their daughters and her husband's increased working hours at a time when she would have appreciated seeing more of him, not less. Trying to use the advantages of having more time on her hands she arranged to meet friends for coffee and offered more hours at the charity shop she worked in as a volunteer. This was her perfect job and one she really enjoyed; it gave her the opportunity to meet new people and make new friends. The banter with the customers and the other staff helped the hours to pass quickly but after her shift was over the time seemed to drag and her life lacked purpose and meaning. She began to wish she had pursued a career of her own, feeling that her full potential had never been realised. The area manager of the charity shop, Tim, had more than once hinted that he felt Angela would be suited to a management role in one of their local branches but she had never taken him seriously. Although Tim was several years younger than her, he flirted quite openly, making it difficult to know how serious he was. Flattered by his attentions she eagerly anticipated his visits, hoping one day for the opportunity to raise the subject with him to find out if he really did think a full time job was feasible.

Rachel's graduation was to be the next major family event and Angela was trying to organise a holiday for the four of them and Jane's husband. It was in her mind that this may be the last time they holidayed together as a family as Rachel was applying for positions all over the country and Jane would shortly be a mother. Their family dynamics were changing, an unwelcome prospect and one which she did not relish at all.

Both girls went along with the holiday idea, mainly for the sake of their mother, although they agreed it would be a good opportunity to be together as a family. So a cottage was booked in Cornwall for two weeks almost immediately after the graduation ceremony. The date seemed to suit everyone although Peter wasn't too enthusiastic about taking a full fortnight off when things were so busy at work.

Angela Lloyd was simmering, working up to anger, which wasn't like her at all. She had tried to be reasonable and understanding when Peter put all those hours in at work but he didn't seem to notice her much on the rare occasions he was at home making her feel like a housekeeper and an unappreciated one at that. True she had friends and was kept busy working at the shop, but she desperately craved more from life. When their silver wedding came along she had had thoughts of a second honeymoon but an evening meal with a couple of friends was all that materialised. She missed her daughters and her husband, but his priority was work, his conversation was work, it was becoming a demanding mistress keeping him away from her and one he was only too happy to indulge seemingly unaware of her feelings and now even grumbling at the idea of two weeks holiday. What some people would give for such a wonderful family as theirs and the chance to spend time with them. She was nursing resentment and anger, yet she couldn't express how she felt to her husband, and he was completely oblivious.

The graduation day arrived, after which a celebratory meal was booked and the family intended to spend the night in a hotel before travelling on to Cornwall. Angela was delighted at the way her plans had come together; even Peter seemed keen now the event had actually arrived. It was a perfect day. The mood was light and relaxed with Peter's focus for once solely on his family and Angela experiencing a glimmer of hope that this time away together could be just what they both needed.

A late evening phone call soon extinguished the hope that she had dared to feel. A very apologetic Charles Brown interrupted their nightcap in the hotel bar, needing to speak rather urgently with Peter.

After a lengthy conversation, Peter returned to his family with the news that he would have to delay his going with them to Cornwall due to an emergency at work. His wife's face spoke volumes and even when he tried to tell her how important the situation was, she just didn't seem to understand the firm's predicament. A valued client who generated a great deal of business for them had made some significant changes to a development in the planning stage. Charles and Stephen were working flat out to accommodate him and as contractors were booked, time was short and they needed Peter's input with the changes in costing. Although promising to join them in a couple of days, he could tell that his wife was livid and the previous good mood of the day was shattered.

Perhaps this was the point when Peter realised how shaky his marriage had become. He couldn't ever recall Angela being so angry. When they were alone in their room she vented her feelings, not just about the present situation but going back for the last couple of years. Words poured out vehemently with her tears, prompting him to try and comfort his wife, but she wouldn't let him touch her, something had snapped inside her and it finally dawned on him just how critical things had become.

With hindsight, Peter knew he should have put his family first but he returned home, which was probably the worst thing he could have done, leaving Angela to go on to Cornwall with their daughters. Once caught up in work, he became single minded and a week flew by before the problems were ironed out. On the telephone his wife was cool and indifferent, even when told that he could finally join them for the second week of the holiday.

'The beginning of the end,' was how Peter now thought about that time. He had tried to make it up by being particularly attentive, but the damage was done and she seemed to have no desire to improve their flagging relationship. On returning home, Angela announced that she had secured a full time job as a shop manager. That was the first time she mentioned Tim, but not the last.

Looking back Peter could see signs he should have noticed at the time but no, he had carried on with his work centred life whilst his wife began to build her own future and the gulf between them had widened daily.

Why then it came as a shock when Angela declared she was leaving to move in with Tim, he couldn't explain. Perhaps it was the ostrich syndrome and Peter had assumed it was just a phase but whatever it was, it hit him hard. A black cloud of depression descended, threatening to crush his spirit. Sleep became impossible and he was unable to function properly at work or in the simple chores of his day-to-day life. A couple of beers in an evening to help him relax soon turned into three or four, followed by a whiskey or two to help him sleep. When asleep, he wasn't hurting but when he woke the hurt returned, exacerbated by a hangover and feelings of guilt, shame and self-loathing.

Jane and Rachel were naturally concerned for their father. They tried to spend time with him but both had commitments of their own. Jane was by then a full time mother to a lively ten-month-old girl and Rachel had a teaching post in York, her first position and one that proved to be totally demanding. She did however manage to visit during school holidays, not entirely sure if the visits were a help to her father or an intrusion into his downward spiralling world.

Peter had moved into a flat shortly after the split and the marital home had been sold with the profits divided equally. At least there had been no bickering over finance. Angela had just wanted her half from the sale, a few of the contents and a clean break so she could start again with Tim. Peter, however, found it difficult to let go. His wife refused to meet him face to face claiming there was nothing to talk about and she was decidedly cool on the telephone. Once, on impulse, he had turned up at her new home but could remember little of the episode, as he was completely drunk. Angela was disgusted, closing the door in his face. He remembered to his shame sitting on her doorstep and actually crying. Peter had been taken home by a very irate Tim and told emphatically never to go there again. Throwing up in Tim's car hadn't helped the situation either. Perhaps it was a blessing that the events were such a blur the next morning.

In his sober moments, Peter knew things couldn't continue as they were. He was embarrassed to think that his daughters may have guessed he was drinking too much. They tried to understand but became frustrated when he didn't seem to want their help, or even to help himself. Work now brought with it feeling of guilt knowing that he wasn't pulling his weight. His partners were supportive yet couldn't carry his workload as well as their own and they too began pushing him to do something about his problems.

Evenings were the worst. Peter became maudlin after the first couple of drinks and with nothing to distract him it was easy to drink more than was healthy, sinking into drunken oblivion in an effort to blot out his despair and his increasing sense of self-hatred.

It was on one such evening, a particularly low point, that the phone rang pulling him back from the point of wishing he could just go to bed and never wake up, Peter no longer wanted to live.

It was an effort to answer the phone and many evenings he wouldn't have bothered but something prompted him to pick up the receiver.

'Hi Dad.' came Jane's chirpy voice from what seemed to be very far away. Just hearing her speaking brought a lump to his throat.

'How're things?' she asked.

Peter could barely answer, conversation was a heavy chore these days so he resorted to what he usually did, turning the question around and hoping to set his daughter off on her favourite subject, Emma.

'Oh Dad, you should see her.' Jane happily took charge of the conversation, 'She's so mobile, crawling around, into everything and now even pulling herself up to standing. I swear she'll be walking before her first birthday. I know I go on a bit but she's just so clever gurgling on to herself in that sing-songy way of hers, always happy, except when it's feeding times! I could eat her I really could. I never thought I'd feel like this but Emma's just the whole world to me… and to Brian of course. She has another tooth coming through but doesn't complain. Her little cheeks are hot and red but she just finds something to chew on, and gets on with it. She's a little miracle Dad. I know its early days, but we're trying for another baby, I just love being a mummy and can't wait to have another. We'll be lucky to have one as good as Emma I know, but I feel as if I could have a dozen at least.'

As he listened to the enthusiasm of his elder daughter, Peter could feel hot tears running down his cheeks. His beautiful Jane, it seemed like only moments ago that she was a baby herself; when had she grown into this competent young woman? Had he been such an enthusiastic parent? He couldn't remember, but perhaps that was the alcohol clouding his mind. He focused on a photograph on the mantel of his daughter and granddaughter. It was taken at Christmas, beside the tree. Jane looked radiant and Emma's little face was turned up, gazing adoringly at her mother. She was such a natural earth mother, enjoying each moment of her child's life. Peter's tears flowed freely; he made a few appropriate responses during the rest of the conversation, barely able to hold himself together. Saying his goodbyes, he lay down on his bed and wept until sleep finally came.

****

Thursday morning found Maggie on a home visit to a client she had become very fond of. Walter was eighty-three years old, widowed ten months ago and still finding it hard to cope. Her involvement with him had begun about five months previously when the doctor decided that time alone was not the great healer it should have been. Walter had been married for over sixty years and it wasn't going to take just a few weeks to bounce back from that kind of loss. Apart from the war years and stays in hospital giving birth to their two children, he and Iris had never been parted. He was still relatively active for his age, but learning new skills, such as cooking and operating the washing machine were proving to be a trial. Iris had been one of those wives who had done everything for her husband and therefore her loss presented him with practical as well as emotional issues.

By the time Maggie began to see him, Walter had moved through the first stages of bereavement, those of shock and grief. After the practicalities of arranging a funeral and notifying all the relevant authorities, he became depressed and was overtaken by an inevitable sense of loneliness and isolation. It was at this stage that he sought help from his doctor who for a while concentrated on relieving some of the physical symptoms of his distress but later referred him for counselling. Over the next few months Maggie had worked with Walter to enable him to accept his loss, and acknowledge and cope with the pain. Although not a religious man, emotionally he began to relocate Iris in his mind to a place where they would eventually meet again. This helped him adjust to the reality of life as a widower whilst taking comfort in the memories he had. Only then could he begin to move on with his life. Walter had called Maggie his rock and would always be grateful for her time and patience during his mourning.

Initially, she had visited weekly but recently this had dropped to fortnightly in an effort to 'wean' him off her support and encourage greater independence. A home visit for N.H.S. patients was unusual, except in the case of physical problems that prevented a client from coming to the surgery, but in Walter's case it was more a concession to his age and to save him a lengthy bus journey. From Maggie's point of view it gave her chance to get out of the office and free up the room for her colleague's use.

They both knew it was now time to bring their sessions to a close. They had discussed it together and he understood the reasons, admitting that he had turned a corner with her help. Still, he enjoyed her company and would have prolonged the visits if he could. Maggie arrived to find Walter leafing through an old photograph album and was pleased to see that he was enjoying the memories rather than becoming depressed by them.

'I'm going to put the kettle on now and I know you don't usually have one but I also know that I won't be seeing you much longer, so I want to show off my new talents.' Walter winked as he left her with the invitation to browse through the album. He and Iris made a handsome couple, their happiness almost leaping out from every page, documenting their life together, the birth of children, family holidays, birthdays and so much more. Maggie could barely begin to understand what sixty years of togetherness would be like. There were so many more memories in this one book than she would ever have of her marriage. A strange feeling… a pang of something, momentarily gripped her. Envy perhaps, or just sadness, she didn't know but she experienced a degree of understanding of his loss and was grateful for having played a small part in helping him to adjust.

Walter returned with a tray of tea and homemade scones.

'Wow this is a treat.' Maggie was delighted. 'You haven't been baking these have you?'

'I certainly have. Thought it was time I learned to do a bit for myself. They won't be as good as Iris's scones but I hope you like them.'

She accepted one from the proffered plate, they did look good.

Walter poured the tea and sat down opposite her. Biting into the scone, she was aware of him watching her reaction. Maggie smiled and then giggled.

'What…?'

'Have you tried them Walter?' she asked.

He took a bite, and then he could see the funny side. Instead of sugar he had used salt and the scones tasted awful.

'I think a little more practice would help,' he laughed at his mistake. 'But you could have pretended they were delicious.'

The tea dispensed with, Maggie began to broach the subject of how Walter would manage without the visits. He understood that it was time to let go of his counsellor's support.

'You've been very patient with a silly old man, but before you leave I want to give you these.'

Walter produced an expensively wrapped box of chocolates that Maggie recognized as being from her favourite shop in the high street. She didn't quite know what to say. Professional ethics prevented her from accepting gifts from clients, but the sentiment behind the gift was genuine and the last thing she wanted to do was to cause offence. He seemed to sense her dilemma.

'My Iris was always partial to chocolates and I loved to treat her once in a while. It'll mean a lot to me if you'll accept these, just as a little something to say thank you.'

Maggie had to blink back tears. Of course she would accept them in the spirit they were offered and confess to her supervisor at their next meeting, by which time the evidence would almost certainly have been eaten. Walter saw her to the door, smiling and nodding.

'You know where I am if things get too much?' Maggie always liked to leave the door open for contact to continue if necessary. She would miss him, but helping him through his bereavement was what her work was all about.

Chapter 8

Maggie sat in her office, cocooned from the chaos in the rest of the surgery. The computers had failed; causing mayhem for the reception staff who were rendered unable to take new appointments, repeat prescriptions and most of the other day-to-day functions of the practice. The medical staff too couldn't access patient notes, setting everything back to the pace of days gone by.

Sue was caught up in the panic. She'd hoped to catch Maggie and maybe share lunchtime with her today but now it looked unlikely. The cavalry had arrived in the form of 'Technical Support' but they would have to work miracles to get the system up and running by the end of the morning. Sue buzzed through to see if they could share a coffee break. Taking two steaming mugs into Maggie's office, she made herself comfortable and looked directly at her friend.

'I've decided to take you in hand, so you can either help me, or trust me, what's it going to be?'

Maggie was wary of the twinkle in Sue's eyes.

'I'm getting that same feeling I have when you tell me you've had a good idea. Is there time to make a run for it or have you got all the exits covered?'

'You know me too well, but, as always I have only your best interests at heart.'

Sue took a newspaper from her bag. It was opened at the classified section and red circles highlighted some of the entries.

'You're not serious,' Maggie exclaimed, realising Sue was holding the lonely hearts section, 'No way. Don't even think about it!'

'It's not such a bad idea. You hear some really romantic stories about couples who meet like this. Just listen, *'Knight in shining armour seeks damsel in distress.'*'

'More likely big bad wolf seeks little red riding hood. Anyway I'm not in distress.' Maggie protested.

'Well how about this one, '*Fancy a spring roll? Genuine male, 49 seeks loving lady to enhance his life. N/S, solvent, GSOH.'* Sounds perfect.'

'I can see that he's genuine, he's certainly setting out what he wants. Sue, this is one of your wind ups isn't it?' She couldn't believe her friend was serious.

'Why not just think about it? You could do with a bit of masculine company.'

'I've got Ben.'

'But he's a dog. When did he last give you a back massage or bring you breakfast in bed?'

'We're working on it.' Maggie laughed.

Sue was content; the seed had been sown in her friends mind. Now all she had to do was nurture it and hey presto, she could be looking for a new outfit at last. She left the temporary haven of the office to see if 'Technical Support' worked any quicker on a cup of coffee, although she doubted it.

****

Maggie couldn't help but smile at Sue's attitude to life, and although the idea of responding to a dating advert was ridiculous, she appreciated her friends concern for her situation.

In the months and years after Chris had died her grief had been so overwhelming that had anyone suggested another relationship, even in the context of her future, Maggie would most probably have exploded. The memory of Chris would have to suffice if she couldn't have him. His presence was with her spirit, he was still so much a part of who she was and yes, at times she still spoke to him as if he was physically with her. Holding fast to his memory kept him alive in her heart. Yet Sue was right in a way, it was fourteen years ago and she was a different person now, older, wiser she hoped, and her life had taken a different direction than it would have if Chris had still been alive. She was forty-three, Chris would always be thirty. As a counsellor she knew the dangers of living in the past and not embracing the present. Perhaps a few sessions talking to herself would be in order?

Checking the time, Maggie pushed away the empty coffee mug and turned back to the paperwork she had been reviewing and trying to fit a couple of days holiday into her very full diary.

****

Paul Rea was every bit in love with his wife as he had been on the day they were married. His life had been built around Janet and their two children, Anna and Graham, and he had always assumed they would continue to live happily together into old age. But now he was not so sure. The woman he had married seemed no longer to exist and his fear was that she may be lost to him forever. It was nearly a year now since the changes had begun, changes he at first put down to hormones, symptoms of the menopause. Knowing little of such things he did what most men would do, he ignored it and waited for it to pass. It had been his suggestion that his wife should see her GP, hoping that some magical prescription would restore his beloved wife to him, but she stubbornly refused, becoming distressed if he pushed the matter. Things had changed at home too; the children were living independently, Anna now a young mother of a baby boy, and Janet was bound to miss them. His own situation had also changed, he'd taken early retirement from the solicitor's practice where he had spent the whole of his working life and was fulfilling a lifetime's ambition of writing freelance. Janet had also retired from the role as matron of a large nursing home and it had been his hope that this new found freedom would bring them closer together with opportunities to travel and enjoy life before they were much older. It had therefore been an absolute bombshell when his wife eventually broke down and poured out all those appalling childhood memories which had been bottled up and repressed for so many years. Paul was bereft not knowing where to turn to help her and facing feelings of his own which were proving difficult to cope with. He had never been an angry or over emotional man but this revelation stirred up such powerful emotions which he knew wouldn't help Janet if he released them. If the bastard who did this had still been alive, Paul didn't know if he would have been able to control his anger. How could people do such things to a child? But the evidence was all around, since Janet's revelation, every newspaper he opened and every news bulletin he heard seemed to be full of such atrocities. It was hard to think about, but he was so glad Janet had confided in him, at least her moods were understandable and his help could be offered with a degree of insight now. She did eventually see the GP and was now receiving counselling, but it seemed as if there was very little progress in what seemed such a long time.

Paul had to admit that he didn't fully understand all the whys and wherefores of his wife's problem. Why she had kept it secret for so long, how her family had not known it was happening and why now, when their lives had never been easier, it had all come tumbling out? They had everything going for them, financial security, freedom from the nine to five grind of employment, wonderful children and a beautiful new grandson who he knew Janet adored. But he could only ask so many questions and only when he felt his wife was strong enough to talk; there had been times when she seemed like an automaton, just going through the motions of life, existing rather than living and buried somewhere in a silent world of her own. Paul felt completely adrift, his own life on hold and having absolutely no idea how long his wife's recovery would take. There were times when he wondered if she ever would recover. Each day he tried to reassure her of his love and that their home was a safe place where she would be looked after but he wasn't even sure if his words registered anymore. All he was certain of was that he loved his wife with a fierceness which was almost frightening and he would do anything for her.....if only she would let him.

****

Karen Jenkins was characteristically early for her appointment, choosing a seat at the very back of the waiting room where Maggie's office was visible but where it was unlikely that she would be seen by other patients. She was feeling ambivalent about her last visit, Maggie was certainly an easy lady to talk to and had seemed keen to help but could talking make any difference? The first session had left her feeling quite exhausted with probably more questions than when she started. Her memories of that awful time of her mother's death had come flooding back with the news that her father would shortly be released and her head was stuffed with so many imagined scenarios that she couldn't think rationally. Would her father try to make contact? Would Mike do something stupid? And would this ever be behind her so that she could live a normal happy life?

After her mother had died, Karen had channelled every ounce of energy into holding the family together. Her grandmother had tried to be supportive, but she was, like them all, devastated by the loss of her daughter in such shocking circumstances. Karen had watched as her gran aged before her time, becoming an old lady almost overnight although not yet seventy. They had no extended family to fall back on and her friends were so shocked by the murder that they didn't know how to react, which was understandable, they were Karen's age with little life experience to draw upon. Although the family were all devastated she had somehow felt that her brother Mike was the one to suffer mostly. His friends were teenagers and their way of dealing with it was to avoid him, not from any malice towards the family but simply out of embarrassment. He had learned the hard way that teenage boys don't discuss feelings and so for him the whole event had been worsened by virtual isolation. When he did return to school, his peers were unsure of how to handle the situation and so avoided the issue as if it had never happened. With hindsight Karen realised that her younger brother had bottled up his feelings and his reactions now betrayed the unhealthy anger still simmering below the surface, yet she felt totally inadequate to help.

And now for brother and sister it was resurfacing again, the pain cutting as deeply and feeling every bit as raw as it had done twelve years ago. Karen felt that perhaps she missed her mother even more now; there were times of incredible loneliness in her life when she craved a mother's wisdom and love. It was exhausting facing the burden of responsibility yet again and although older and perhaps wiser she struggled as much as ever, feeling like a drowning swimmer fighting to keep her head above the water, but what was even more frightening was that at times Karen wanted to sink below the surface, to let it all engulf her and plummet into oblivion.

Maggie was almost toe to toe with her client before Karen was aware of her presence; obviously she had been far away with a deep frown confirming her state of mind.

'Hi Karen,' she smiled. The younger woman was visibly startled but recovered composure sufficient to return the smile. Once seated in the office and having been reminded of the confidentiality contract, Maggie asked what kind of week it had been.

'Not so good,' Karen admitted having decided during the week that complete honesty with her counsellor was the best way forward. There was no one else to share problems and anxieties with so she was determined to make full use of these appointments. Had Maggie known of this resolve she would have been delighted. Many clients wasted valuable time trying to be strong or polite or whatever other facade they chose to hide behind. Karen's attitude was one to be applauded and would certainly be of benefit during their time together.

'I'm not sure what I hope to get out of these sessions really, last week was good, I think I felt better for talking, but I don't want to come here just to have a good moan and go over the same ground each time.'

'Actually having a good moan can be really helpful. I'm an outsider to your situation so you don't have to worry about how it will affect me. Sharing with friends and family bring their own set of problems in that you are always conscious of their feelings as well as being concerned about what they may think. You also may not be able to speak freely to those closest to you due to loyalties to other family members. I hope that this makes sense, it can be a little confusing?'

'No, I think I get it and you're right about talking to those close to me, they've heard it all before, well, maybe not all, I do try to be tactful.'

'Exactly, so these sessions are completely for your benefit. There is no way I'm going to judge you or try to persuade you into doing something you're not comfortable about. If I ask any questions you don't want to answer, then don't. My only reason for asking is to clarify that I understand what you've said, or to help you to understand your own thoughts and feelings. Is that okay?'

'Yes, I think I got the gist of that last week although I probably talked too much, it was such a relief to get it all out of my system.'

'You certainly didn't talk too much; talking's a good thing here. And you were very clear in telling me your story which is what I needed to understand what you've been through and to know how best to help you. How did you feel after we met last week? Did it bring any issues to mind that you'd like to start with today?'

'Well yes and no really. As I said it did help to get it all out of my system but I've still had some pretty awful days this week. Everything's such an effort at the moment, I feel as if I want to curl up into a ball and sleep until I feel better. I suppose that's how depression affects people isn't it?'

'It certainly can cause those feelings but what about the medication, I know you weren't keen on taking them, have you thought any more about it?'

'I've had the prescription filled, but as yet I haven't taken any. It's a comfort to know they're there if I get really desperate but I want them to be a last resort.'

'That's good, and a sensible thing to do; it gives you a kind of safety net to fall back on. So, do you want to talk about any of these bad days?'

'If I'm honest, I don't really know what I want. I feel so mixed up lately that I hardly even know who I am anymore...' Karen turned her face away from Maggie, biting her bottom lip in an attempt to stop the tears from falling. They sat in silence for about a minute, which to the younger woman seemed much longer. Eventually turning back to her counsellor she continued, 'I'm so confused; I'm struggling with all sorts of feelings which I've never experienced before. I can be angry one moment then incredibly sad the next. I have whole days of feeling sorry for myself and then it turns to guilt at being so self absorbed, but the worst thing I feel is loneliness. I feel as if I'm so completely alone.' A large teardrop escaped from her wide blue eyes and dropped onto her hand. Maggie's heart went out to this young woman who was obviously carrying burdens from the past and the present, and even anticipating the problems of the future. After a few moments silence she spoke gently.

'Karen, I think it may help you if we looked together at your life as a whole. You've gone through so much pain and heartache in the past which is weighing heavily on you at this time and is obviously exacerbated by the news of your father's impending release. What I suggest we try, is drawing up a time line of your life to date. We can set it out on paper and focus on major events, not only the bad stuff but the good too. How would you feel about giving it a go? If it doesn't prove helpful we can drop it and try something else, or if you'd like to think about it for a while we can decide next week, what do you think?'

Taking a tissue from the box Maggie had gently pushed her way, she blew her nose and dabbed at her damp cheeks. Her interest was aroused, this sounded like something to really get into and she was keen to know more.

'How do you think it will help?'

'Well, it's a way of exploring who you are, that is who you really are, not who others think you might be or who you think you should be. By looking at major events in our past we can see how and why we reacted as we did and what the consequences were. You might find that patterns have developed in your behaviour, for good or for bad. Through this intensive kind of soul searching we'll hopefully find the real you, your strengths and weaknesses. We're all multi-layered, our layers having been acquired from our experiences in life and the influence of the people around us; for example, a child will generally take on his parents' values in life as they are the ones closest to him. By this scrutiny of our history we can see how we have become the person we are today. We can also see ourselves a little more objectively and learn what we need to make us happy and whole, and on the flip side, what we need to avoid, for our well-being.' She paused to let her client process this idea.

'It sounds like a plan.' She smiled and at that moment felt anything but alone. In Maggie there was an ally, someone to share her innermost thoughts, someone who would walk with her through the mess which was at that point in time Karen Jenkin's life.

Chapter 9

Julie had wavered over what to do all week and now it was time to make up her mind. Jim had been decidedly cool since the beating on Wednesday and it felt as if he was watching her all the time yet the incident was mentioned by neither of them. Simon had asked about the bruised and swollen jaw, obviously shaken when he first saw his mother, but she laughed it off, putting it down to her usual clumsiness and telling him she had tripped over the step in the yard.

'Mum, you must be more careful,' he sounded anxious. 'You fall over more times than Chloe.'

Moved by her son's concern Julie hoped he believed her, but he was growing up quickly and was a bright boy. Simon was also a gentle child, not rough or rowdy, except perhaps on the football field where he was proving to be quite talented. He did well at school with his reports carrying phrases such as 'Always tries his best' and 'Simon is a pleasure to teach', making her proud of her son. It hadn't been easy for either of them. When Jim was around she couldn't give him the attention he deserved, her husband objected to what he called 'fussing' the children, he had to be the centre of the household and their children came very much at the bottom of the ladder. Still, Simon was a joy and despite his father's attitude he was growing into a fine boy. The children were the best part of Julie's life.

But now it was Sunday and she was due to see Maggie again tomorrow, an appointment she really wanted to keep. Jim would be out, Julie was sure of that and Sally over the road would be only too happy to have Chloe again. Having a little boy of the same age, Sally swore it was easier to have the two of them rather than just her own.

Dare she risk it? Surely Jim had just found out about her visit last week by chance. Someone must have seen her and told him, but she couldn't think who.

'I'm going,' Julie told herself decisively. 'What's the worst he can do if he finds out, beat me? Heaven knows I'm used to that now. Yes, I'm going.'

Her resolve was equally as strong the next morning. Jim left at his regular time, and as usual Julie had no idea where he went and didn't dare to ask. Over the years of their marriage she had learned that it was better to remain silent; it had become part of the peace keeping strategy. Half an hour later taking Chloe over to Sally's and feeling that her neighbour deserved an explanation, Julie told her that she was seeing a counsellor.

'A shrink,' Sally almost laughed until she saw Julie's face.

'If you ask me it's that husband of yours who needs to see a shrink. I don't know why you put up with it love. It doesn't go unnoticed you know.'

Julie didn't ask what, there was no time to get into that discussion and she also didn't correct Sally about the 'shrink' she was just grateful for her help.

'I won't be much more than an hour or so thanks Sally.' Then kissing Chloe's cheek, she left to make her way to the surgery.

****

It seemed so peaceful in Maggie's little room. Julie felt soothed and relaxed as if stepping into another world, a world where people cared about each other and were unafraid to show it. Sitting down, she was aware that the bruising was still evident on her face but Maggie made no comment although it hadn't gone unnoticed.

'How have you been Julie?' Maggie began.

'Okay...... No, not okay, it's been awful.' A desire to be open with

Maggie and not hide things from her prompted her truthfulness. There was something about this counsellor that instilled confidence and Julie felt she could trust her.

'I felt better after seeing you last week, but I wasn't altogether honest with you.' She tried to hold back the tears that pricked her eyes.

'Do you want to be honest with me? You know you don't have to tell me anything you don't want to, but I'm here to help. If talking helps, that's great but if there are some things you don't want to share, then that's fine too. It may be that some things will come out later when you feel you know me better, but we all have the right to keep our thoughts and feelings to ourselves. It's really more important for you to be honest with yourself.' Maggie spoke softly and slowly, giving Julie time to collect her thoughts and regain her composure.

'Thank you Maggie, I think I know what you're saying. It was hard for me to come here today and I do want to tell you why. The things I talked about last week were true but only the half of it. I have been feeling low and emotional but the real reason is this.' She touched her swollen face.

'I'm not as accident prone as I make out, you've probably guessed, I'm sure Dr. Williams has. My husband has quite a temper and when he loses control, I take the brunt of it. Jim's not really a bad person, he just finds it difficult being a family man. Neither of the children were actually planned you see, so it's been hard for him to accept.'

'So those bruises were caused by your husband?' she reflected what Julie had told her to make sure the facts were right.

'Yes'

'Has he always been like this throughout your marriage?'

'Oh no.........he's always been, well... moody, but I could usually handle that. It started when I was pregnant with Chloe, four years ago. I was shocked at first but put it down to his reaction to another baby on the way. He didn't want children at all. But after Chloe was born he started to hit me regularly. It's only when I've done something to annoy him......although sometimes I don't understand what, and never in front of the children, he wouldn't do that.'

'Can you hear what you're saying Julie?' Maggie wanted her to think about her attitude to the violence.

'You said it only happens when you've done something to annoy him. Do you really think that being beaten is your fault, or that you actually deserve it?' Maggie said this very quietly and slowly, without emotion giving Julie time to think about her own words. After a few moments of silence, she continued, 'Do you think the children are aware that he hits you? Simon is, what, eleven now? Could he know what's happening?'

'I don't think so, although this last week he seemed very concerned for me...but he wouldn't suspect that, I'm sure'

'Julie,' Maggie hesitated, 'I'm afraid I have to ask this. Has Jim ever hit either of the children?'

'No, never. I make sure they don't annoy him and he doesn't really see that much of them.' Another peace keeping strategy. Julie sighed and looked out of the window. She looked tired and drawn almost as if the effort of the day's revelations had completely drained her.

Waiting for a few moments to give her time to think, Maggie knew it couldn't have been easy keeping this to herself for four years and coping with physical pain and injury as well as the emotional torment it would bring. It was bound to catch up with her sometime. The young woman seemed to have no family support, and the role of protecting the children from what was happening around them fell squarely on her shoulders alone. Maggie admired her strength and in a strange way, the loyalty to her husband. It wasn't of course up to her to say that this loyalty was misplaced, this was one of those occasions when the client would have to reach her own conclusions and if that was to stay with Jim then the decision would have to be respected. But while Julie was still her client she would offer all the emotional support possible in helping her to explore her own feelings and reach the best possible outcome for herself and the children.

During the rest of their time, Julie related details of the beating Jim had inflicted upon her last week. At times she was understandably emotional, especially when describing how Chloe had been left alone, probably only for a few moments, but it was obvious that this had had a profound effect, a wakeup call to the dangers in her own home. By this time both women had tears in their eyes.

Before the end of the session, Maggie ensured that her client was in possession of contact numbers to call for help in an emergency. Julie was quite horrified when the police were mentioned but was reassured that this was only a last resort. Foremost in both of their minds was the safety of the children and Maggie felt confident that Julie would put their welfare first, loyal though she may be to her husband. And it was gratifying that Julie seemed determined to continue with her appointments. After only two visits she felt comfortable in Maggie's presence as if being with a trusted friend of long-standing and when it was made clear that her counsellor would be happy to see her at any time without an appointment if the need arose, she left with a lighter heart than she'd had for a long time.

****

Maggie used the time before lunch to catch up on some paperwork. The afternoon would bring another new client, Peter Lloyd, for his second visit. As her thoughts moved from Julie to Peter she found herself wondering about the man himself. He had come over as open and fairly confident but could that have been an act? He had spoken honestly about his marriage, seemingly able to accept his own part in its breakdown. Her curiosity was aroused and not for the first time she wondered how this man's problems would work out and what her role would be in this situation.

Peter was also anticipating his next visit for counselling and reflecting on the first appointment. In his mind's eye he had pictured a matronly, gray haired lady, frumpily dressed in tweeds and brogues. Not so Maggie Sayer. Early forties he would guess, three or four inches shorter than his own five foot eleven, a good figure with short dark curly hair and brown eyes. She was stylish in her dress, the sort of lady who wore clothes which suited her rather than blindly following whatever was in fashion. He had a clear mental image of her wearing an emerald green blouse, brown layered skirt and suede boots, the green complementing her olive skin and shining curls. Why he should remember such detail he didn't know. He wasn't great at remembering such minutiae but Maggie had made an impression and not just with her appearance. She had a quiet, soothing voice and pleasant manner, holding eye contact, not in an intimidating way but with interest and understanding. Warmth and sincerity emanated from her, immediately putting Peter at ease, finding himself surprisingly open and sharing even very personal feelings. One thing he did hold back was a concern over his drinking. Yes, he realised she was a professional and her ability to help depended largely on his honesty, but for some reason he had kept this information from her. Dr. James knew that he was relying on alcohol but Peter didn't think this had been passed on to the counsellor. It was stupid really, it wasn't as if he was an alcoholic; he could probably stop drinking if he wanted to and it was just to get him through this difficult time, a kind of release from the depression. 'Medicinal purposes,' he thought, but why hadn't he told Maggie? Her opinion of him was for some reason important to him, but he also wanted to be honest with her. Perhaps he would bring it up that afternoon when they met. He was surprised to find that he was quite looking forward to this next appointment.

****

Maggie grabbed a quick lunch at home and an even quicker walk with Ben before going back to the surgery for the afternoon appointment with Peter. Pausing to check her reflection in the mirror at the entrance to her office she decided a comb and touch more lipstick would be in order, not something she would usually bother about but for some reason she needed a boost.

Peter was prompt and followed purposefully into her office when invited. Watching him sit down, Maggie thought he looked different from their last meeting, tired perhaps and as if he had lost weight, which seemed ridiculous in only a week. Still he did not look a picture of health, rather more like a man on his own who wasn't looking after himself properly.

'How have you been Peter?' Maggie took the lead.

'I've been better, but I've been a lot worse too.' Peter made the effort to smile and shifted in the chair to find a comfortable position.

'Did our conversation last week bring up anything you'd like to continue?' She returned his smile.

'Well… I think I told you the bones of the situation and how things have been getting me down; I don't really know where we go from here. Do you wave a magic wand or something, or give me some home spun advice to get me back on track?'

'No, and no.' she smiled again. 'My magic wand's in for its MOT at the moment and I'm not here to give you advice.'

'So I've had a wasted journey?' he continued the banter.

'Let's hope not,' her tone was a little more serious now.

'I have been thinking a bit about where I went wrong. Talking about Angela and the girls last week brought it all back to me.' Peter had in mind the recent telephone conversation with his elder daughter, Jane, and the emotions it had aroused.

'I have regrets. Some going back a long way, but I do see now that things aren't going to go back to how they were. Angela has moved on and I can't say that I blame her. I wasn't prepared to give her the time she needed, I can see that now and I really do wish her well. She deserves to be happy and at some point I hope we can be friends again, after all we have children together and a granddaughter.'

Maggie noticed the light in his eyes and the way he sat more upright as he mentioned his granddaughter.

'Do you think that by working on these family relationships it might help your present feelings?'

'Yes. I think perhaps it could.'

Peter began to talk more about his daughters with an obvious pride. The infrequent contact seemed to be the fault of both sides, they all had their own busy lives but Maggie sensed that he had kept the girls at a distance for some other reason. She began to probe gently,

'It must be difficult with a grown up family leading their own lives and your divorce from their mother adds more complications, but could there be another reason you don't see much of them? I get the feeling that perhaps you discourage them a little, which is strange when you obviously care so much about them?' Maggie rarely challenged her clients so early in the counselling relationship but on this occasion she sensed Peter was holding something back.

His face took on a more solemn expression. She held his gaze, noting the flicker of indecision in his eyes as he thought about whether or not to continue. For one awful moment, Maggie wondered if he was going to get up and leave the room but he didn't. Sinking back into the chair he lowered his eyes.

'There is something else.' he said, avoiding her gaze. 'I have been drinking rather more than usual since Angela left.' Peter sighed and his shoulders slumped. Lifting his eyes, he was unsure what reaction he would get.

'Is this something you'd like to talk about?' Maggie showed no shock or horror, which in itself surprised him.

The answer was yes. He went on to talk quite openly about relying on alcohol, initially to relax and help him sleep but he was becoming increasingly aware of how unhealthy the situation was, a situation which could possibly get out of hand. He still maintained that he could stop drinking if he wanted to but was at a loss as to why he hadn't. Embarrassed at his own weakness Peter admitted that he had been avoiding his daughters, ashamed that they would see him at his worst. His vulnerability touched Maggie; feeling his pain, she wanted to give some measure of encouragement as their time was rapidly coming to an end.

'Peter,' she began, 'Thank you for trusting me enough to share this concern. I have a few ideas that I'd like time to work on, so assuming you want to come again next week, can we pick up on this where we must leave it now?'

Yes, he did want to come again. This session had perhaps been more of a strain than their first one but it was a relief to have spoken so openly to someone about his true feelings. He already had enough trust in this lady to feel comfortable with sharing his problems. The concern appeared genuine and her perception impressed him. It almost felt as if she was entering into his situation with him. Next week couldn't come quickly enough.

Chapter 10

The second half of March brought welcome signs of spring. Trees were budding green, some with early blossom, and a weak sun was making the effort to warm the stone cold earth. It was a time of year that Maggie loved. Unlike her parents she wasn't really a winter person; hibernation would have suited her well, but spring and autumn were her favourite seasons, particularly spring with the rich promise of new life within grasp.

Maggie had made plans to visit her parents for a long weekend. It was mothering Sunday and being an only child, she always made the effort to visit, usually taking them both out to lunch. It would be good to see them again and catch up on their news.

George and Helen Price had moved to Scotland three years earlier when George had retired from his job with the post office. They had always loved the rugged beauty of the Scottish borders knowing it well from countless holidays there in the past. Even the harsh winters held an appeal when the heathers were covered with snow, the ice crunched beneath their feet and each breath froze in the biting air. Helen's retirement dream had been one of a stone built cottage within a small community where they could make new friends and become involved whilst they were both still active. A cottage appealed to George too, just so long as it had a modern interior and a garden for his vegetables and flowers. Remarkably they had found their perfect home after only a few months of searching. It ticked all the boxes, was relatively low maintenance and they were now three years happily settled into their new life. Naturally a visit from their daughter was anticipated with relish, even though she complained that they made more fuss of Ben than of her.

The weather was cold but bright as Maggie drove north on the A1. Feeling the wind playing on the steering made her grateful that it was dry and not icy. Snow was forecast but mostly in northern Scotland rather than the border regions. Ben was sitting in the back seat, clouding up the rear windows with his heavy breathing. He adored travelling and always amused her with his excited antics as he watched her load up the car and it finally dawned that a journey was in the offing. She was always happier when he could travel with her. Being away from home and her dog was a little too much for Maggie's liking. Ben was after all her baby. 'People and their pets,' she thought, 'where would we be without them.'

Ben began to bark noisily when he sensed their arrival, his long tail thumping on the back seat as his mistress manoeuvred the small car to the side of the garage. George and Helen came out to greet them and he wasted no time in jumping from the car to initiate his search for biscuits, homing in on Helen, sniffing and wagging his tail in unison.

'He knows you spoil him.' Maggie laughed, hugging first her father and then her mother.

'Well I did bring just half a biscuit to say hello.' Helen replied, rewarding Ben's enthusiasm. The biscuit disappeared in record time and the four of them hurried inside out of the cold wind.

As usual, her mother had laid out an enormous meal. In the tradition of all mothers she worried that her daughter didn't bother to cook properly and took it upon herself to feed her up each visit.

'Mum,' she exclaimed; 'I always have to go on a diet after coming here.' But she really loved slipping back into the role of a child again and letting Helen fuss. In the single life she led and also at work Maggie assumed the part of being the strong, capable, in control professional, which indeed she was. But it was hard at times in her personal life when there was no one to help her make even the smallest, day-to-day decisions and hers was the shoulder on which others cried. It wasn't that she minded, this was her choice and her work was incredibly fulfilling, but just sometimes she longed for something more. Someone, other than her mother, to look after her for a change, a bit of excitement maybe, and yes, perhaps Sue was right, a little romance would be welcome too.

Maggie had inwardly vowed never to marry again after Chris died, but over the years had mellowed to the idea that there could be closeness to someone in the future.

'Never say never,' was more her philosophy now and just lately her attitude to another relationship had become desirable rather than a possibility. Still she certainly wasn't desperate enough to consider Sue's idea of the lonely-hearts column. 'Save me from that,' she thought.

The family spent a pleasant evening together catching up on each other's lives, laughing at day-to-day trivia and being content to be together. Maggie let Ben out for a last sniff around the garden then said goodnight to her parents and made her way to the guest bedroom at the back of the house. The room was warm and cosy, untouched by the modern facilities her Father had insisted on throughout the rest of the house. The original beams and a small cast iron fireplace were true cottage features and Helen had unapologetically decorated the room with flowered wallpaper and chintz fabrics. The overall effect was delightful. There were two tiny windows in the room, one to the back of the house and one to the side, overlooking a small stream that bordered the garden. The back of the cottage looked onto a wooded area, which sloped upwards as far as could be seen. Maggie loved the tranquillity of this area and although she had never lived here with her parents, it felt very much like home.

Leaving the curtains open, she switched out the lights, settled down into the big double bed and looked out at the sky. It was so much clearer here than in town, a rich velvety black studded with diamond bright stars. There were no street lamps here to invade the cocoon of darkness and the silence was almost tangible. Maggie closed her eyes and sank into a deep, restful sleep.

At six thirty in the morning Maggie was woken by the sound of ducks and after a moment's confusion remembered where she was, looked at the clock and rolled over to go back to sleep. The duck quacked again, four rasping quacks which she ignored and began drifting off to sleep again, until four more quacks.

'Does it think it's a cockerel?' she muttered, flipping her pillow over and snuggling down into the cool softness, when the wood pigeons began their call; the start of the dawn chorus. Ben was wandering around the room by then so she gave up on sleep, dressed in warm clothes and quietly took him off to enjoy an early morning walk.

They took a familiar route leading down the road and over a bridge to a path which bordered woodland on one side and fields on the other. Snow capped the hills in the distance, but on lower ground it was milder with just a hint of frost. The field was full of sheep with their early lambs. Maggie paused to watch them skipping after their mothers and nudging their way in to suckle as if saying 'hey, don't forget me.' Ben was too busy taking in all the unfamiliar scents to bother with the sheep. They walked for about an hour, a circular route which brought them into the village and back to her parent's home from the opposite direction. Signs of life came from the lighted kitchen window and walking through the doorway the aroma of coffee and toast made her realise how hungry she was. Helen was making porridge.

'Very native.' Maggie laughed.

'Your father has become rather fond of his porridge. I've made enough for us all so give him a shout and we'll eat together'

Maggie couldn't remember when she had last eaten porridge. Her mother had made it with full cream milk and she ate two helpings drizzled with honey and was too full to eat the toast, much to Ben's delight.

A lazy Sunday morning was exactly what was needed. She started a novel she had wanted to get into for ages. George sat opposite with the Sunday papers whilst her mother busied herself in the kitchen, mixing a fruit cake for tea, as if there wasn't enough food in the house to feed an army. By the time Helen came through with morning coffee, she had read four chapters. As her mother sat beside her, Maggie put the book down.

'How's that friend of yours doing?' Helen asked 'The one who works with you at the doctors.'

'Sue? She's fine mum. I thought maybe in the summer I could bring her to stay for a few days. We'd thought about a few days holiday in Edinburgh so we could combine it with a couple of nights here as well.'

'That would be lovely darling. Your friends are always welcome and we can look after Ben for you while you're in the city. Are there any other friends you might like to bring? You know how we love visitors.'

Maggie's dad coughed from behind his paper, turning the pages in an exaggerated fashion so he could peer at his wife over the top.

'There's no one else Mum,' she smiled at her mother's attempt at subtlety. 'You'll be the first to know.'

'So…' continued Helen, not wanting to let the subject drop, 'Is Sue still single then?'

'You're becoming a nosey old woman Helen.' interrupted George.

'Well you're obviously listening in too.' she replied rather smartly.

Maggie smiled at her parents; it was good to be with them. They weren't really nosey, she knew how much they cared but she didn't want them to worry, which naturally they did from time to time.

'There's no man in my life, I honestly would tell you if there was, so don't worry, I'm perfectly fine as I am, really.'

'I know dear,' Helen went on, 'We only want you to be happy.

You've been through such a lot and we're really proud of how you've coped, but it has been a long time now and Chris would want you to find happiness, I'm sure'

Maggie appreciated the concern. She knew Helen had had reservations about leaving their daughter alone when they moved to Scotland and it had taken a lot of reassurance to persuade her that she would be all right. It wasn't as if they were leaving a teenage daughter who had never been away from the security of the family home before.

'Yes Mum, I know. I'm not totally against the idea of meeting someone else; I just don't want to begin a campaign of looking for Mr. Right. If he turns up, fine, I'll let you know, but I really am happy on my own. You're beginning to sound like Sue. Do you know, last week she even picked out some adverts in the lonely hearts column for me.'

'Well that's not such a bad idea love. It's a lot safer than this Internet dating. I've heard there are all sorts of perverts out there, preying on lonely women.'

'Mum. I can't believe you've just said that. I'm not going to do either. Dad, help me out here will you?'

'Far be it from me to interfere with one of your mother's ideas. Has she mentioned coffee with Mrs. Taylor tomorrow morning?'

'No? What's this?'

'Oh nothing dear, Mrs. Taylor just said if we haven't any plans in the morning perhaps you and I would like to go down for coffee.'

George was having trouble with that cough again.

'What's the catch?' Maggie asked

'A six foot two computer geek who can't string two sensible words together if they're not about gigabytes or whatever.' George answered her question for her.

'George, that's not fair!' Helen defended her neighbour's son. 'He's just shy, but quite brilliant by all accounts. His mother and I thought it would be nice for them both to have younger company whilst Maggie was here, that's all.'

'Well thanks mum but I'm afraid I'll have to disappoint Mrs. Taylor and her son. I wanted to take you to town tomorrow. You've both got birthdays coming up before I'll see you again and I'd like you to look for something you would like.'

'That's a shame; she'll be upset, perhaps afternoon coffee?'

'No Mum, I'll be leaving late afternoon and I'd rather spend the time with you and Dad.'

Helen just had time to make an apologetic phone call to her friend and then they were off out for Sunday lunch. Maggie had asked her father to book somewhere special for them, it was her treat and she wanted to spoil her parents; she had learned never to take her loved ones for granted.

The lunch was excellent, all three of them eating far too much. An afternoon stroll filled in the rest of the day with an evening playing scrabble, reminiscent of a childhood passion to score higher than her Father, which as ever, she didn't.

Monday morning was bright yet still cold. The trip into town was quite a treat for her parents who rarely bothered other than for their weekly grocery shopping. George chose to look around the bookshops whilst mother and daughter trawled the woollen mills. Helen wanted a cashmere scarf in a particular shade of turquoise, which they eventually found in the fourth shop they tried.

'What would Dad like do you think?' Maggie asked.

'Goodness, he never knows himself. We might be better calling in at the garden centre on the way home, he'll be much happier in there.'

George approved and chose a young apple tree that he fancied for a particularly bare corner of the garden.

'He's only thinking of the apple pies,' teased Helen.

All too soon the visit to Scotland came to an end. With affectionate farewells, she and Ben began the journey home. Helen packed a box full of home baked treats, an infinite number of irresistible calories that she knew her daughter would enjoy.

There would be an hour or so of daylight for the start of the journey after which the roads would be familiar to Maggie, who felt refreshed and relaxed from her short break but as ever, she would be pleased to return home and settle back into some semblance of routine.

Chapter 11

Maggie opened her desk drawer and pulled out an A4 sized pad of plain paper. Turning it to the landscape position she took a ruler and a thin black pen and drew a line along the centre of the paper from left to right. This was repeated on the first four sheets in the pad and placed together with a selection of felt tipped pens, on the coffee table in her office. Karen Jenkins was due in almost fifteen minutes and Maggie wanted to be well prepared. She re-read her notes from their last session then opened the door of her office in order to see her client arriving.

Karen was again a few minutes early and noticing Maggie's open door moved quietly towards it tapping it gently. Maggie looked up and smiled and the two women were soon seated in the easy chairs by the coffee table.

'What kind of week have you had?' She asked her client.

'Oh, so-so,' Karen replied, wiggling her fingers to illustrate her words. I haven't heard any more from the police or the probation service so there's nothing new there. I've seen Mike a couple of times but he still avoids talking about the release. I can tell he's brooding though, he never could hide his feelings and I'm aware of the anger eating away at him, it scares me to think how he would react if dad tried to get in touch.'

Maggie had been expecting her to bring Mike into the conversation and felt it needed to be clarified that Karen was the client and she couldn't counsel Mike by proxy.

'I understand your concern for Mike, but in some ways he's not your problem. I'm sorry if that sounds callous, but he is an adult and capable of making decisions for himself. You can't be responsible for his happiness.' Maggie could see Karen's shock at these words and tried to explain what she meant: 'Our meetings are for your benefit Karen. I'm here for you. Of course Mike will crop up in our discussions, he's an important part of your life but you're the focus of these sessions and my priority is your well being. Perhaps you could talk to him about seeking counselling himself?'

'I'm not sure he'd want to do that.'

'Does he know that you're seeing me?'

'Yes, I told him but he shrugged it off as he does with most things he doesn't want to talk about. I'll mention it again though; he could really do with some help.'

'Good, it's always worth another try. I'm sorry if it seems a harsh thing to say and I know your problems are closely bound with your brothers' but it's you we need to concentrate on to find out what's best for you, can you understand that?' Karen nodded and Maggie smiled as she continued,

'That's great, thank you. Have you had chance to think any more about working on a time line yet?'

'Yes, I'd like to try, although I don't know what to expect from it.'

'It's probably best if you don't have any expectations from this kind of work. We'll just take it a step at a time and see how you feel. Initially we're aiming to enhance your understanding of who you are and how past experiences have moulded your personality.' Maggie lifted the pad of paper from the coffee table, turning it so Karen could see, and then began to explain,

'What I'd like us to do is to make a chart of major events in your life, starting as early as you remember. As you recall instances, we can discuss whether they were positive or negative events, putting the positive ones above the line and negative ones below it. Does that sound okay?'

'It sounds easy but I've a feeling it won't be.' Karen gave a little smile as Maggie went on,

'What's the earliest memory you have? That's probably the best place to start.'

'Gosh, it's hard to pinpoint the chronology of memories, but probably the first thing I remember is Mike being born, I was three and really excited about my new little brother or sister. Mum talked about him coming, telling me I would be a big sister and would be able to help her look after the new baby.'

'So, that was a positive memory?' Maggie asked.

'Oh yes, definitely. We went shopping for little clothes and I helped Mum to sort out my old pram and cot. I hadn't been long in a 'big' bed and it made me feel quite grown up knowing my little brother or sister would be sleeping in my room with me. I must have told anyone who would listen that I was going to be a big sister, it was a new status for me but I must have bored everyone silly with my little girl chatter.'

'It sounds as if your Mum did a good job of involving you in the preparations,' Maggie commented as she wrote '*Birth of brother*' above the line on the first page.

'She really did, I can never remember feeling any jealousy of Mike during his early years at all. She was a great mother and treated us equally throughout all those early years.'

'Is there anything else you remember about that time?'

'Yes, the day he came home from hospital. Mum had been in for about a week and I was missing her terribly. Dad took me in to see her every day and there was such a sense of excitement about them coming home. We put up blue balloons and I helped Dad to clean the house, or as much as a three year old can help, it was probably more of a hindrance, but it made me feel involved in the whole event. When they eventually did come home, Mum asked me to sit and hold the baby while she sat down and had a cup of tea. I've a photograph somewhere of me sitting beside Mum on the sofa with Mike on my lap with such a ridiculous grin on my face, but it was one of those priceless moments and the photo always makes me smile.'

'It sounds as if you were a very happy family in those days?'

'We were. I adored my parents yet the memories are more of Mum than Dad, which is probably natural as she was the one I spent the most time with.'

'Well, I'm glad we've started on a positive note. You've had such a lot of negativity in your life but you can always look back on the happier experiences. Your Mum's efforts to involve you with your brother probably laid the foundation for your close relationship with him today.'

'I've never thought about it like that but yes, you're right. We had the usual sibling rivalries, but mostly we were, and still are, very close.'

'What else can you remember from those early years?'

'Starting school was the next milestone.' Karen paused, lost in thought for a few moments. Maggie waited for her to break the silence.

'You know, now that I think about it, Mum made that such a positive experience too. We had a visit to the school before term started. I was rather shy at first, but Mum held my hand and kept pointing out things in the classroom. She told me that I was a really big girl and how much fun school would be with lots of new friends to play with. She knew all the right things to say, starting school was such a magical time, I loved it.'

'So that's another positive,' Maggie said passing the paper to Karen for her to continue the notes. Karen picked up a bright orange pen and wrote '*Starting school*' above the line then began to embellish the words with little doodles as she thought.

'I've got one for below the line next... it was in the first or perhaps second year of school when I had appendicitis. I felt so poorly and the hospital ward seemed like a prison. Mum stayed with me every day while Gran looked after Mike, but when she left each evening I was a real baby and screamed and cried. She must have felt terrible. There was a round table in the centre of the ward where we all sat to have our meals, it's still set it in my mind and I can almost smell the ward when I think about it, a mixture of disinfectant and semolina, awful.' Both women smiled at the thought.

'Is this okay Maggie, am I doing what you want,' Karen asked, choosing a gray pen and writing below the line.

'You're doing fine, but it's not for my benefit, it's your time line, add whatever you like. As we get further along the line you'll hopefully pick out patterns which could be of help in the present. For now it's enough to remember those early days and it's good that it's mostly positive.'

'I remember sport's day at school, when I was about seven or eight and was a really competitive child, everything I did I had to do well. In that particular year Mum and Dad were both there, I remember because Dad won the father's race. Mum, Mike and I shouted and cheered, jumping up and down on the side lines and feeling so proud when he won. That must go on the positive side, we were a really a happy family then.' Karen again went quiet as if the memories of happier times magnified the bad and she couldn't recall one without comparing it to the other.

Maggie listened as she recounted more early memories, mostly good, but with the occasional negative event, like the death of her Grandfather when she was twelve. Generally Karen's early time line would concur with most children of comparable age and she was able to talk about events with ease and clarity. But Maggie knew there was much to follow and as they left the exercise to continue at their next session, both women were well aware that the time line would plunge dramatically before too much longer.

****

Her first day back at work since the visit to Scotland, had passed in its usual flurry of busyness and Maggie found herself looking forward to a long walk with Ben followed by a quiet evening flopped in front of the television. Ben certainly agreed with those plans and intended giving his mistress no peace until after the walk.

'Come on then boy,' he didn't need any coaxing, 'it's a lovely evening; a long walk will do us both good.'

Maggie had parked her car outside the front door only a few minutes earlier. Another car had pulled up behind; well more of what Sue would call a 'rust bucket on wheels,' to which she had paid little attention. Now stepping outside with Ben, the car was still there with its male driver sitting at the wheel watching as Maggie locked the door and set off towards the fields where Ben could run free.

The driver climbed out of his car and began to follow at a distance, down to the end of the row of houses and over the stile into the fields. He kept at a reasonable distance behind them to avoid being noticed until Maggie was well away from the streets and approaching a copse, Ben's favourite spot.

Bending down to let him off his lead, she threw his rubber bone into the trees for their customary game of fetch. It was only then that she became aware of someone approaching from behind and she stepped off the path to let him pass, assuming it was another early evening walker, minus a dog.

The man stopped, uncomfortably close. Maggie took a step back; he stayed on the path, staring at her with a look of contempt on his face.

'Was there something you wanted?' She forced herself to sound calm even though her heart was pounding high in her chest and fear beginning to throb in her head.

He did not respond but continued to stare, his hard eyes as cold as steel. The silence was even more frightening than anything he could say.

'Ben, Ben!' Maggie's voice trembled with mounting fear.

The man lunged forward and grabbed both of her arms. She screamed and tried to pull away as his fingers dug into her arms in a vice like grip.

'A warning,' the man broke his silence with a growl, gripping her so tightly she wasn't sure if the tears welling up were from pain or terror.

His acrid breath assaulted her nostrils and his hard stare seemed to hold her as tightly as his hands.

'Leave Julie alone. Keep your bloody nose out, bitch. Do you understand? A warning, d'you hear?' At this the man pushed her to the ground then turned to hurry back the way he had come.

Maggie twisted her knee as she fell, landing in a heap on the ground, shaking and stunned at what had just occurred.

Ben came running from the trees, his tail wagging, the bone in his mouth. Sensing something was wrong he sniffed and whined then sat close beside his mistress as she clung to his neck and wept.

The incident was over in just a minute or two but it felt like an hour. Managing to stand to assess any damage she found she could walk although in pain. Her arms were sore and she still trembled. There was no sign of the assailant so she put Ben's lead back on and keeping him close, made her way back home.

Maggie felt physically sick. A hot sweet drink would be the sensible thing but she couldn't face it. Sitting, still in shock and with her eyes closed, the whole scenario replayed in her mind. Feeling the cold and turning up the fire, she started to reason with herself. 'Be practical Mags. You're all right, not really hurt. It was only to scare you.' Then she burst into tears again and reached out to grab the phone.

Sue's voice had never sounded so good and as she tried to tell her friend the words wouldn't come. Her friend heard the emotion in Maggie's voice and said simply, 'I'm on my way.'

'Let me call the police,' Sue pleaded after hearing the story.

'No, please…it won't help and it might make things worse.'

'Worse, for whom?'

'You know I can't tell you Sue. Please don't ask.'

Sue didn't need to ask, already putting two and two together.

'If you can't tell me then it's to do with a client and last time you 'couldn't tell me' it was that madman who came to the surgery.'

Maggie said nothing: she couldn't think logically but was grateful for Sue's presence.

Sue had arrived within minutes of the phone call and insisted on the hot sweet tea and put a cold water bandage on her knee to stop the swelling, then had listened to her friend's garbled account of events.

When Maggie was calmer Sue again suggested calling the police.

'It was an assault; you've been injured as well as shocked.'

'No…it would only be my word against his and I don't want all the hassle, really.'

'Well at least take the day off tomorrow. I can tell Dr. Williams and you can have a quiet day to get over it.'

'No, really I'll be fine. I'd rather go into work instead of moping about here thinking about it and I don't have a heavy workload tomorrow.'

'We'll see how you are in the morning, but for tonight I'm staying in that spare room of yours so I'll just go and make the bed up while you finish your tea.'

'You make a good job of it,' Maggie managed a smile.

'What?' Sue asked

'Acting like my mother.'

'Huh, and here was I going to suggest a bottle of wine and some chocolate, both medicinal of course.'

'The wine's in the fridge and I've got just the thing,' she replied, reaching for Walter's chocolates.

****

Maggie slept better than expected. Having Sue in the next room was a comfort but she didn't really think that Julie's husband would risk confronting her again, yet the thought that he knew where she lived was unnerving. A hot shower helped to relieve some of the aches and pains but noticing the bruises on both arms made her shudder. Her knee was better than it might have been, still a little swollen but not as painful, Sue had done a good job with the bandaging.

Over breakfast Sue agreed that perhaps it would be better for Maggie to go into work, it would distract her thoughts and she promised to have a chat to Tom Williams about it.

As expected, Tom was horrified and like Sue wanted to ring the police immediately.

'Please, no,' Maggie begged, 'I really don't want to make a fuss. It probably sounds worse than it actually was.'

'But this man is dangerous and he knows where you live. What if he comes back again?'

'He won't, I'm sure. He just wanted to scare me off but I will be more careful now.'

Tom examined her knee and the bruises on her arms. Satisfied that the injuries were not serious, he looked sternly at her,

'I'm going to have Jim Chambers taken off our list. He can go elsewhere to find a GP now.'

'Wouldn't it be better to wait? I don't want any of this to fall back on Julie. I need to see her again and try to find out exactly what the situation is. I'm not sure even she knows how volatile he can be.'

'When do you see her again?'

'Next Monday. I'm sure she'll come, she seems quite determined.'

'Well keep me informed won't you? When you feel the time's right I'll have him removed from the practice list.'

Tom left, and almost immediately Sue appeared.

'How are you now?'

'Just the same as when you saw me fifteen minutes ago.'

'Okay, okay. Now you're not going on any home visits today are you?'

'No, like I told you last night, I've got an easy day today, a few phone calls to make and one or two bits of paperwork. I'll be fine,' she smiled at her friend's concern.

'Right, I'll bring you a nice cup of coffee and then you know where I am if you need anything.'

'Thanks mother.' Maggie laughed, feeling grateful for such good support.

Most of the day was, thankfully, uneventful and the previous day's encounter with Jim Chambers was already becoming a memory. She was determined not to be intimidated in any way by Julie Chamber's husband.

Chapter 12

'Hi Tony, its Maggie Sayer here. Remember me?'
'Hey yes, of course I remember, how're you doing?'

'Oh I'm just fine thanks. You sound pretty chirpy yourself, how are things with you?'

'I'm doing really well, all credit to you of course.'

'No, mostly your own doing but thanks anyway. Tony… I have a favour to ask but feel free to say no if you want, I'm not sure if it'll even pan out yet.'

'Intriguing, tell me more.'

'It involves a client, so I can't tell you anything much, you know that, but I'm pretty sure he'd benefit from meeting you and perhaps going to one of your meetings. Do you think that's possible? I haven't suggested it to him yet so feel free to say no. It's a bit unconventional but he's having problems which I think you could help with more than I can, or even a specialist counsellor come to think of it.'

Tony didn't need to consider it.

'Sure Maggie, my pleasure. Give this bloke my number and he can get in touch directly. There're meetings every day so we should be able to fix something up.'

'Tony, you're brilliant, thanks ever so much. If he doesn't want to go for it I'll let you know, but I hope he will. I see him again in a couple of days so his call could come any time after that. Bless you Tony, bye.'

Putting the phone down, Maggie's thoughts turned to Peter. If he wasn't already an alcoholic he was very close to becoming one. Hopefully Tony could help him. Although they had only had a couple of meetings, there was something about Peter that Maggie liked. His company made her feel almost nervous there were one or two rather unprofessional thoughts which, although Sue might approve, horrified

Maggie.

For most of the day, which had thankfully been uneventful, Maggie had managed not to think about her encounter with Jim Chambers and when leaving for home she was determined not to let it upset her. As a precaution she would take Ben on a different route that evening, but would in no way let Julie's husband intimidate her.

****

Julie Chambers seemed to be nervous and on edge when they met that afternoon. Maggie thought it could be reaction to their last meeting when Julie had been so open but there seemed to be no signs of regret at having shared so much of herself previously. Indeed Julie was again very honest about her situation and expressed feelings with a certain new insight that hadn't been apparent before. Maybe it was the fact that their session was on the afternoon, she could have been anxious to get home for her children. Maggie felt it best not to challenge this apparent nervousness or to tell her client about her own encounter with Jim Chambers; it was history now, she had decided to put it out of her mind and forget it ever happened, telling Julie would only add to her already heavy burdens.

When Julie left, Maggie didn't feel they had made a great deal of progress except in the strengthening of their bond. The two women had reached a point of mutual trust and respect, which could only enhance the counselling relationship.

When the day's work was at an end, Maggie left for home. The evenings were noticeably lighter now and her thoughts turned to plans she had for her little garden. A trip to the garden centre was on the agenda for the weekend to buy a few bedding plants to brighten up the borders, and perhaps one or two shrubs suitable for the patio pots.

Opening her front door, Maggie knew instinctively that something was wrong. A sickly smell filled the house together with an unusual silence, rather than the boisterous welcome which Ben never failed to give. Her attention was drawn immediately towards the little bay window where Ben lay on his side, whimpering softly and trying unsuccessfully to rise and greet her.

'Ben!' she exclaimed, running to him and kneeling beside her beloved pet, stroking his head to soothe him. His breathing was rapid and shallow and his muzzle was wet with a white frothy substance. He had obviously vomited and by his agitated state seemed to be in considerable pain. Running outside to the car she opened the door, then hurried back to lift Ben and carry him awkwardly to the car. Maggie struggled to get him on the back seat, then swiftly locked the house and set off to the vets, all the way talking to Ben, reassuring herself as much as him.

Maggie's obvious panic on bursting through the door at the vets, spurred the staff into immediate action, they helped to lift him from the car and within only two or three minutes, Ben was laid on the vet's examining table being thoroughly checked over. Not wanting to hamper the vet's progress Maggie stood back against the wall with a pale face and tears streaming down her cheeks. She couldn't understand much of the jargon they spoke to each other, but their expressions and the speed with which they worked told her it was serious. One of the nurses eventually turned to guide her out of the room. Taking her into a small anteroom, away from the main waiting area she offered a box of tissues.

The badge on her tunic read 'Helena, Veterinary Nurse' and she spoke quietly, slowly choosing her words.

'It looks as if Ben has eaten some kind of poison.'

Maggie gasped.

'The vet is going to give him a saline fluid orally, to try to make him vomit some more. We don't want to give any kind of anaesthetic at this point as we can't tell what poison is already in his system, so it's better if we can manage without.'

'Will he be alright?' Maggie asked the inevitable question, fearing the answer.

'It's a bit early to say, but we don't think he can have ingested the poison too long ago, as he's still conscious, so let's take that as a positive sign shall we?' Helena seemed to know what she was talking about, which inspired some hope.

'Will you be alright if I go back in?' Helena asked, 'I'll let you know as soon as I can how things are.'

'Yes, thank you.' The nurse silently slipped out of the room leaving Maggie trying to work out what on earth could have happened.

After what seemed like an age the door opened and the vet himself came in to talk to her.

'You can relax Mrs. Sayer, Ben's going to be fine.'

The tension drained from her body but she still trembled, this time with relief.

'I'd like to keep him overnight to monitor his progress but I'm pretty confident he'll be as large as life in a couple of days.'

'Can I see him?'

'Of course, Helena's just cleaning him up then she'll be straight in to get you. Poor chap will probably feel sorry for himself for a while; we've had to be quite rough on him to make him vomit. There were signs of raw meat and a strong acid smell suggesting it was poisoning. Has he been out alone today, perhaps he could have eaten poison set for vermin?'

'No....I never let him go out alone, he's been in since lunch time while I was working and I don't give him raw meat.' Maggie was thinking of the smell at home when she found Ben, realising that someone must have deliberately pushed poisoned raw meat through the letterbox.

'Well I really think you should report this to the police. Had Ben been alone for much longer it would almost certainly have been fatal. It was lucky that you found him when you did.'

Just then the nurse came back into the room smiling, 'He's ready for visitors now.' Maggie wasted no time in following on.

Poor Ben was looking quite doleful. Most of his upper body had been washed, a procedure hated at the best of times. Laying still he gallantly managed a couple of tail thumps when he saw Maggie, inviting sympathy and a fuss which made them both feel better.

After thanking the staff, she left the vet's to go home, but first she would call in at Sue's flat. Her mind was spinning; she needed someone to talk to and who better than Sue.

Chapter 13

Sue was outraged when Maggie finished her story. 'It's that bloody Chambers bloke again!' she railed.

'I'm inclined to agree with you, but we've no proof. Is it worth going to the police?'

'Yes is the short answer to that… and we tell them about last time too.' Sue was insistent and after giving a lecture, colourfully outlining what punishment she would inflict on Jim Chambers, she went back to the house with her friend to help clean up the mess left in the panic to get to the vets. Sue stayed well into the evening, sharing a mountain of hot buttered toast, ideal comfort food, and not going home until Maggie insisted she didn't need a babysitter. The next day was Saturday and they arranged to meet to go to the police station before going to the vets to pick up Ben. An early phone call had assured them that he was doing well and could be taken home later that morning.

Maggie felt a little self-conscious walking into the police station, even though Sue was beside her. They told the desk sergeant briefly why they had come, and then waited for someone from CID to come and hear their story.

Sue's eyes were everywhere.

'Wow, this is the place to be on a Saturday morning. Don't you think a uniform does something for a man?'

'Shh,' Maggie giggled, 'Someone will hear you.'

'Hmm, with a bit of luck.'

Sue's face fell however when a short, slightly overweight officer came to invite them into an interview room. He had a round face with a pleasant smile and friendly manner but Sue, who had hoped for nothing less than a George Clooney look alike, couldn't see past his shape, emphasized she thought by a comb over hairstyle, hiding his premature balding.

'What a disappointment,' she sighed, prompting a swift dig in the ribs from her companion.

Detective sergeant Hurst, as he introduced himself, proved to be anything but a disappointment, professionally at least. Far from making Maggie feel as if she was making a fuss over nothing, he took her story very seriously, making notes of both incidents. He asked about any injuries received during the attack and if a doctor could verify them. His main concern however was that there had been no witnesses to either event.

'I think it would be almost impossible to take any prints from your letter box, so unless a neighbour saw this man at your door there's little we can do. The same is true of your own encounter with him. If there were no witnesses who saw him approach you, we have no evidence and the CPS wouldn't agree to proceeding with any kind of case.'

'So really I'm wasting your time?' Maggie asked, 'And unless he does something else, in front of witnesses, there's nothing that can be done?'

'That's not quite what I'm saying,' DS Hurst continued, 'As far as charges go we're not going to get anywhere, but I fully intend to visit this man, just to let him know we're aware of what he's up to. Sometimes that's all that's necessary and he'll back off. You've certainly done the right thing in reporting it and if there is anything else then let us know straight away won't you?'

'Yes, thank you.' she felt better knowing that something would be done.

'Perhaps you'd feel safer carrying a personal alarm when you're out dog walking?' DS Hurst suggested.

'She's got one.' Sue interrupted, 'but doesn't use it.'

'I'll search it out and keep it with me,' she promised, thanking him again as they left.

****

The vet's surgery was full of Saturday morning patients. The room was noisy with anxious meows, low threatening growls, panting, and the sound of paws skidding on linoleum. Maggie felt much calmer than on her visit yesterday and waited patiently with Sue for the nurse to fetch Ben. They heard his bark as he approached a welcome sound after the shock of nearly losing him the night before. Ben added considerably to the din in the waiting room almost pulling the poor nurse over in his hurry to reach Maggie. He looked so much better it was amazing. After brief instructions on his care for the next few days and making another appointment for a week's time, they set off home. Plans for the rest of the weekend had now changed. They both needed a quiet day or two, lazing around the house enjoying each other's company. Sue complained that she felt like a gooseberry even though she too could hardly stop fussing him.

With her faithful dog home and the police looking into her troubles with Julie's husband, Maggie could relax again and settle back into some kind of routine.

****

Jim Chambers was away from home as usual. He went out every day, but particularly Saturdays when the kids were at home, he couldn't stand their whingeing on. Sundays were better, the mornings were spent in the pub with his mates, and then after a good roast dinner he invariably slept the afternoon away while Julie took the kids out to the park or wherever, he didn't really care. Today, however Jim was at his garage, his own space, a secret place where he didn't have to put up with anyone he didn't want around. It was a cheap little lock–up, probably because it was so run down and in a rough neighbourhood, but that didn't bother Jim. It served its purpose, not to garage the car, but to keep stores in. His own little empire...well, not all of it, most of the stuff was stored for his mates but he was creaming off his own share little by little, and why shouldn't he? It was one thing helping mates out but they got to expect it and Jim didn't like being taken for granted. So it was only fair that he took his share of the goods as well as the paltry sum they gave him for all his hard work, he deserved more. And there was always a ready market for the cheap booze and cigarettes not to mention the pirated DVD's. Supply and demand, that was the name of the game, it was providing a service really which one day he intended to expand. This was okay for now but it was becoming boring. Jim wasn't one to put much effort into anything for such little profit and the time was coming when he would go it alone. He'd built up a few contacts now so why shouldn't he use them and widen his horizons at the same time? The travelling appealed to him. Driving to the continent to pick up the stuff himself could be a laugh and the profits would all go into his pocket, then he could start living. The thought of leaving Julie and the kids was appealing, he'd done his bit by marrying her when she got pregnant, but it was time to think about himself now, he deserved a better life. Who knows what heights he could have reached if he hadn't been tied down so early in life. Julie had been a looker then, now she was dull. He could have had any girl he'd wanted with his looks, but the old man had put the pressure on to marry Julie and 'settle down.' Well a bloke has a right to a better life if the opportunity comes along he reckoned. The family thing wasn't for him and now Julie was seeing this counsellor bitch too. He was fairly sure his wife knew nothing of his little sideline, but he didn't like the thought of an outsider sniffing around, asking questions. Of course he was pretty sure he'd scared her off now, she'd be too busy crying over that stupid dog to interfere in other people's business.

Jim opened a bottle of whiskey, just sampling the goods. Smiling he lit the gas heater at the back of the garage, there was no electricity supply, another reason why it was cheap, then he settled down to plan his future flicking through some of the magazines he kept there, just a taste of the good things ahead.

****

It was still cold for spring and Janet Rea was swaddled in winter woollies for her trip to the supermarket. It was a chore she no longer enjoyed; making simple decisions, even what food to buy seemed such an effort, but she'd forced herself to get out of the house if only for an hour or so to get the weekly shopping. The car park was almost full, the only spot available was in the farthest corner. Before leaving home Janet had made a list, but typically for her these days, it had been left on the kitchen table so she began to steer the uncooperative trolley around every aisle in the hope of not forgetting anything, if only to avoid a second visit. It wasn't as busy as it might have been and Janet felt pleased that she had completed a full circuit of the supermarket and was in the queue within an hour. Standing in line behind a young woman with a small boy, she began to unload her purchases onto the conveyor belt when from behind, a male voice took her by surprise as a man pushed past her to get to the woman and child in front. He had brushed against Janet's arm and was standing uncomfortably close. Almost immediately the dizziness began. His appearance automatically registered in her mind; a shaven head and tattoos on his neck and bare upper arms, she felt nauseous, but what was more evocative was the smell clinging to him, a distinctive mixture of sawdust and putty, presumably he had come from some kind of work as a joiner. It made her head spin, taking her back to her childhood and those harrowing memories of her abuser. Common sense told her that it was nothing to do with this poor man, but inside she was screaming like a cornered animal. Janet felt the heat rising to her neck and face and loosening her scarf, a burning sensation swept over her as if hundreds of hot needles were puncturing her skin. She couldn't breathe properly; the air was dry and hot and for one embarrassing moment she feared she might pass out. Leaning heavily on the trolley she tried to concentrate; the symptoms had caught her by surprise before and she now recognized them as a panic attack. Closing her eyes, she tried to think what Maggie had told her to do in this situation. Occupy your thoughts on something mundane, like counting. Opening her eyes and forcing herself to turn away from the man to look at the checkout shelf, she began counting the packets of chewing gum on a rack. 'This is ridiculous,' she told herself as another wave of nausea swept over her. 'He just happens to look like *him*. It'll pass, I can cope, the poor man has done nothing….it's a trigger, that's what Maggie called it, it'll pass.'

The man and his wife had paid for their shopping and were moving away from the checkout.

'Are you all right love?' The girl on the till asked, 'You look quite flushed.'

'I'm fine, it's just rather hot in here, I'll be okay when I get some air.' Janet didn't want a fuss, she could barely remember packing her trolley but somehow she managed to get outside where the blast of cold air was a welcome relief. Sitting in the car feeling angry with herself and rather stupid, it was several minutes before she could even think about driving. It wasn't only that the man had looked so much like him, she saw many men with shaven heads and tattoos, it was more the smell, it had taken her right back in time to a place she didn't want to go or even think about. When her breathing had settled and she felt calmer, Janet was exhausted. It was all she could do to turn on the car engine and head for home.

Chapter 14

She was standing in a windowless room; the only light from a faint dusty bulb hanging from the ceiling, obscured even more by a heavy shade. Dust motes floated in the beams of light and the still, airless space made her heart beat rapidly. The man had his back to her. She knew him… but she did not know him. Maggie moved towards him. Her legs felt solid, as if made of lead and her progress was slow. The man didn't move. He was taller than she remembered with broad shoulders and fair curls reaching down to his collar. She raised her hand to touch his hair. It was soft; she had always thought such hair was wasted on a man. He didn't turn as she expected he would, so Maggie slowly moved around to face him. He was very still and his eyes were closed.

'Chris…' her voice was a whisper. Touching his cheek, it felt cold as ice yet it almost burnt her fingers.

His eyes opened and she gasped. Behind his eyelids instead of those laughing blue eyes, there was nothing, darkness; a vacuum. A muted scream began to form in the pit of her stomach but before it could escape from her lips, there was suddenly no oxygen in the room and she struggled to breathe. She was collapsing onto the floor, dissolving, she could no longer see Chris; she needed air…

Maggie wasn't as disturbed by the dream as she would have expected. Curiosity as to why it had come again was what was on her mind. It was the same dream she had for a year or more after Chris had died. Pouring her cereal she decided it was probably just the stress of the last few days and the unpleasant happenings catching up on her. A lazy day was in order. Ben had slept soundly but was now wandering around looking for food.

'A light diet for you, vet's orders, your tummy will be delicate for a while you poor old thing.'

He was unimpressed but settled down at her feet as she ate breakfast.

The dream wouldn't go away. Maggie had never put much store in dreams or interpretations. Although eclectic in her approach to work, she was very much a fan of person centred counselling and a disciple of Carl Rogers and his humanistic theories. Yes, she had studied other approaches to counselling and their theorists but felt most comfortable working with the conscious mind rather than the unconscious. Freud had placed a lot of emphasis on dreams and their meanings and although Maggie had respect for much of Freud's work, there was a big proportion of his theories that she couldn't subscribe to. She decided not to struggle with this one any longer. There had been enough thinking about it in years gone by. A dream is, after all only a dream. Maggie would leave it at that. Ben seemed almost his usual self, remarkable, considering he had nearly died. Before leaving for work in the morning she would ring a joiner and arrange for a box to be fitted inside her letterbox. Ben was too precious to take any risks and until it was done, she would leave him shut in the kitchen with his bed against the radiator so he didn't have too much to complain about.

****

Without consciously realising it, Karen had colour coded her time line and looking at the events recorded the previous week, she could see a pattern. Her early childhood memories were noted in yellow, orange and sky blue, positive memories of happy times, written in her neat fastidious handwriting, the words uniformly half an inch above the line in bright colours. Below the line she had changed to a gray felt tipped pen when writing about an unpleasant stay in hospital and the death of a much loved Grandfather when she was twelve. Looking at her handiwork now she realised she had only just scratched the surface and the exercise had prompted many memories over the last week. Lying in bed at night, sleep eluded her even though she was weary from the physical activities of the day, which she readily admitted was used as a distraction. Childhood memories would take over, tumbling into her mind like long lost possessions unearthed from a dusty attic. She told Maggie of this, asking if it was part of the exercise.

'It's not a planned part of this kind of work, more like a by-product, inevitable as you trawl your mind for past memories.' Maggie smiled at the younger woman, concerned that she was able to continue.

'Are you sure you want to carry on with this? We could try something else if you wish?'

'No,' Karen replied, 'I'm quite happy to go on. It hasn't upset me, just made me sort of reflective I suppose, but then I haven't got to the upsetting parts yet have I?'

As if to emphasize her determination to continue, Karen picked up a thick black felt tipped pen, pulled the pad towards her and began to write below the line. Carefully forming the letters she said, 'I really want to get this done today Maggie. These thoughts have been rattling around in my head all week, a bit like one of those cheesy tunes that you hate but can't stop singing over and over. It was when I reached my teens that things started to go wrong...I've thought about it all week and I just have to get it all down.'

Both women were silent for several minutes, the only noise the scratching of the pen on paper. Karen wrote steadily at first but her speed increased to keep pace with the words flowing through her mind. She was writing more than notes or headings of her memories, Maggie could see the expressive words spreading down the page as Karen frantically raced ahead as if the thoughts would evaporate if she didn't write them quickly enough. In her mind's eye she could see her parents but not in the happy, early years. They were constantly bickering, often over money but often over things Karen couldn't understand even in her early teens. She wrote about her father's drinking and how unpredictable he became after a night at the pub. Many times her mother asked if she would take Mike out to the park or upstairs to play where she would put on her little transistor radio so he wouldn't hear the noise of their parents' shouting downstairs. It was only when bruises appeared on her mother's face and body that she became afraid, before that it had been a sadness, a worry perhaps that there might be a divorce, but the bruises signified a change in the family dynamics. From loving both of her parents, Karen moved into a period of having a very real fear of her father, not only for herself but for Mike and her mother too. She had often wondered if she was somehow to blame, or if there was something she could do to turn the clock back to happier times.

And now, years later, here she was sitting in Maggie's office writing down things that had been pushed to the back of her mind, scribbling furiously now as if all the hurt, anger and sadness flowed through the pen and onto the paper.

As Karen paused to think, Maggie took the opportunity to draw her client back to the present day.

'If you want to continue the writing that's fine, but perhaps you'd like to take the pad home with you and work with it there?'

'Yes, I'm sorry. You don't want to sit here and watch me write I'm sure.'

'It's not that Karen, the writing's certainly a good tool for you to express your feelings, but I'm a little concerned that you're moving too quickly.'

'I suppose it is getting rather frantic. Gosh, look at my writing, I can hardly read it myself. Did you want to read it Maggie?'

'Only if that's what you want?'

'Oh yes, it'll probably make more sense than my rattling on all the time.'

Maggie smiled and offered,

'I could make a copy for myself so you can take the pad home if you like? I'll keep it under lock and key, it'll be quite secure.'

'That's fine...so what now?'

'Well, last time we looked at some of the events above the line but they seemed to have tapered off and we're well below it now. How about telling me about this gray time when things began to change. You were what, thirteen or fourteen then?'

Karen nodded; putting down the pen which she had been gripping so tightly her hand was almost fused onto it, and allowing her thoughts to drift back to her early teens and the dark days when her life began to change.

****

Maggie's next client that morning was Peter Lloyd, a man who had been in her thoughts quite often during the last week. His candour had impressed her and the acknowledgment of his increasing reliance on alcohol was a good sign. Hopefully this problem could be resolved before it became any worse but Maggie knew she was no longer the one to help him.

The phone call to Tony had secured the option she hoped Peter would take. Tony had been a client after his own lengthy struggle with alcohol and the picture he had painted of his spiralling downfall had been a testament to how this addiction could ruin lives. Tony had already lost his wife and children. The alcoholism had put him into debt and his home was repossessed. When he first came to Maggie he had been dry for several months and living temporarily in a hostel where he was being encouraged to make plans for the future. Some help was still necessary in the early days of his new life, to build confidence where none existed. Maggie had had the privilege of being able to provide that help. Now Tony was deeply involved in Alcoholics Anonymous, giving generously of his time to help others get the support they needed. The way he had turned his own life around was admirable and if anyone could help Peter, Maggie felt it would be Tony.

It was over two weeks since Peter had seen his counsellor. His last appointment had been cancelled as it coincided with a meeting at work. Peter would have much preferred to see Maggie but his partners had been so good to him and flexible of late that he felt duty bound to give his work commitment priority. Now waiting rather nervously for her to appear at the office door, he was unsure whether his revelations at their last meeting might have changed her attitude to him. For some reason Peter wanted this lady to like him, or at least not to dislike him.

Her welcome seemed genuinely warm and friendly as she asked how he had been and remarked that he looked in better health than at their last meeting. Peter did feel better but last time they had spoken had been rather an emotional encounter, he was more in control today, surprisingly so.

Peter felt almost duty bound to justify the issues they had discussed previously and quickly realised that he was talking too much, without making a great deal of sense. Maggie listened attentively for a while but eventually felt the need to interrupt.

'You don't seem as focussed today. Is there something bothering you?'

'Yes,' came the rather abrupt reply followed by a few moments silence in which he seemed quite agitated.

'I don't know if I want to continue our sessions, I know we're only just beginning in a way, but I've already felt the benefit of talking to you, I feel I need to pull myself together now. No, I feel that I'm able to pull myself together, that's different isn't it?'

'Yes quite different. I was actually going to make a suggestion today about seeing someone else…'

'Don't take this personally Maggie, I don't want to see another counsellor, I think perhaps this isn't the kind of help I need at the moment.'

'I agree,' she smiled, 'But it wasn't another counsellor I was going to suggest.'

She then began to tell Peter a little about Tony, explaining that what she was suggesting wasn't in anyway an official referral, and was in fact, a little unorthodox. Tony however was a trustee member of AA and therefore an informal meeting between the two men could perhaps help Peter's situation.

'Do you think I'm an alcoholic?' Peter sounded horrified.

'No Peter, I don't, but I think it's a fear that's in the back of your mind. You have talked about your growing dependency on alcohol and you're obviously concerned about what might happen if you don't come to terms with this. Have I got that right?'

'I suppose you have really....'

'Then I'm not the one to help you in this. I think we both recognise that. I'll give you Tony's phone number and leave it up to you whether you'd like to contact him or not. I haven't told him anything about you at all, so you don't have to worry on that score. All he knows is that a man may call him and mention my name. It'll be up to you to take it from there.' Maggie didn't want Peter to feel that she was washing her hands of him, even though it had been his suggestion that the counselling sessions should end, so she emphasized that she would always be available to see him again if he wished, telling him he could make an appointment directly without having to get another referral from his GP.

Peter seemed more relaxed and asked a few more questions about Tony, which Maggie did her best to answer without breaching any confidentiality. Before their time was finished, he seemed resolved to ring Tony to pursue this avenue further. He thanked Maggie for her time and patience, seeming a little reluctant to leave. Maggie also felt unusually awkward, eventually offering her hand as they stood to say goodbye. Peter held her hand in both of his, studying her expression as if looking for something. She smiled, wishing him well and feeling unexpectedly sad to think this would probably be the last time she would see him.

Chapter 15

Maggie was in a strangely sombre mood for the rest of the day. Joining Sue in the staff room over lunchtime the conversation inevitably turned to their visit to the police station.

'I know it was only on Saturday but do you think I should ring DS Hurst to see if he's seen Jim Chambers yet?'

'No point,' Sue answered, 'Alan's off until Wednesday.'

'Alan, who's Alan?'

'Whoops.' Sue grinned at her 'I know something you don't know' look.

'Out with it.' Maggie demanded.

'Well I was going to tell you, but there's hardly been chance has there?'

'There's a full twenty minutes left of your lunch break, so come on, all the details.'

'Okay, if you're twisting my arm. After I left you on Saturday I had a bit of shopping to do and I had to go to the post office to tax my car. Well you know how long the queues are on a Saturday and I found myself standing behind your DS Hurst. After exchanging pleasantries, I had to be nice to him since he's dealing with your case, we began chatting in general and he's really not all that bad. We stood for nearly thirty minutes in that queue and we were both gasping for a coffee after that, so Alan asked if I'd like to join him at that little café over the road. It wouldn't have been polite to refuse, so I went.'

'You are a fast worker. So did he look any more like George Clooney out of office hours?'

'Ha ha, he's really quite an amusing guy. And he's not that short when he's sitting down. I thought he was quite cute really, so when he asked me if I was doing anything on Sunday, I freed up my social calendar to go out for lunch with him.'

'I do believe you've got a twinkle in your eye Sue. Are you seeing him again?'

'Well I did feel obliged to offer to cook for him in return for Sunday lunch, so he's coming at eight tonight.'

'Three days on the trot. My my, your mother will be buying that hat after all.'

Sue's only response was a wistful sigh as she appeared to drift away into her own little world leaving Maggie speechless.

****

Peter wasted no time in contacting Tony. As Maggie had promised Tony knew nothing about him except that he would be ringing on her recommendation. Peter took an instant liking to this man. His voice and manner over the phone were both relaxed and affable, so when he invited Peter to attend one of the AA meetings as an observer, he readily agreed.

The two men shook hands. They were of a similar age and height, although Tony had the presence of a much older man: confident and cheerful, with a wisdom gained from life experience. It was early evening with over an hour before the meeting. They had agreed to meet in a coffee shop close to the church hall where AA leased a room. Peter didn't quite know where to begin so was grateful when Tony took the lead and began their conversation by mentioning Maggie. He obviously thought highly of her and spoke openly about the part she had played in the rebuilding of his life. Peter was surprised that Maggie hadn't mentioned the fact that he'd been a client, he'd assumed that she knew him through her work contacts. Tony spoke about himself almost objectively, without emotion and in no way seeking sympathy or indeed any other reaction. His story was related concisely and clearly, as fact and without embellishment.

Peter studied the coffee cup he was hugging, surprised by the honesty and also the similarities he could identify with in his own life. There were questions he wanted to ask but held back, not wanting to appear intrusive. Almost as if telepathic, Tony invited him to ask any questions about what he had told him or about AA in general.

Peter responded gratefully and was impressed by Tony's clarity and wisdom in explaining a little of the history of AA and its present day functioning. It was an organization grown out of the desperation of alcoholics in the 1930's to seek help in changing their ways. He described how sympathetic medical practitioners had promoted the disease concept of alcoholism and how religion played a major part in successful recovery. The organization was founded with a word of mouth program and later formalized by the writing of the book 'Alcoholics Anonymous,' known affectionately today as the 'big book'.

Tony asked if he had heard about the 'twelve step program' of AA

'I've heard of it, but I can't say I know what it's all about.' Peter replied

'I won't bore you by reciting all of the steps,' Tony smiled, 'But the main points include making an admission of powerlessness, some kind of moral inventory of your life and the asking of help from a higher power. These are three of the things all members of AA must do, their responsibility if you like. No one can change them except God, or whatever higher power they choose to believe in, and it's worked for countless alcoholics over the years, including me.'

This was perhaps the only point at which Tony displayed any emotion; his former life was obviously a painful memory. After a moment or two's silence, Peter asked, 'You said you lease a room but where does the money come from. Is AA a charity?'

'No, not as such, it's an autonomous and self-supporting group. Having said that, there are no membership fees either, we rely on member donations but obviously no one is barred if they can't contribute.'

'Well, what about leadership?'

'We have trusted members, men and women who are usually long term members of a local group and have the desire to give back some of the help they've received. We also have a system of sponsors, where a new member is partnered by a sponsor, usually someone who has been dry for a considerable time. The sponsor can pass on his experience and provide valuable support, particularly in the early days. We very much take one day at a time in AA.' The meeting was due to start and despite their lengthy conversation, Peter was still unprepared for what he was about to experience.

A group of seven or eight people were standing in the church car park, smoking and drinking coffee. Tony was greeted with enthusiastic hugs and handshakes from this entire group and when he was introduced as a friend, Peter too was grasped by the arm or embraced by both men and women of all ages. Mugs of steaming coffee were pressed into their hands as they entered and made their way towards a couple of empty chairs in what was already becoming an overcrowded room.

By the appointed hour, every seat was taken and people were standing or half-hitched upon tables at the sides of the room. There was a friendly buzz and enthusiastic greetings continued to be made over heads and along the rows as friends spotted each other, all of which contributed to a warm and relaxed atmosphere. Order was called for and an immediate silence settled over the group. The day's meeting was a general open meeting with opportunity for all members to share experiences and ask for advice, or give a word of encouragement. Peter couldn't ever remember seeing such an eclectic group of people gathered in the same room, yet there was such an obvious unity and genuine friendship. Well-dressed middle-aged ladies sat beside teenage girls with piercings and tattoos. Unshaved men in worn jogging suits and trainers, who looked total strangers to soap and water, slapped the backs of white-collar workers, sharing a joke or an animated conversation.

When a member spoke, respect was shown, whoever he or she was. What they said was digested and commented upon in the most sensitive of ways, giving encouragement, praise or just a 'well done' for having the courage to share.

Yes, he did hear that phrase 'My name is…and I'm an alcoholic.' and he was almost moved to tears in every case.

At the end of the meeting the members dispersed with the same enthusiasm as they had arrived. Peter was stunned. Tony's participation in the meeting had been authoritative yet gentle, increasing Peter's regard for him, and leaving him at a total loss for words. They sat on a bench opposite the church in the fading evening light and for a few moments neither man spoke.

'Awesome,' Peter eventually said. 'I feel privileged to have been there, thanks Tony.'

Tony smiled, not knowing much of the other man's circumstances but recognising the obvious impact the evening had had upon him, was glad to have helped.

Throughout the meeting Peter's attention had been frequently drawn to a little man, sitting nodding and smiling and cheering for all those who spoke. The man was younger than he was and there was something familiar about him. He asked Tony if he knew who he was.

'His name's Ken. A super little chap but it's nothing short of a miracle that he's still around. You may have seen him wandering the town a couple of years back. He was a homeless drunk, a harmless man, but his condition became so bad that he was difficult to help. In his younger days they say he'd been some kind of executive in the finance world, hard to believe now isn't it? Ken was an amusing character for a couple of years and most people accepted him for what he was. Then his drinking got worse. Sleeping on the streets didn't help and even the charitable institutions had to ban him because he became so unpalatable to be near. He was unwashed, unshaven and incontinent. It really was difficult to look at him without retching and the smell….diabolical.

It was obvious that he wouldn't see another winter through; in fact I think he was probably in his last few weeks when the Salvation Army took him in. He had frostbite in both hands and feet, lucky to still have them, and was all but malnourished. The Army cleaned him up and looked after him. They have a hostel in town, great work they do there, and they took Ken in, nursing him back to health and sobriety. It would be a happy ending except for the fact that he's now permanently brain damaged with so many years of alcohol abuse. But he's happy and he feels at home in AA meetings, he's one of us, a brother who's trodden the same road we all have. In many ways he's a kind of mascot. We support and protect him and Ken looks upon us as his family.'

Peter was more grateful than it was possible to say. The things he had witnessed today had been a real eye opener and had given him plenty of thinking to do. His own situation was more in perspective now than it had been for a long time. The men parted with Tony giving an open invitation to ring again at any time, an invitation he may well take up. Peter went home with his mind reeling from the evening's events and more than enough to occupy his thoughts.

Chapter 16

Janet had begun her counselling session by relating the panic attack she had experienced in the supermarket.

'Did you try any of the tools we had talked about?' Maggie asked.

'Yes, and there were thirty two packets of spearmint chewing gum and twelve boxes of throat pastilles on the rack next to the till,' Janet smiled. 'But you were right, expecting the symptoms and understanding what it was really did help. Before when I've had a panic attack it's been so scary, but I felt sort of prepared for this latest one, does that sound silly?'

'Not at all, this whole experience is a learning curve for you and the more we understand our feelings and emotions, the better equipped we are to deal with them. How about the cards we tried last time, did you feel they had helped at all?'

'Oh yes. I've looked at them most days and even added one or two ideas to some of them, look…' Janet brought the cards out from her bag and spread them on the table, as Maggie had done at their last session. On the card they had worked with last time, guilt, Janet had written, '*It is not and never has been my fault.*'

'Amen to that.' Maggie grinned. Perhaps Janet was going to respond well to this more pro-active approach to her problems. A photograph was among the cards, of Janet as a child. The likeness was obvious, the red hair brighter than the adult Janet, and braided into two plaits but the same pale skin, peppered with freckles in the child, now a smooth ivory, emphasizing the high cheek bones and wide green eyes. Gazing for a few moments at the pretty five year old smiling at the camera, her heart ached for her client; even with all her training and experience it was still hard to comprehend how people could treat a child in such a way, knowing how wrong their actions were and how devastating it would be to that child's future.

'Before we move on from the subject of guilt, I think I mentioned last time that it was closely linked with another of the issues you identified, self loathing.'

Janet nodded; there had been times in the last year when she had truly hated herself with a passion. It wasn't easy to explain why, but it had been a powerful emotion and she was keen to hear what Maggie had to say about it, hoping to gain an insight into why she should feel like this.

'I've mentioned the 'inner child' before,' Maggie went on 'and I'm glad to see that you've found a photograph from your childhood. We're all a product of our upbringing and are moulded by what we encounter along the way. The most common analogy we use is that of an onion. It consists of several layers and we too acquire 'layers' as we grow into adulthood. At the centre is our core self, our true self if you like and the layers are added as we grow, shaped by our experiences and the people we are close to, usually parents and other care givers. We have our own core values, but we also absorb from those around us, taking on board their values. These are 'introjected values', they are what others think of us and expect from us, but this is often where problems begin. For example, if a child is constantly told he is stupid and worthless, he will absorb that opinion into his system of values and have a low self esteem. To personalise this for you, the way you were treated as a child has affected your own opinions of yourself. Your system of values has been distorted and consequently you have a very low opinion of your worth as a person. I'm hoping that by understanding what has happened in the past and the reason why things are affecting you now, you will be able to overcome the symptoms you're having at present and move on with your life, taking new values with you.' Maggie stopped speaking, allowing the words to sink in. Janet's brow was furrowed with concentration trying to understand all that she had just heard and after a few moments of silence she nodded, smiling at Maggie, wanting her to continue.

'Have you thought which issue you'd like to work on today?' Maggie felt it was right to move on, aware of their time limitations.

This time Janet picked up the card with *anger* written on it.

'You talked about channelling anger; I think I need to be able to do that. It's very frustrating when I'm angry and not something that's been part of my make up before, but now I can fly off the handle at the least little thing and it leaves me feeling quite bitter. I don't want to turn into a bitter old woman; it's such a destructive emotion.'

'That's good, the very fact that you want to deal with your anger and understand how destructive it can be means that you're part of the way there already. Anger is an emotion that's not only self destructive, it can destroy relationships too. Let's think of a few ways to channel these feelings appropriately shall we?'

Janet nodded, so Maggie picked up a cushion from her chair.

'This cushion is Billy,' she said, noticing her client flinch at the name of her abuser. Pulling up a chair in front of Janet she placed the cushion on it.

'Now, you can tell Billy what you really think of him. We're at the end of the corridor here, so no one can hear and I'll gladly join in with you if it helps. I don't like him much either.'

For a moment Janet looked hesitant.

'You can thump him if you like…this is your opportunity to tell him just what he's done to your life. You're in a safe place here Janet, just you, me and Billy.'

Janet looked directly at the cushion and began. A torrent of profanities, words so alien to her streamed out of her mouth, then standing up and picking up the cushion she thumped it and began wringing each corner in turn.

'You've ruined my life…' Letting rip, hot tears ran down her face and after several minutes of lashing out, she flung the cushion across the room then slumped down exhausted. The tears flowed, but Janet was laughing more than crying. What she had done was so unlike her, a woman usually in control of every emotion, but now there was a rich satisfying feeling of exhilaration, as if she had achieved a great feat, climbing a mountain or running a marathon. Maggie sat, not breaking the silence, waiting for Janet to think about what had just happened and how she felt about it. Eventually Janet turned and grinned.

'I feel like a naughty schoolgirl caught out playing truant.'

'Did it help?' Maggie asked simply.

'Yes, I think it did. It's not something I could do every day. It's a rather silly feeling talking to a cushion like that, but it certainly gets rid of the tension.'

'Good. Perhaps this is something you can do when you're completely alone and in a safe place, another tool for your collection if you like, and I'm glad you felt free enough to try it here with me.' Maggie grinned in a conspiratorial way as if they were partners in crime, then went on, 'There are other ways of channelling anger, some of which can be not only emotionally rewarding but have a constructive element too.'

'What do you mean?' Janet asked.

'Well, a former client once told me how she took her frustrations and anger out on her garden. Taking a firm grip on her pruning shears she would literally attack a shrub, pruning it to within an inch of its life. While doing this, the shrub actually became her abuser, her imagination took over and ran riot.'

Janet chuckled at the thought.

'Other people have found release in physical exercise. Jogging can be quite therapeutic and gives the added benefit of a toned, healthier body. Listening to soothing music as you jog may help to focus on pleasant thoughts. Most exercise can be used in this way; it's a well documented fact that exercise releases endorphins into the system, which are the body's natural 'feel good' hormones. If you're not up to aerobic exercise, even brisk walking can help, again with the side effect of being good for your general health.' Maggie paused, looking at her client and as if reading her thoughts she continued,

'I know, sometimes even getting out of bed can be an effort and that's okay. But if and when you do feel able to tackle some kind of exercise I think you'll find it helps.'

Janet nodded slowly and thoughtfully, experiencing a strange sense of peace running through her body she noticeably relaxed deeper into the chair.

'Are you okay?' Maggie was concerned, 'Do you want to stop now?'

'No,' Janet replied, 'I just have this incredible feeling of becoming lighter. It sounds silly I know, but it's as if I'm waking up and for the first time in months, I really want to get on with my life and put this all behind me.'

****

There was something therapeutic about cleaning. Julie had always enjoyed housework and took pleasure in mundane, repetitive tasks, listening to the radio as she worked. Simon was at school and Chloe asleep upstairs, presenting her with the opportunity to turn out those kitchen cupboards which had been on her 'to do' list for ages. The lemon fragrance of the detergent filled the room and at that moment she felt content, enjoying the peace and quiet whilst pottering about in her little kitchen.

The doorbell made her jump. They had very few visitors, so assuming it to be a salesman or perhaps her neighbour, Sally, Julie opened the door.

Two men stood outside flashing identity cards. When it sank in that they were policemen, her first thought was that something had happened to Simon or Jim. The shorter of the two smiled reassuringly asking if they could come in. Stepping back to allow them to enter, the men seemed to fill her tiny lounge. It was Jim they were looking for, but she couldn't tell them where to find him, rarely knowing that herself. She was aware that the policemen didn't fully believe her, perhaps thinking her obstructive. It perhaps did seem strange that Julie could almost guarantee the hours Jim would be out and when he would return, yet she had absolutely no idea where they could find him. Julie's questions about why they wanted to see her husband were evaded, instead they moved quickly on, asking about his whereabouts on particular days last week. She really could tell them nothing. Julie imagined how pathetic they must have thought her: not many women would be happy to let their husbands go out so often without knowing where or why, but for her, ignorance was bliss and she was only too grateful for the time alone when she didn't have to be on edge or worried about one thing or another.

The police left a card for Julie to pass on to Jim, asking for him to telephone them when he returned. Now that was something to worry about: not so much why they wanted to see Jim, but what his reaction would be to their having been there.

****

Karen had taken the note pad home when she left the surgery, reminding Maggie to make a photocopy for herself, which was essential to Karen who, although she didn't know why, had a strong desire for her counsellor to share in everything written on the time line. Having someone to trust during this whole experience was crucial, and her counsellor already made her feel comfortable enough for her to be that person. Someone else being involved and sharing the burden somehow validated her feelings.

Karen automatically put a frozen meal into the microwave, setting it to defrost. She didn't feel like cooking tonight and would settle for the easy option. After the visits to Maggie she always felt physically drained, almost as if she'd been for a workout at the gym, but her mind was still churning, seemingly packed full of memories she could not erase. Pulling the book from her bag and curling up on the sofa Karen found the place she'd left off earlier. Writing was something she'd never tried before but now found that it gave her a kind of release and at times she could hardly write quickly enough to keep pace with her thoughts. The microwave pinged but went unheard, she was a teenager again completely focussed on the events of those dark years.

There were more bruises the next morning. Mum's face was a mess yet as usual she told us she'd fallen down the stairs. Mike might have believed that one but surely she realised that I would know differently? I wanted to do something to stop my father from hurting her so much but was afraid. It was easier for me to take Mike out for a walk or upstairs to play than to stand up to my dad. It was also easier for me to go along with mum's stories; we were both pretending that I believed her when she must have known differently. By this time 'O' levels had begun at school so I must have been sixteen. I remember the morning of my French oral exam. Mum was busy in the kitchen and Mike was eating toast at the kitchen table swinging his feet and with every swing tapping the opposite chair. I don't know why I remember silly little details like that but I do. Dad hadn't gone to work and was still in bed. We heard a loud thump from upstairs and mum suddenly froze. Mike looked at me and I could tell he was scared. The next thing we knew Dad burst into the kitchen and lunged straight at Mike, slapping him on the side of his face. Mum tried to intervene but he turned on her then. Mike was crying so grabbing him away from the table we went outside into the back garden where I hugged him until he stopped crying.

There was a terrible row going on in the house with the sound of furniture being knocked over and dad shouting at mum. I was trembling with cold and fear, I really thought dad was going to kill her, so I grabbed Mike's hand and we ran up the side of the house and into next doors garden keeping my finger on their doorbell until Mrs Adamson came to answer. My words were hardly coherent but she could see our predicament and I kept repeating that dad was killing my mum. Taking us inside, she phoned for the police. By the time they arrived Mrs Adamson had seen dad leave the house and we went back in to find mum, to see if she was okay. She wasn't and was barely conscious. The policeman called an ambulance. Mike screamed when he saw the blood but one of the police officers was brilliant with him, taking him into the lounge to calm him down. Our neighbour called my grandmother who came straight over to look after us. Mum had left for the hospital by then with one of the police officers in the ambulance with her, the other one stayed and asked us questions.

At the time I thought that was the worst day of my life! I missed my exam which seemed trivial and I felt physically sick all day. It was only after Gran had taken us to see mum in hospital that evening that I could relax a little, seeing her cleaned up a bit and making an effort to be chirpy reassured me that she wasn't going to die. I don't know quite what happened with the police and dad, but Gran said he wasn't coming home anymore and I felt so relieved, yet guilty at the same time. Mike seemed to get over it all very quickly and mum was home after a couple of nights in hospital, so for a while things were settled. Mum explained that she had an order from the court to say that dad couldn't see us anymore and wasn't allowed to come to the house. That was the beginning of a peaceful summer when our world seemed normal again, but that awful day wasn't to be the worst of my life, there was one even more terrifying still to come.

Chapter 17

For the first time in months Peter's thoughts were centred more on other people's problems than on his own. The visit to AA had given him an insight into the lives of those who were unquestionably addicted to alcohol. Tony had been patient in explaining it all and honest in answering questions. He had admitted how his own drinking had led to the break up of his marriage and alienated his children, and also confessed to sinking so low as to steal money from his elderly mother and sister to support his drinking habit. Peter was shocked and would never have believed it looking at how Tony seemed today. His story was an example of how a broken man could have a second chance at life, as well as a tribute to the AA group with which he was involved.

Then there was Ken. He too had overcome his addiction but, unlike Tony, alcohol had left a permanent mental scar and his life would never be the same. And what about those who didn't get as far as AA? Peter knew there were many for whom alcohol had been the road to complete destruction, sport stars and celebrities came to mind whose lives had been ruined or cut short due to the excesses of drink but, closer to home, what about himself? He too had lost his wife although not through alcohol. His children were still there for him but would that always be the case if he didn't sort his life out?

The brief counselling sessions with Maggie had helped to put his thoughts into some semblance of order and to accept the recent changes in his life and the permanence of them. It was now time to put in the hard work. Peter didn't feel that he was addicted to alcohol as yet, but he knew deep inside that that was the way he was heading. He felt like Scrooge in Dickens's 'Christmas Carol' having a glimpse at what could be his own future and alarm bells were ringing at what he could see. Is this what people referred to as a light bulb moment? Was his resolve really strong enough?

'Yes.' He spoke the word aloud into the empty room then in a burst of sudden energy repeated,

'Yes, I can do this!'

****

Simon and Chloe were having tea in the little kitchen when Julie heard the front door open. Her heart seemed to leap into her throat. Jim. Should she tell him about the visit from the police now, or wait until the children were in bed?

'Best to get it over with,' she thought, it was only 4.30pm and maybe the sooner he contacted the police station the better.

Leaving the children in the kitchen she went into the lounge, closing the door in between. Her legs were shaking and her heart pounded in her chest. Glancing at his wife, Jim's expression was more of a scowl and she could tell from his half closed, hooded eyes that he had been drinking again.

'You had a visit from a couple of policemen today.' There was no way to dress up the fact.

'What?' he snarled.

Julie didn't need to repeat it, he had heard.

'What the hell did they want?'

'I don't know, they wanted to talk to you…they gave me this card and asked if you would ring them as soon as you could.'

He snatched the card,

'They must have said something woman. And what did you tell them?' He moved closer to his wife, speaking through gritted teeth, his hands working, clenching and unclenching as his mind tried to work out why the police wanted to talk to him.

'The children,' she began, 'They're in the kitchen…' Julie spoke softly in the hope that her husband would keep his voice down too.

'What did you tell them?' he repeated, his voice rising.

'Nothing, honestly. There was nothing I could tell them....'

The first blow was always the worst. Jim went straight for her head, the palm of his hand slapping the left side of his wife's face. Pain shot through her ear and she could taste blood in her mouth but before Julie could move out of the way, his fist rammed into her stomach. Doubling up with the pain, she fell onto the carpet in front of him. His right foot came in first, taking her by surprise. He didn't usually use his feet; always seeming to get more satisfaction from slapping and punching his wife.

'Jim...no...the children, please.'

But he was in a frenzy now, out of control and kicking her with both feet, almost as if she was a football he was trying to move along the floor.

Julie tried to keep quiet, but inevitably the kitchen door opened and Simon came running in, hot tears streaming down his face.

'No, no. Stop it... leave her alone!' He flung himself at his father who pushed the boy aside, laughing.

'Oh yeah, and who's going to stop me then? Mummy's little boy?'

Julie tried to get to her feet but the kicking had disorientated her and her eyes wouldn't focus.

Simon was up again, his face red as he screamed at his father,

'Stop it, stop it!'

She saw her son launch himself at Jim again,

'No,' she screamed, but couldn't reach him in time. Jim slapped the boy with the same force he had used on her and Julie could do no more than watch in horror as Simon fell to the floor, hitting his head on the stone hearth. She was aware of blood, Simon's blood, and she stared transfixed at his slight body lying motionless on the floor. Jim too looked at his son, a wild expresion on his face. A frantic banging on the door was the last thing Julie remembered and then the world went black.

****

Maggie had only just put the phone down when Sue appeared.

'Are you free at lunch today?' She pressed her palms together in an attitude of pleading,

'I need your help choosing some new shoes.'

'But you have more shoes than Clarks,' Maggie reminded her friend.

'Yes, but there's a reason...I'll tell you later, twelve okay?'

'Fine, but I'll only have an hour and I need something to eat first.'

At ten past twelve, Maggie found herself sitting in McDonalds eating a cheeseburger with a hot apple pie to follow.

'Why the need for more shoes?' she asked Sue.

'For Alan of course.'

'What? We're looking for shoes for Alan?'

'No, silly, but all my shoes are sexy high heels, which, don't get me wrong, I love, but I tower above him in them. I want some flatties but still sexy ones of course. Perhaps some of those cute little kitten heels as well, for special occasions.'

'Talking of Alan, didn't I see him in the surgery yesterday? I hardly recognized him, he's changed his hair style hasn't he?'

'Yes you did, he just popped in to see me as he was passing, and yes again, he has changed his hairstyle. I persuaded him that the comb over look was a bit dated and shaved hair is very 'in' at the moment.'

'So, if you can't have George Clooney, you'll settle for Bruce Willis eh? Things are going well between you I take it?'

Sue sighed, leaving her friend to draw her own conclusions, but not content with that, Maggie pushed a little harder,

'It's getting serious then? Do you think he's Mr. Right?'

Maggie was taken completely by surprise when Sue's eyes suddenly filled with tears.

'Oh I'm sorry.' She quickly apologised, 'Am I being too nosey... I'll mind my own business shall I?'

But her friend laughed,

'No, I'm not crying because I'm sad, I'm happy; I think I might be in love.'

'Wow, already, you've only known him a couple of weeks.'

'It's enough, Alan's all I think about; he makes me laugh but he can be so romantic. I get that wobbly feeling in my stomach when I think about him; we really seem to fizz together.'

Maggie could only conclude that love was expensive as in the next half hour Sue bought four new pairs of shoes, basing her choices purely on the size of the heels, but she was delighted for her friend and hoped the relationship would work out for them both.

Toting several carrier bags, they returned to work that afternoon to find Dr. Williams waiting to see Maggie.

'Bad news I'm afraid.' As was his way he came straight to the point, 'Julie Chambers and her son are both in hospital.'

'Both of them?' she gasped, 'Why, what's happened?'

'They were admitted yesterday, early evening I believe, after some kind of domestic. A neighbour found them both unconscious and rang for the ambulance and the police. I've had notification from the hospital this morning. Julie is going to be fine, she has a slight concussion and bruising consistent with an attack. The boy however is still unconscious, he has a nasty head injury and as yet there's no sign of him coming round. The doctors can't assess how serious it is and when, or if, he does come round whether there'll be any brain damage.'

Maggie's heart sank as the energy and light-hearted mood of earlier drained from her. Had she in some way contributed to this awful situation by going to the police? There was no doubt that it was Julie's husband who had inflicted the injuries but where was he now? What would happen to Julie and the children?

Tom Williams knew what Maggie would be thinking.

'Have you any clients this afternoon?' he asked.

She shook her head, ‘Only an appointment with my supervisor, do you think I should cancel and go to see them?’

‘I assumed you’d want to and I’m sure the poor wee girl could do with some support at the moment so off you go and see what you can do. But be careful not to get too involved here Maggie.’

Stopping only briefly on her way out she asked Sue to ring after work, hoping to find out from Alan what, if any, involvement the police had in these latest events.

Heading towards the hospital with a heavy heart, her mind swam with questions and doubts about her own part in this latest development.

Chapter 18

Early afternoon was a bad time to find a parking spot at the hospital. Visiting would be starting for most of the wards and all the convenient spaces were taken. Maggie found a gap eventually but only after driving around for several minutes. After feeding coins into the ticket machine she began the lengthy walk to the main entrance.

Hospitals were not her favourite place: they brought back memories of Chris, particularly this one which was where he had died. Walking gave her time to compose herself and deliberately focus on Julie; this was about her, not Chris. Hurrying down the corridors leading to the ICU, Maggie found them to be every bit as long as she remembered and just like before, she was unsure of what might be found at the end.

After a brief word with the ward sister, Maggie was directed to the room where Julie and her son were ensconced. Simon was unconscious on the high, single bed; wired up to various monitors, with tubes taped to his thin limp body. His mother was sitting alongside in an armchair, leaning forward to hold her son's hand, anxiously searching for any sign of life. The trauma and strain of the last twenty-four hours was visibly etched on the young mother's face. Turning at the sound of someone entering, Julie expected to see a nurse, so the sight of her visitor was such a relief, that her tears spilled over, allowing the pent up emotions to be released at last. Maggie moved forward, kneeling beside the chair to wrap her arms around the younger woman and silently holding on to her trembling body. A nurse looked in the doorway then quietly moved away, deciding that this was probably the best thing for the boy's mother. There had been no other visitors apart from the police officers assigned to the case and she had given them no details of family or friends to contact. The nurse was pleased that she had some support at last.

Several minutes passed before Julie managed to compose herself and turn her attention back to her son. Maggie pulled up a chair; sitting close to them both and for a while they sat in a comfortable silence, each with their own thoughts and feelings, the only sound being the rhythmic noises of the machines. Julie was the first to speak, with a quiet, strained voice.

'Thank you for coming…' the whisper trailed off, lost in the silence.

'I wanted to come, but if I'm at all in the way I won't be offended if you say so.'

'No. Please, don't go. If it's no trouble to you I could do with some company. Everything feels so unreal, as if I'm trapped in a dreadful nightmare. I can't think what to do for the best and I don't even want to think about what might happen.'

Maggie was happy to stay but felt that it was practical help which was needed at the moment so, not wanting to pry but realising Julie had no one else, she asked, 'What arrangements have you made for Chloe?'

The tears streamed again as Julie replied, painfully recalling what she could remember of the previous evening.

'She's with my neighbour, Sally. I must have blacked out and didn't come round until I was in the ambulance. Apparently Sally heard all the noise and came across to see if we were all right. Jim ran out of the house, nearly trampling her down and poor Sally was left to call the ambulance and look after Chloe. It must have been quite a fright, finding both Simon and me unconscious, but Sally's a brick really. When the police arrived she insisted on taking Chloe, even though they wanted to bring in social services. The police came to see me last night to get my consent for Sal to look after Chloe. I'm so grateful; I couldn't bear the thought of them putting her in a foster home. I've spoken to Sally on the phone and she's insisting on keeping her for the next few days until we see what's going to happen…I want to be here with Simon until he wakes up…'

Maggie's heart went out to Julie who hadn't mentioned her own injuries which must have been painful, her mouth was cut and swollen and the whole left side of her face was bruised, with an angry looking black eye. Dark bruises were visible on her arms too. Goodness knows what the rest of her body looked like.

'Do you think it would be a good idea to contact your parents or your sister? Some of your family around you now could only help?'

'I'd love to see them, but what if they don't want to? I've pushed them away so many times.'

'If you like, I can get in touch with them for you.'

'Would you? That would be wonderful, if you could tell them what's happened and …tell them I'm sorry too, will you?'

Julie wrote down the address and phone number. They agreed that it would be better to visit the house rather than breaking the news over the phone, which Maggie would do straight after leaving the hospital. Staying only a little while longer, she left when a nurse appeared to check on Simon and to remind them that Julie was also a patient and should try to get some rest.

Driving to the outskirts of town in search of the address, Maggie reflected on what Julie had told her. This latest assault had been unnecessary and brutal; having the effect of finally making her aware that Jim would never change and opening her eyes as to how dangerous he really was, to the children as well as herself. Julie typically played down her own injuries, although admitted to how severely she had been kicked; naturally she was more focussed on Simon's condition. Initially telling the police he had hit his head on the hearth, she eventually had to agree that it was the result of his father pushing Simon with unnecessary force. The police apparently couldn't find Jim Chambers, he hadn't returned to the house and his wife could shed no light on where he might have gone. Maggie rather hoped he would disappear for good, they would all be far better off without him. Hopefully, Julie would realise that now and begin to build a new life for the three of them without Jim. This was of course assuming that Simon pulled through.

Mr. and Mrs. Spencer lived in a neat little semi in a quiet cul-de-sac in a popular part of town. This was where Julie had grown up, a pleasant leafy area on the edge of town with good schools, wide grass verged streets and very little traffic to disturb the peace and quiet enjoyed by the residents, a far cry from the little terraced house she occupied now. A lady in her late fifties answered the door, the same build as Julie with the same features and high cheekbones. She smiled pleasantly as Maggie introduced herself and asked if she could come in to talk to about her daughter. Denise Spencer's wide smile switched immediately to a look of concern as she quickly enquired if Julie was all right, stepping aside for her visitor to enter. Maggie chose her words carefully, not wishing to cause alarm but wanting Mrs. Spencer to know how desperately her daughter needed her. Seated in the comfortable lounge Maggie explained that mother and son were both in hospital, briefly outlining their injuries. She then asked if her husband was at home, feeling that Denise would cope better with the news if she had her husband there for support.

'He'll be home any time now. He works out of town, but leaves early to miss the traffic. Shall I make some coffee? He'll probably be here by the time the kettle's boiled.' Denise anxiously twisted her watch around her wrist, checking the time

'Thank you, I'd like that.' Maggie accepted the offer.

While Mrs. Spencer went into the kitchen Maggie took in the surroundings. The large lounge had a picture window overlooking a well-manicured garden. The house was at the head of the cul-de-sac, looking down the road, so not overlooked by neighbouring properties. It was an immaculate room, as neat and tidy as Denise Spencer herself. Photographs were carefully arranged on top of a well polished piano, several of two young girls whom she assumed to be Julie and her sister

Sarah as children. There was also a picture of a laughing baby whom she wondered at first if it was Simon or Chloe, but it was obviously an expensive studio portrait, which suggested that it wasn't.

A car pulled into the drive and Maggie watched as a man she assumed to be Mr. Spencer got out, a tall man of similar age to his wife, possibly a few years older, he was smartly dressed in a well cut suit over an immaculate white shirt. Graying hair was cut short and he carried an expensive looking briefcase, the very picture of a successful businessman. Glancing in the direction of Maggie's car he paused momentarily before heading to the house. She heard his wife hurry into the hallway and their anxious voices before they both entered the lounge.

'This is my husband, Malcolm,' Denise Spencer introduced him to their visitor.

'How's Julie?' Concern was evident from his expression, 'and the boy?'

Maggie went over the same ground she had covered with his wife while Denise left the room to fetch coffee. When they were all seated nursing cups and saucers in their laps it became Maggie's turn to listen and piece together Julie's story from her parent's point of view.

'We had such hopes for her as a girl,' Malcolm began, 'Always a very bright student, could have easily gone on to university, but she changed overnight when she met *him*. We tried to guide her when she told us she was expecting, encouraging her to do the right thing, you know? And we would have supported her too, with the baby I mean, to help her continue her studies…but it didn't work out as we thought. Jim didn't want her to see us anymore and as it seemed to make life difficult for her, we kept in the background. We've never stopped loving her though.'

The pain was evident in both of their faces.

'Julie needs you now.'

'I'll get my coat.' Denise jumped up. 'We can go straight away can't we?'

'Of course.' Maggie smiled.

Within two hours of leaving Julie and Simon in the hospital, she returned to witness an emotional family reunion. Feeling like an intruder to what should be a private moment, Maggie took her leave, promising to call in the next day to see how they were doing and offering herself as available if there was any way in which she could help.

It was too late to go back to the surgery so Maggie headed for home. Ben gave his usual, and more than welcome, rapturous greeting, looking with expectation at his lead hanging on the kitchen door. There was a message on the phone from Sue, who was home from work and waiting for news.

'You first,' she patted Ben's head, 'then we'll ring Aunty Sue shall we boy?'

Ben seemed to concur with the plan so they set off for a long walk, hoping to blow away some of the cares of the day.

A good walk, a cheese and tomato sandwich and a welcome mug of tea later, Maggie settled down with the telephone to ring her friend.

Sue had heard about Julie and Simon on the surgery grapevine and had spoken to Alan after work, but still knew no more than anyone else.

'He's as tight lipped as you about his work,' she grumbled 'If I sign the official secrets act would you both admit me to your working lives?'

Maggie laughed; talking to Sue always lifted her mood.

'He did tell me that the police are looking for a man in connection with a domestic assault. It's pretty obvious who it is and it seems to me that you've already stepped beyond your remit of counsellor and become personally involved in the situation. I'm not blaming you in any way, in fact, in my opinion Jim Chambers made it personal when he intimidated you and poisoned Ben. I'd like to get my hands on the little bastard. He's started on children now, eh?'

Maggie had to agree that her involvement was now on a personal level. Julie had become more than a client and her own concern was beyond that of a professional interest. It was a relief to be able to share some of her afternoon's experiences with Sue, there was a gnawing feeling at the back of her mind that she was somehow responsible for these latest events, perhaps if she hadn't gone to the police? Voicing these thoughts to her friend, Sue launched into one of her little lectures.

'Utter rubbish Maggie, you should know better! That man had it coming to him. He could have killed his wife and son, no one knows what would have happened and seeking help is probably the best thing that poor girl ever did. I'm surprised at you sinking into the 'what if' pit. Isn't that something you're supposed to discourage? Live for the moment and all that?'

Sue was obviously worked up and always one to speak her mind, but her blunt words held no offence to Maggie, she had to agree with the truth of the facts and her friend's concern was touching even if it did come out in anger.

'You're right,' she conceded, 'But don't bite my head off will you?'

'Sorry, but sometimes you're too nice. Call him what he is and don't make excuses for him, you'll feel better if you let off a bit of steam. And as for blaming yourself, that's ridiculous, that creep deserves a bloody good hiding.'

The rest of the conversation was in much the same vein. A little of Sue's indignation rubbed off and she did feel somewhat better for having a good old moan. After replacing the phone, Maggie felt suddenly hungry again. Prowling restlessly around the kitchen to find comfort food she eventually decided to make an omelette…which she did, with the most well beaten eggs she had ever used.

Chapter 19

Not surprisingly, Maggie hadn't slept well that night. Thoughts of Julie and Simon kept her awake well into the early hours. At two am she settled down with the latest John Grisham novel, hoping to divert her mind to the plot, but Ben's snoring made it virtually impossible to follow the complicated legal proceedings Grisham's hero was embarking upon. Eventually a restless sleep overtook her until six am when Maggie showered and prepared for whatever the day ahead would bring.

Before leaving for work a quick call to the hospital only told her that Julie and Simon had had a 'comfortable' night.

'Could mean anything,' she told Ben, 'but I suppose I'm not family so that's the best I'll get.' Ben twisted his head to one side offering a look of sympathetic understanding before settling himself down for his morning snooze.

****

After the first of the day's clients had left, Maggie went out into the reception area and almost collided with Sue who was dashing out, struggling into her coat and holding the straps of her handbag in her teeth.

'Hey.' Maggie deftly avoided being mown down. 'Where's the fire?'

'Early lunch,' Sue answered in passing, 'shopping to do. Want to tag along?'

'No thanks, I've a client coming in soon.' She watched as Sue disappeared around the corner, heading towards the town centre.

The client in question was a young man seen on four previous occasions over the past couple of months. Matthew West's appearance was quite imposing, at easily two or three inches over six feet with broad shoulders and an athletic body. Although twenty-seven, he had a boyish face capped with a mass of thick wavy red hair that most girls would die for. He had been referred through his G.P. at the request of Victim Support, a charity dedicated to helping victims of crime. At the time of their first meeting, Matthew was recovering from major surgery to reconstruct his face after an unprovoked and brutal attack from a group of teenagers. A volunteer from Victim Support had been visiting him for a few weeks after the attack which had helped considerably through the process of pressing charges, liaising with the police and providing emotional support as far as they could.

Unfortunately, his state of mind worsened as time went on and now, four months after the attack he was entering Maggie's office for his fifth visit.

'Hi, you're looking better each time I see you,' she greeted him. 'How're you doing this week?'

His face had certainly improved, the lumpy swelling which he was beginning to think would be permanent was now almost completely gone although scars from the operation were still visible.

'I'm getting there thanks, and you?'

'Fine. Want to tell me the latest doctor's report?' Maggie was genuinely interested in Matthew's physical progress as well as his emotional recovery. During his first sessions he had, as was fairly common, been able to talk more readily about his treatment and physical progress rather than his feelings and the psychological effect the assault had. She found this was a good way to begin each session as it kept her up to speed with his progress and broke the ice a little, freeing his reservations about talking.

Maggie had been aware from the beginning how difficult he found it to put his feelings into words. Matthew was embarrassed about the assault. His height and build gave the appearance of strength but he was a gentle young man to whom violence was alien and abhorrent. He had difficulty in admitting to his friends exactly what had occurred, anticipating that their reaction would be to ask why he hadn't got the better of them, they were just kids. The reality was that his friends probably wouldn't have expressed or even thought that but Matthew was feeling guilty, branding himself a coward and giving himself a hard time with such thoughts. By his third visit he had come to understand that this was what he was doing and had broken down, pouring out his fears of going out alone, his panic when the doorbell rang and his guilt at being such a big man and feeling so afraid.

Maggie had her work cut out in helping him to understand where his feelings were coming from. Having always been 'a big boy' people's expectations of him, even as a child, were that he should be responsible, mature and strong. In many ways he was, but an attack by five teenage thugs would be devastating to anyone and the injuries he had suffered were quite horrific, not to mention painful, with the prospect of more prolonged and uncomfortable treatment to come.

Matthew could now smile again, although that in itself was difficult as his jaws had been pinned during surgery and temporarily wired.

'The wires come out this week,' he proudly told her.

'Ooh, painful,' she sympathised.

'Not really, I still have no feeling below my cheekbones, although it would be just my luck for it to come back before they take them off. No more soup after that, I'm sick of sloppy foods and if I never see another rice pudding again it will be too soon.

Maggie grimaced at the thought.

'But what I really feel good about today is that I came here on my own.'

'That's great. And was it okay?'

As he began to tell her, she felt that he was certainly beginning to make progress, looking at the assault more objectively now and although the effects would be with him for a long time, he had a greater understanding of his emotions and feelings. She had helped him to see just how normal they were, and also encouraged him to look upon himself as a survivor rather than a victim. He readily latched onto this, feeling it was a much more positive attitude and one in which he could take some small measure of pride rather than the shame and embarrassment he had initially felt.

Content with his progress, in the next visit or two the subject of ending his counselling could be broached; his recovery was underway. Perhaps they could meet every two weeks soon and hopefully he would begin to feel able to manage without her support.

When Matthew had gone, Maggie left her door open in order to see Sue returning to reception, curious as to why her friend had been in such a hurry to go shopping, and also to interrogate her for all the latest news on her romance.

Sue returned, positively glowing and when she saw the open door, popped her head around to see if Maggie was busy.

'Aha.' Maggie's eyes flashed at her friend, 'Come on in and tell me all.'

A grin spread across Sue's face.

'Alan's asked me to go away with him for a long weekend.' Her excitement was obvious as was the fact that the shopping had been successful looking at the number of carrier bags her friend was holding.

'That's great, so come on, all the details please.'

'Well… he's being a little secretive really. I know it's in the country and we'll be away Friday until Sunday. He said the accommodation's great and good food too, although this is all on a friend's recommendation, Alan hasn't actually been there. And I'm to take some outdoor, casual clothes so it's probably a country hotel with log fires, four poster beds…. the works.'

'Lucky old you. So what's in the bags?'

'Oh yes, you're going to love these.' Sue opened the first bag and shook out a beautiful satin nightie. It was pale green with a lace trim around the plunging neckline and a lace trimmed split high up one side.

'Wow, that'll do justice to any four poster bed. It must have cost a bomb.'

'Yes, but it's an investment of course, what else?'

Next she unpacked a pair of coffee coloured trousers and the most beautiful cream cotton jumper Maggie had ever seen, a delicate weave of soft cotton giving texture to a simple but elegant style.

'I'm so jealous,' she said looking at the designer labels.

'Good,' laughed Sue. 'You will think of me enjoying my luxury weekend while you're worming the dog or whatever treats you have planned, won't you?'

'Out, now…' Maggie made to chase her friend out of the office and they both returned to work, each with their own thoughts about the coming weekend.

****

Janet Rea opened her front door, stepped inside the hallway and leaned heavily on the wall. She had just completed a rather long, brisk walk and felt physically shattered but emotionally exhilarated. Kicking off her shoes she padded to the kitchen to put the kettle on. Paul was out interviewing a local businessman for one of his articles and she would have the house to herself for at least another hour. Stirring the tea bag in her mug, she couldn't help but smile to herself, a smug sort of smile but deservedly so. Janet had walked for at least half an hour each day that week and today had managed almost a full hour which made her feel pretty good about herself. So…it was just walking, but it felt like a real achievement. Maggie was right about the endorphins or whatever. It really did feel better, making the effort, and the more she walked, the less of an effort it became. Taking the tea into the lounge, Janet flopped down on the sofa and picked up her journal. Skimming over the first few pages, which were now so familiar she could recite them verbatim, the latest entry read:

Wow, what a session I had with Maggie last week, the time just flew by, I could have stayed much longer, in fact I really wanted to stay longer. She's teaching me a bit about psychology, apparently we're like onions with all our layers, but I can see where she's coming from and I actually find it all quite fascinating. The things we're talking about now seem so much more relevant. I think I was in danger of becoming self-absorbed and wallowing in my misery and desperate feelings, but this more practical approach is great. I've tried to do a bit of walking too and have found I really like it. There's something about being outdoors, when there's no ceiling to restrict your view everything is put into a different perspective. Looking at the vastness of the sky makes me feel so small, no…better than that, it makes my problems seem so small.

I feel more relaxed too and I'm sleeping better. Even Paul has noticed a difference. He's been a brick; I don't know what I would have done without him, crumbled under it all I suppose. Anyway, I hardly dare say it but I think I've turned some sort of corner. There are positive thoughts swimming around in my head, which is a wonderful change to all those negative ones over the last year. I find myself thinking about the future and things I would like to do which is amazing really because I've hardly wanted to leave the house or even get out of bed for so long…

Janet put her book away as she heard her husband's key opening the front door and jumped up to greet him.

'Hi, you're early. I thought you'd be another hour at least.' Reaching up to kiss his cheek she smiled, enjoying the surge of pleasure she felt in seeing him. Paul returned the kiss and the smile, noting how animated his wife looked.

'I'll make you a coffee,' she offered, 'and you can tell me all about your interview, then I thought we might go out for lunch, just the two of us?'

Paul Rea could have wept with joy. Okay, it was a pretty ordinary greeting and a suggestion of lunch out, but for him it was a welcome sign of hope, such pleasant exchanges with Janet had been few and far between lately. His concern for his wife over the last year had been a painful, almost tangible burden. This little breakthrough was balm to his aching heart, he felt lighter in spirit than he had in months. Just this one little sign of normality gave him such hope. 'Please God' he silently prayed.

Chapter 20

Alan arrived at Sue's flat on Friday, promptly at two thirty, the appointed hour. Her excitement level was off the scale by then, having packed and re-packed several times, changing her mind about one thing and then another, and adding things that might be needed. Dashing to open the door she almost tripped over her case in the lobby. Alan was beaming, taking in every detail of his girlfriend from top to toe. As she blushed, he reached over to kiss her cheek; they both moved in the same direction ending up with more of a nose rub than a kiss.

'Calm down girl,' Sue thought, 'Be cool.'

Alan lifted the rather large case.

'We're only there until Sunday,' he groaned, feeling the weight of it,

'Yes, but you haven't told me much at all about where we're going so I need to be prepared for every eventuality.'

Alan rolled his eyes as he packed the case in the car, then they set off. He switched on a country music CD while Sue began to question him about their weekend.

'Did I mention that we're meeting up with a couple of my mates and their girlfriends?' he casually asked.

'No, you didn't.' Thoughts of a romantic weekend suddenly evaporated but she tried not to sound too disappointed as he began to talk about his friends, both of whom had trained with him at Hendon.

'Should be fun,' it was suddenly difficult to sound enthusiastic, the idea of sharing him with his old college buddies did not appeal but he seemed excited at the thought so Sue resigned herself to going along with his plans.

The journey took nearly three hours. It seemed as if everyone was heading towards their destination, which she now knew to be 'somewhere' in north Wales. It could still be a great weekend she thought and at least they would have time to themselves on an evening, all was not lost.

The landscape was becoming quite remote. Beautiful yes but rather isolated and the traffic had thinned down considerably.

'Here we are,' Alan announced as they turned a corner into a large gravel car park. The building facing them wasn't quite what Sue had anticipated. A long single storey building, stood before them, brick built rather than stone, old but reasonably well maintained if lacking in the charm and character she had expected.

'Looks like the others are here,' Alan sounded excited like a schoolboy let out for the holidays. He grabbed their bags from the boot and hurried towards what looked like the entrance where a large square hall served as the reception with rather stark furnishings. No log fires or cosy armchairs, in fact the seating resembled old pews from a church. There was a desk near the door, but Alan made straight for a group of people seated at the far end of the room, already in animated conversation.

Whoops of greeting and backslapping took Sue by surprise. Alan was enfolded in bear hugs by the two men, and then hugged warmly by their girlfriends too. He introduced Sue to his friends, bringing her into the group with his arm affectionately around her shoulders making her smile as she tried to take in their names. There was Mike and Dave, Claire and Lisa, but who was with whom wasn't quite clear. Mike took off to find the new arrivals some coffee, then the interrogation about their relationship began. Alan laughed it all off, telling his friends he'd met Sue in the police station, giving an exaggerated wink and leaving the reason she was there open to speculation. Sue enjoyed the banter, they appeared to be easy going people; she could see why Alan enjoyed their company. Both girls were friendly and she warmed to them instantly, although feeling rather overdressed. They both wore jeans, sweaters and trainers, a stark contrast to her smart trousers with her new kitten heeled boots and beige mohair cardigan over a cream blouse.

After coffee Alan wandered over to the desk to register while the girls offered to show Sue to her room.

'But what about Alan?' she asked, not really wanting to leave him.

'No worries,' Lisa replied, 'The boys will take care of him and we'll meet up later.' Sue thought this rather odd, but followed on, not wanting to offend them.

'Here we are,' Claire announced opening a heavy door at the end of a rather long, gloomy corridor.

Stepping inside, Sue gazed around in horror, as the reality of an eight bedded dormitory hit hard. A couple of young women sitting at the end of the room smiled and waved a greeting. Claire and Lisa exchanged glances as they watched Sue's reaction. Unable to disguise the shock on her face, she obviously hadn't expected this type of accommodation.

'We got here early, so grabbed the beds by the window.' Claire steered her over to three beds at the window end of the room.

'Room with a view eh?' Lisa added, then gently sat Sue down on the bed asking, 'Just what did Alan tell you about this weekend love?'

'He said it would be a weekend in the country with good accommodation and great food. He didn't mention you four until we were on the way, not that I mind or anything…. I just sort of got the wrong idea.'

'What about the activities?' Claire asked.

'What activities?' A look of raw panic crossed her face.

'Oh dear, he has dropped you in it hasn't he? This is a multi activity weekend... with a great choice on offer. There's canoeing, archery, paintball, rock climbing, quad bikes, you name it.'

Sue was mortified. She silently lifted her heavy case onto the bed, opening it up to reveal its contents to the other girls.

'I'll kill him,' she hissed through gritted teeth.

'Obviously not the kind of weekend you were expecting.' Lisa grinned as she lifted out the gorgeous new nightie, 'Bet this cost a packet.'

Sue's face was burning with a mixture of anger and embarrassment. She had only just met these girls and felt foolish in front of them, not knowing what on earth to say as they gawped at her smart, sexy clothes and totally unpractical footwear. Claire took charge. 'Men,' she tutted, 'but don't you worry, dinner's not until eight and there's a twenty four hour Asda about three miles down the road; we can be there and back in no time.'

Without bothering to find the men and tell them where they were going, they set off on a mission to save face for Sue. All the way there Claire quizzed her as to what she had packed and in no time her two new allies compiled a list of the essentials to see her through the weekend. They returned in record time having purchased jeans, trainers, socks, a couple of sweatshirts and a cagoule. A pair of winceyette pyjamas completed the ensemble; she would feel extremely silly in her new nightie in a girl's dorm. Grateful to her new friends, and to Asda's prices, she told herself that one day she would laugh about this…if she survived the weekend.

By the time she saw Alan again the desire to throttle him had waned a little and she decided to give him the benefit of the doubt, assuming he had not deliberately neglected to tell her what kind of weekend it was to be, but if that was the case, she thought him pretty dim for a policeman.

Dinner was something else. Sue had given up hope of good food, silver service, wine and candles in an intimate restaurant, which was just as well. A canteen would be a better description although she had to admit that the food was good. Not A la Carte, but good old British home cooking: steak and ale pie with chips (not french fries), jam roly-poly pudding and custard, or bread and butter pudding. The men thought they had died and gone to heaven.

'Good job we'll be working off the calories,' said Lisa.

‘Which reminds me,’ Sue turned to Alan, ‘You didn’t mention that this was an activity weekend.’

‘Didn’t I?’ He was the picture of innocence and it was impossible to tell if he’d genuinely forgotten or was leading her on.

‘We’ll have to decide on our options tonight,’ Mike interrupted. ‘A committee meeting at the local should be just the thing.’

The local proved to be a bumpy five-mile drive away. Mike had brought a list of the activities on offer and passed it around the others for their opinions. Sue felt ignorant, not knowing what some of the options involved. She’d heard of things like paintball and abseiling but thinking herself too old for such things and never having been a sporty person, even as a girl, she had little idea about any of them so decided the best thing to do was to go along with Alan’s decisions.

‘I really don’t mind which we do.’

‘That’s my girl, game for anything.’ Alan gave her a squeeze and she relaxed at his approval, thinking she had said the right thing.

It was decided to choose quad biking for their morning activity, followed by an afternoon’s rock climbing, then on Sunday they would abseil on the morning and finish with a session of paintball before setting off for home.

Sue thought it seemed a hefty programme to cram into two days, but at least each activity wouldn’t last too long, after all how high can you climb in just a half day?

Thank heaven for the winceyette pyjamas; they were certainly the right thing among this group of young, sporty females. They were all younger than Sue, except perhaps for Lisa, who’d been Dave’s partner for three years and was probably the same age. Trying to ignore the butterflies in her stomach that thinking about the next day’s events brought, she tried to get some sleep, determined to cope, somehow.

Breakfast was as hearty as dinner. Sue hadn't eaten porridge for years, her mum would be pleased.

Finishing off her toast and marmalade, she asked Alan, 'Are quad bikes those big three wheeler things that go off road?' Alan roared with laughter

'You are a comic!' He planted a kiss on the top of her head and she said no more, figuring she'd find out soon enough.

The quad bikes seemed huge and much noisier than she'd expected but great fun. The helmet wasn't a good look, but they all had them on so hey, who cares?

They had a fantastic time. At the end of the route, it hardly seemed as if they had been riding for two hours. The helmet had given Sue hat hair and they were all covered in mud, but she didn't care in the least. Perhaps if there had been a mirror about? They grabbed a quick packed lunch, doorstep sandwiches, what else, then it was into the mini bus and off rock climbing.

This was definitely much scarier. Sue checked her safety equipment more times than necessary, asking the instructor umpteen questions before allowing Alan to begin the ascent, tentatively following in his steps.

Later he congratulated her, 'I've heard people say they could do it blindfolded, but you're the first person I've seen actually rock climbing with their eyes shut.' A comment which earned him a thump on his arm as she scrambled back into the bus, desperate to get back for a long hot shower.

It was no surprise that the next day the girls were all stiff. Sue perhaps more than the others who were obviously fitter, so she looked forward to a more relaxing day.

As the bus approached the cliff top, Sue was puzzled. Expecting a lake or a river, she began to wonder how they could sail without water and was just about to comment on this when someone pointed out a group already abseiling down a cliff face opposite their site and realising her mistake, her eyes widened in horror.

'Never done this before?' Alan asked. Shaking her head, she wondered if there was some way to get out of it without looking chicken, but he pulled her close and kissed the top of her head, grinning at the expression on her face.

'You're doing great,' he said, 'I'm so proud of you.'

That was it, she was trapped. There was nothing for it but to adopt yesterday's tactics and close her eyes.

Like going to the dentist, it did pass eventually and she clung onto the fact that there was only one more part of this endurance test left. Paintball; surely that couldn't be bad?

The group decided on splitting into girl – boy teams. Sue thought she'd rather be with Alan, until she realised the potential for revenge, splattering him with paint seemed an appealing idea. As they covered up in overalls the girls talked tactics. Claire and Lisa were old hands at paintballing and outlined their objectives, then it was high fives all round as they went out to face the enemy.

Sue loved it from the word go. The adrenalin kicked in and her tiredness evaporated as their team ran around like headless chickens, forgetting the battle plan and just out to get the guys. The hits hurt more than she had expected, but after all she had been through over the weekend she considered herself to be a tough nut now and scrambled, hid, charged and screamed, thoroughly enjoying breaking all the rules to 'get' her man. She hadn't laughed so much for ages. At the end of their time she collapsed on top of an exhausted Alan, kissing his paint smeared face.

'I surrender,' he laughed.

Forty eight hours earlier, Sue would never have believed how reluctant she would be to leave. They had gelled as a group and parted with promises to do it again soon. Claire whispered to Sue that perhaps she should book the next weekend away for herself and Alan, an idea that had already occurred to her. Although tired, they chatted happily all the way home, both delighted at the way the weekend had gone. Alan carried Sue's case inside for her. 'This seems even heavier than when we left,' he said, rather puzzled, but she just smiled and promised to ring him the next day.

It was late, but Sue wanted to ring her friend and tell her about her weekend away.

'Hi Mags, it's me. I haven't got you out of bed have I?'

'No,' Maggie lied, 'It's good to know you're back. How's it gone then, up to expectations I hope?'

'I've been thrown off a cliff, covered in mud, shot at and forced to climb a mountain and it was fantastic!'

'I think you'd better tell me more. Was this Alan's idea of a romantic weekend?'

'Well... it was certainly a dirty one,' Sue laughed.

Chapter 21

Simon had been unconscious for six days which was the longest, darkest week of Julie's life. Most of her time was spent at his bedside, not daring to leave, fearing the worst and half expecting what she couldn't bring herself to think about. The nurses constantly reminded her during those first few days that she too was a patient and Julie appreciated just how marvellous the staff had been, allowing her to sleep on a makeshift bed in Simon's room until eventually persuading her to go home to rest for a while after being officially discharged. Home, however, was a place where Julie was afraid to go to after recent events, so Malcolm Spencer volunteered to accompany his daughter while she frantically packed some clean clothes to move herself and Chloe into her parent's home for the foreseeable future, every minute spent there brought back the vision of Simon; falling, bleeding and lying deathly still. Julie couldn't wait to get out.

Her neighbour, Sally, insisted on continuing to look after Chloe during the day for as long as was needed which proved to be an excellent arrangement, Julie's mother was keen to have her granddaughter but wasn't as familiar to Chloe as Sally was so sharing the care left Denise Spencer free to devote time to her daughter as well; there were several years of catching up to do.

Though desperately worried about her son, Julie could see the silver lining of the whole situation. The reunion with her parents had been emotional to say the least, with regrets and apologies expressed on both sides. Her sister, Sarah, had also rallied round to help, making her realise exactly what the estrangement from her family had cost. What a fool she had been. Why on earth had she had stayed with Jim, protecting him, making excuses for him and pretending it would all work out one day? It seemed so stupid now, perhaps it was raw fear, she'd certainly known plenty of that, but whatever the reason it was most decidedly over now. She was determined to press charges against Jim for what he had done and he would never again be part of her life, or the children's. And now looking at her son she silently prayed for his recovery.

Julie wanted to be involved in caring for Simon as much as possible. The ICU staff had explained the various tubes and wires attached to his body and shown her how to wash him and put on fresh pyjamas. The physiotherapist too had been patient in showing her how to exercise his limbs and massage his muscles which she did now, gently and lovingly rubbing his limp body while talking quietly to him. Julie was aware of the differing schools of thought on how aware coma patients are and resolutely chose to go with the more positive line of thinking, talking to him as if he could hear and understand. She told him about Chloe being with her Grandmother and how the two were enjoying getting to know each other, and she chatted with as much enthusiasm as she could manage about their future when he would be well again. It had been agreed that they would move in with her parents indefinitely. They had made her so welcome and shown such genuine pleasure in having her and Chloe that it grieved her to think of the time she had wasted putting Jim first and depriving her children of their grandparents, as well as denying herself the love and support of her parents.

'You'll love Grandma's house,' she told her son. 'there's a huge back garden with apple and plum trees and enough room to play football. Granddad has a season ticket for the new stadium and he's going to get you one too when you're better. Chloe and I are sharing a lovely bedroom and Grandma's getting the little room ready for you, we'll have so much fun, I promise.'

Perhaps Julie was trying to convince herself as much as Simon. It was a constant strain to keep hopeful, but the doctors' had encouraged her to remain positive, assuring her that the percentage of children who make a full recovery from a coma was much greater than that of adults, but there had been no change whatever in his condition and as she looked at him now it was difficult to stay strong. He looked so small and fragile but was already twice the man his father was. Mentally re-living the way he had rushed to protect her from Jim, her heart ached. Not just once but twice she remembered him running fiercely at his father, tears of anger streaming down his face, shouting at Jim to leave his mother alone. Simon was just a child and didn't deserve any of this. Regrets, sadness, fear and guilt constantly raced around her mind. She was tired from lack of sleep but torn each time she left his bedside, although she knew that Chloe needed her too.

Julie's mother and Sally had slipped into a pattern of care for Chloe, Denise having her each morning, and then taking her to Sally's after lunch, enabling her to join her daughter at the hospital. The little girl seemed quite happy with the arrangement and Julie made a point of being home to give her tea and a bath each night before returning to sit with Simon for a few more hours.

The police had been to the hospital most days to monitor the situation. Julie had managed to give a formal statement but they still wanted to talk to Simon when he came round. Each day they had no news of Jim who seemed to have vanished off the face of the earth and she could give them no help at all as to where he might be. They had spoken to a few of his friends at the pub who also hadn't seen or heard from him.

Maggie hadn't missed a day in calling in at the hospital even if it was only for a few minutes. Julie had come to look upon her as a true friend, sensing that her concern was genuine as was her desire to help. It was a great relief to be able to talk without feeling judged in any way or having advice pushed upon her. Maggie was sharing her pain, walking through this nightmare with her which was exactly what Julie needed at that time.

Sarah came silently into the room bringing her sister out of her thoughts.

'You're early,' Julie smiled.

'Couldn't sleep, someone here is practicing football.' Sarah patted her rounded stomach. The baby was due in three weeks and if the scan was right it would be a boy, a brother for Rosie, completing her family.

'Ooh, feel the little imp.' Sarah took Julie's hand and rested it on her bump.

'Wow, amazing isn't it? Auntie Sarah's here Simon and the baby's due soon so you'd better wake up for the party.' There were tears in her eyes as the sisters began yet another day's vigil.

****

'Hey, Chambers.'

Jim turned to look for who was shouting. He had hardly been out in the last week and until today, only under cover of darkness. Unshaven and unkempt he had ventured out feeling pretty confident that things had probably blown over. Searching the local papers each day had brought no news of his family so Jim assumed they were back at home but he'd been careful, lying low and sleeping in the lock-up, unsure why the police wanted to see him. If they were looking for him and had got involved with his family, there could be big trouble. If only that stupid bitch from across the road hadn't come sticking her nose in. Still, maybe he could risk going home tonight, the thought of a proper meal and a warm bed to sleep in was inviting and Julie wasn't one to hold grudges, she'd want to please him, keep him sweet and all.

The voice belonged to Mickey, one of his friends who ran the little racket with the booze and fags. Jim hadn't wanted to meet anyone but Mickey was okay and wouldn't rat on him.

'Hi,' he called, crossing the road to speak to his mate.

'You're in it up to your bloody neck aren't you?' was the reply.

'What d'you mean?' Jim acted the innocent, on a fishing expedition now.

'The cops have been looking for you. Three times they've been to the pub. Knocking the wife about's one thing but putting your own bloody kid in a coma, well that's a bit much pal!'

'A coma,' he panicked, 'I didn't put him in any coma.'

'That's not what we heard, and anyway, where've you been hiding? We need to get some more supplies; it's time you gave us a bloody key to get into that lock-up. It's our stuff in there you know.'

'Yeah and I'm running the risks for very little reward!' he snapped back, anxious to get away, needing time to think things over, work out a new plan.

'I'll be in touch,' he said, hurrying away.

'Better make it soon pal,' Mickey called after him.

Opening the garage Jim went inside. He badly needed a drink. The first can of beer went down in one go but tasted sour, something stronger was called for. Reaching for a bottle of whiskey, he settled down in the old chair he kept at the lock-up, his mind racing. Why had the police wanted him in the first place? And now, if the kid was in a bad way, he'd be in even more trouble. Hell, the boy might even die, and then it would be a manslaughter charge at the very least. He took another swig of the whiskey, feeling cold and hungry; he hadn't eaten yet that day, but had come back in a panic, forgetting the food he'd gone out for. Jim lit the gas heater. Another swig of whiskey to warm him up a bit and then another. He should have made Julie get rid of the kid, why the hell had he listened to his parents in the first place; it was the last time he ever had! More whiskey, that was better, with the malt and the heat from the fire he felt much warmer. Looking around at the goods in the garage, Jim opened a packet of cigarettes and began to make a plan. Transport was what was needed. He had to get away, far away, and this stuff was his best chance. Knocking off a van shouldn't be too hard, although he hadn't done it since he was a kid. The whiskey and cigarettes were beginning to have an effect. Jim didn't feel so scared now; this could be the break he needed. If he could get the van… but that would have to wait until after dark, then he'd load up and be away, chance to begin that new life he'd always dreamed about. Simple really, he relaxed, telling himself to get some rest and tonight he'd be off. Jim dozed and smiled at the thought of all the good things ahead of him.

****

The nearby school had to be evacuated, as did local shops and houses. The explosion had been at around midday and the fire now seemed under control, but the fire officers couldn't be sure what was being stored in the neighbouring garages and were taking no risks. Spectators were moved back, the press, like a pack of vultures, had been there almost as soon as the fire appliances. No one had been hurt as far as was known, but the garage at the seat of the blaze hadn't been entered yet, so the cause of the explosion was still a mystery.

When it was deemed safe, the fire fighters entered the garage. The door had been completely blown off in the blast and they very quickly discovered the horribly burned remains of a man. The police, already at the scene, took over from the exhausted fire crew and began making enquiries as to who owned the garages and this one in particular. Local residents informed them that they were owned by a landlord who leased them out individually. Within an hour they had traced the landlord and discovered the name of the man who leased the lock-up.

DS Alan Hurst looked at the name on the computer. It must be the same Jim Chambers that he was looking for; there couldn't be two in the same area. He made a quick phone call to his colleague at the scene of the fire, informing him of the connection with his own case, and was told that identification was going to be a problem and looking as if it would be down to dental records which would almost certainly hold things up. Still, knowing the situation of Chamber's wife and family, Alan didn't think there was any hurry in breaking the news to them. He went along the corridor to update his Inspector on the connection. The Inspector didn't agree.

'Take a WPC and inform the wife straight away. We can't make the decision to wait for a positive ID. The man's been missing, she has a right to be kept informed.' Alan knew the Inspector was right, but this was one of the most difficult tasks of his job and he didn't relish the prospect at all.

Both Alan and the WPC had visited the hospital a couple of times during the last week and were recognised by the ward staff. They stopped to talk to the sister on their way in, informing her that he had bad news to deliver to Mrs. Chambers. The sister would be on hand if needed but informed Alan that there was already a family member with Mrs Chambers. They entered the room closing the door behind them. Julie looked up expectantly; she was brushing Simon's hair as he lay motionless on the bed. The officers were grateful for the presence of her sister.

'Any change?' Alan asked, nodding towards the boy.

Julie shook her head saying nothing, her gray eyes nervously searching the policeman's face.

'Would you like to sit down Mrs. Chambers?' The WPC pulled out a chair.

'What is it?' she asked anxiously, her pale face taking on a look of panic.

Alan came straight to the point; there was no way he could make it any easier.

'We've found the body of a man and have reason to believe it could be your husband.'

'A body? Jim's dead?' she repeated the words, not sure if she'd heard or understood what was being said. Julie slumped back into the chair, her sister swiftly kneeling beside her, sliding a protective arm around her shoulders.

'We're not sure,' Alan continued.

'There's been a fire at the garage your husband rented and a body has been found there.'

'Garage?' Julie looked puzzled. 'Jim doesn't have a garage…not that I know of…. could it be someone else?'

'It's going to take time for a positive identification but we are sure that the garage was rented by a man named Jim Chambers. The landlord didn't have an address but there's no one else locally of that name, so I'm afraid it's a strong possibility that it is him.'

Julie was stunned, could it be her husband? It wouldn't surprise her to know he rented a garage; she was beginning to think she'd never really known the man, but dead…burned to death… horrendous! She hadn't wanted to see him again but didn't want him dead. It was an appalling way to die, she wouldn't wish such a thing on anyone and he was her children's father. Strangely though, the tears didn't come, she felt numb; there had been so many tears over the last week. Julie had a surreal sense of being outside of the room, an observer, watching as events unfolded. It wasn't real, it couldn't be real…her son was in a coma from which he might never recover and now her husband was dead…she felt herself drifting away, she was so tired, she wanted to sleep…

'Mum,' Simon's voice, hardly above a whisper, jolted her from her thoughts.

'Mum,' he *had* spoken; his eyes were flickering, trying to open.

The attention of all in the room suddenly focussed on Simon. The WPC moved first, sprinting from the room to summon the sister. Julie jumped up at almost the same time; the tiredness dropping away from her, replaced by a sudden surge of energy. Hugging her son the tears began to flow, but they were tears of elation.

'Simon…Simon.' Tears dripped onto her bewildered son. Julie was crying, laughing, feeling that she would explode with all the emotions spinning around in her head, but by far the most important thing was that her son was awake. Simon had come back to her.

The nurses appeared to be as delighted as the family, hurrying everyone out of the room only allowing Julie to stay. The doctor was sent for and Sarah dashed off to telephone their parents with the good news… and the bad.

For the first time the small sterile hospital room was brightened with smiling faces. The doctor shone a torch into Simon's eyes, checked monitors, instructed the nurses and flicked through charts. Julie couldn't take her eyes off her son. He seemed confused so she reassured him, explaining briefly that he was in hospital, but everything was going to be fine and this time it was said with true conviction.

As Alan and the WPC waited outside they could express nothing but amazement at the timing of the boy's recovery. Perhaps their distressing news had been the trigger that aroused him from the coma? It was almost as if he knew that his mother needed him more than ever. Could he have heard and understood their conversation? They could only wonder and speculate, but they were delighted that the bad news they had brought was balanced with the best news this troubled family could hear.

Chapter 22

Karen held the letter with trembling hands, hardly able to open it, or could it be that she didn't want to open it? Tossing it on the coffee table she turned away to make breakfast thinking that if she ignored it, it might go away. The toast was burnt, she threw it straight in the bin, she had no appetite anyway. Settling for a coffee and going back into the lounge to sit down, her hands weren't shaking quite as much so she reached for the letter again.

'This is ridiculous,' her mind raced. 'It's probably nothing new, I'm being silly.'

Willing herself to open the slim white envelope a single sheet of paper fell out leaving another letter inside, one which was sealed and addressed by hand simply to 'Karen'. Instinctively she knew it was from her father and dropped it back onto the coffee table as if it was a burning ember. Opening the typed letter she read what her father's probation officer had written. It was an update of the terms of license, giving a release date which was little more than a month ahead. It went on to explain that if she wished to reply to his enclosed letter she could do so through their office but if she decided not to reply then that would be the last she would hear from them. They would not forward any more of her father's letters unless requested to do so. It was a relief to receive assurances that her father had not, nor ever would, be given her address.

Karen's heart was beating wildly and she struggled to breathe. Sitting motionless, staring at the handwritten letter, the only sound in the room was that of her heartbeat. She didn't want to read it, yet knew she couldn't go to work without knowing what was inside.

Yes, she would open it; a decision which was to throw her back into the maelstrom she had thought was behind her for good.

****

If anything Peter's resolve had strengthened since his visit to AA. In the following weeks he had worked hard, in his business and his personal life. Stephen and Charles, his partners at work, had noticed the change welcoming it with relief. They had been carrying a great deal of his workload, which realistically couldn't have continued for much longer. The firm was receiving more work than it could handle and their good reputation meant that clients were prepared to wait for their services, putting them in the happy position of having a waiting list but also making it imperative that all three partners worked equally hard, each one pulling their own weight.

Peter again began to spend long hours at work, regaining his enthusiasm which brought with it a little of the self-respect lost of late. Returning to his empty flat was, inevitably, the worst part of the day. Having paid scant attention to his living accommodation, the flat had become little more than a base and the drabness of it was unnoticed in the alcoholic haze that accompanied his hours there. Now when he really began to take notice of his new home he could see how soulless it was. Sundays became his DIY day. This too was new to him; Angela had always looked after their home, employing trades people and decorators when necessary. Surprisingly he found the unfamiliar practical jobs tackled to be enjoyable, perhaps even therapeutic. Replacing the bathroom suite, a rather dated avocado plastic affair which his youngest daughter had declared 'Gross,' it was necessary to employ the skills of a plumber, but Peter attempted the tiling himself after purchasing the necessary tools to make the job easier. He found himself relishing the challenge of learning a new skill. It wasn't rocket science, but to someone who had never tried before, it was an achievement and passed the time with pleasing results to show for it. The lounge and bedroom had also been decorated, more skills to add to Peter's CV. Jane, his elder daughter offered to help shopping with him to choose new curtains and bedding. She had been delighted to help, leaving her husband, Brian, in charge of baby Emma one Saturday, saying it would be good bonding time for them, and throwing herself into the project wholeheartedly. Needless to say they came home from their expedition with more than just curtains and bedding.

'You need an accent colour Dad, to brighten up the neutrals of the décor.' A good excuse, Peter thought, to spend someone else's money on frivolities. But he had to admit that the finished result was pretty good. Jane knew what she was doing and his little flat now looked homely and welcoming, somewhere to feel comfortable in and enjoy rather than just a place to lay his head. He had also rediscovered his love of jazz music, playing CD's constantly, Ella Fitzgerald's rich warm voice filling the empty spaces. What little spare time Peter had was becoming pleasant, satisfying time which was enjoyable and used to the full. As well as practical things in the flat, he made the effort to go out more, accepting the odd invitation to events he wouldn't have considered even a few weeks ago. But the best change of all was in making time for his family, visiting Jane who lived just half an hour's drive away and Rachel too in York, although more often she was the one to visit, combining seeing her mother and sister too. It was good to have his daughter sharing his flat, perhaps staying overnight with the two of them cooking dinner. Little Emma too was a real joy to her grandfather. Peter so enjoyed seeing her face light up with recognition when she saw him and the way she reached out her plump little arms to be picked up, snuggling into his neck murmuring 'aah, aah.' and patting his back as her mother did to her.

Another first for Peter was exercise, not that he considered himself unfit, but regular exercise didn't normally feature in his routine. At Charles's invitation, he took out a trial membership at the new gym near their office and was now hooked, finding exercise invigorating. Two evenings a week were now spent there, using much of the available equipment for at least an hour, finishing with a relaxing swim before heading home on an endorphin high, feeling completely alive.

Peter now considered himself to be back on track. Yes, there would always be regrets, but life moves on and his attitude was to go with it now and be positive. Visiting the doctor a couple of times since the counselling sessions had ended, resulted in coming off the medication which had been prescribed. The doctor had seemed impressed to hear about his change in lifestyle and this new, positive outlook. Peter was quick to ascribe much of the credit to Maggie Sayer, whom he hadn't seen often, but had offered a listening ear and steered him in the right direction by the introduction to Tony and AA.

Peter had really taken to Maggie, having assumed that a counsellor might frown on his problems as being self-inflicted, she had been completely unbiased, treating him with respect and genuineness making it very easy to talk to her. He had surprised himself at how honest and open he was able to be, particularly to a woman and an attractive one at that. Peter would always be grateful for her help, and the understanding of his friends and family who didn't give up on him. The only fly in the ointment now was the headaches and dizziness he had been experiencing lately. At times his vision was blurred, episodes which never lasted for long but were a nuisance he could do without, particularly when working. When reading text it seemed as if clouds were swimming across his vision, rather like a kaleidoscope in monochrome, but he was sure it would be nothing; it always passed in a fairly short time. He pushed it to the back of his mind, ascribing it to coming off the medication or even the alcohol, or perhaps it was just his age catching up with him. This was a new beginning and he would not let it slip away.

****

Maggie had to look twice as Janet Rea arrived at the surgery that afternoon. There was a noticeable difference, nothing physical but her demeanour had changed for the better with more colour in her cheeks, a healthy glow and even the appearance of being taller, which could be down to a more confident posture. As the two women sat in their usual seats Janet grinned as if reading her counsellor's mind, but almost teasing, waited for Maggie to speak first.

'Okay. What is it?' Maggie capitulated.

'Absolutely nothing,' Janet replied, 'I just feel….. happy, I suppose.'

'Well that's fantastic. Do you know why you feel so much better? It certainly shows.'

'Hmm, I've been keeping my journal, using the cards and the photograph and I've even begun a regime of brisk walking. It must be a combination of them all, I can't really explain it myself, but I'm sleeping better too, and I'm not as crabby and miserable as I've been lately, even Paul's noticed and naturally he's delighted. We went out for a meal together the other day for no reason in particular, and then on to the cinema, it was great.'

'You don't know how pleased I am for you Janet, and for Paul. It's wonderful that you're feeling so much better but please, don't expect too much of yourself. Remember it's a journey and you've really only just begun. There'll be times when you feel you're going backwards and losing some of the progress you've made but if you're aware that this can happen it'll be easier to cope with but I'm really delighted. Today is actually our eighth session and normally we should be preparing to bring them to an end. I was thinking of suggesting that we meet only once a month for a while, so I'll still be in the background if you need me and we can touch base each month. How would you feel about that?'

Janet looked thoughtful for a moment making Maggie wonder if she had knocked her back with the thought of bringing their relationship to an end, so quickly added, before Janet could reply, 'Of course, if you're really struggling at any time, we can pick up more regular appointments again but you're a strong woman Janet, you can do this, you've made remarkable progress already.'

'It's okay, I understand. I know your time is precious and you have other clients to help, but I like the idea of you still being available if I get desperate again?'

'Of course, I'm not going anywhere and my door is always open, but for now we've still got work to do, so let's crack on shall we?'

Janet began telling Maggie about the small achievements she'd made since they had last met; the walking and the exhilaration it seemed to bring and her better moods at home with her family, then pulling the cards from her bag she spread them on the table to give a focus for the rest of their session. 'Guilt and 'Self loathing' were pushed to one side as Janet decided she now had a good understanding of these emotions and was learning how to cope with them. A few of the other issues they had identified now also seemed partially resolved. Tearfulness was no longer a major problem, Janet happily announcing that there had been no soggy pillows at all during the last week. Panic attacks were also no longer an issue, not that they hadn't occurred, but during the last one at the supermarket, she felt she had taken control and would be able to do so again. Yes, the symptoms had been very real, but using the tools they had discussed to good effect, they no longer held fear for Janet. The nightmares too were less regular, another achievement and another card to skip over.

'You are doing so well Janet,' Maggie commented, 'But I think you could perhaps benefit from being a little kinder to yourself.'

'What do you mean; this is all very positive isn't it?'

'Oh yes, it's great, but I don't want you to be hard on yourself expecting to be back to how you were before this all came out. The danger is that your expectations will be so high, that you will lose sight of the fact that you are still on a journey. By all means set yourself goals, as you've done with your walking, but make them small achievable goals. Your journey is a marathon, not a sprint, and you have to take care of yourself during this time. We talked about loving the inner child which is particularly important for you because you lost so much of your childhood, it was taken away from you in such an awful way. I suppose I really want to give you permission to indulge yourself. Or perhaps you need to give yourself permission to be self-indulgent. Be a child again and enjoy this childhood, you deserve it. I've known clients who began to collect teddy bears, and why not? If you find comfort in having a soft toy, then buy yourself one. Teddies are awfully good at keeping secrets too, so go ahead, talk to him. Indulge yourself in a new hobby, take up painting, or learn a language, there are so many things to try in life and you're fortunate enough to have the time to try them. And from what you've told me you have wonderful family support, so use them too.

You are a remarkable, strong lady Janet and should be proud of who you are. I feel very privileged to have met you and I hope you'll go on from strength to strength.'

Maggie and Janet parted after their session with Janet making another appointment for four weeks ahead hoping there would be heaps more progress to report and she left the surgery feeling quite light-hearted.

****

Maggie was surprised to receive Karen Jenkin's request for an extra appointment but had free time after lunch so the short notice wasn't a problem.

The young woman arrived, noticeably tired and from the puffiness around her eyes, had also been crying. Maggie noticed a slight trembling but was unsure if it was from the cold or anxiety. Offering her client a coffee was not usual practice but it seemed appropriate and was readily accepted.

'Take your time Karen. A few minutes to drink your coffee should help.'

Her response was just a nod as she sipped the warm liquid whilst cupping both hands around the mug, drawing comfort from its heat. The quiet was a peaceful haven and both women relaxed, then Karen began.

'I feel rather stupid now, coming running to you when you must be so busy.'

'I'm never too busy, and whatever it is that's brought you here must be significant, I'm pleased you feel I can help.'

'I've had a letter.' The words came out like bullets in quick succession. Maggie nodded as Karen continued,

'It's from my father; it arrived with a letter from his probation officer giving me the release date. I should have expected something like this but it really knocked me for six. To see his handwriting made me feel physically sick, yet at the back of my mind I knew he might try to contact me.'

'Do you want to tell me about the letter?'

'Yes, if that's okay.' Another brief nod encouraged the young woman to continue.

'He wants to meet me, and Mike, although I know what he'll say. The letter is full of apologies; he blames the drink and goes out of his way to tell me how much he's changed. He's claiming to be a different man now and wants me to forgive him.' This last phrase was spoken with incredulity and Maggie silently had to agree that this was certainly a tall order. The issue of forgiveness was often a stumbling block to many of the clients she saw week by week. It was something, admittedly, that she herself would struggle with if in some of the circumstances of her clients. But to a young woman whose mother had been murdered by her father, she couldn't begin to imagine how forgiveness would fit into this situation.

'Do I have to forgive him Maggie?' Karen looked desperate.

'The short answer is no, but that's really too simplistic. You may find that forgiving such a brutal act is impossible, but on the other hand if you could bring yourself to forgive, there could be some release in it for yourself too. Your father committed a horrendous crime by killing your mother, but he also let his children down by robbing you of your mother, and putting you through all kinds of trauma which is still affecting your life today. You need time to think about all the implications and I'm sure your father will understand that and won't be expecting an immediate answer.'

Tears were rolling down Karen's face; it was an impossibly difficult situation and Maggie knew that at some level she must be considering meeting her father, or more likely felt that she ought to meet him because it was the 'right' thing to do. If there was absolutely no chance of some kind of reconciliation, Karen would probably not be sitting in her office at that moment and the letter would most likely have been destroyed, perhaps even unread.

'They say a leopard can't change his spots, what do you think Maggie?'

'Well, I've always thought that to be a strange analogy. Spots are a physical attribute and so yes, perhaps a leopard can't change them anymore than you or I can change our height or eye colour. But I have known people to change, in some cases quite dramatically, in behaviour and attitude; so I would have to say that in my opinion people can change. Really though, what I or anyone else says doesn't matter, you are the only one who can make this decision. By all means talk it over, either here in our sessions together or with a close friend or maybe even your brother?'

'Goodness no, I wouldn't dare tell Mike, he'd go ballistic! I'm only hoping he hasn't received a letter like mine, there's no way he'd entertain the thought of a meeting.'

'This is going to be a difficult one for you Karen. Forgiveness in itself is an act of kindness, a gift if you like, often given to those who least deserve it, a category your father certainly falls into. If you do decide to forgive him it won't be easy, but you're obviously considering it or you wouldn't be here today. You need to look inside your mind to try and grasp how you would feel about forgiving him and perhaps building some sort of relationship. On the other hand you need to consider the implications of not forgiving him. I have known people who wouldn't entertain the idea at all, and very often that decision has had a negative effect on their own lives. Keeping hold of grudges can result in bitterness which has a knock-on effect on our emotional well being and sometimes even our physical well-being.'

Karen looked totally bewildered and Maggie wondered if she had understood what she'd said or even heard it. Waiting for a while she then asked, 'Do you have to go to work today?'

'No. I should be there but after the letter came I couldn't face it. I've rung in sick, not something I like doing but I knew I'd never be able to hold myself together.'

'It's probably been the best thing for you today. Why not go home or have a wander round the shops, whatever you want to do. Spoil yourself with a little treat, chocolate, a magazine, something like that and try to put the letter out of your mind.'

Karen's face told her how hard that would be.

'I know it's virtually impossible to put something like this completely out of your head, but churning it over and over will only serve to make you anxious. You could try putting the letter away for the rest of today and even tomorrow, then read it again when you feel a little more relaxed. Give yourself plenty of time to consider this, it's a very big decision and needs to be well thought out before you decide.'

Karen looked tired, having paced around like a caged animal since receiving the letter she'd now like to sleep for a week. Her counsellor was right, she needed time and still had a month before the release date, the decision needn't be rushed into.

'I'll go home Maggie. I'm really quite tired so perhaps flaking out in front of the telly watching something mindless will help. Thank you for seeing me at such short notice, I really appreciate it.'

'No problem Karen, I just hope you feel a little better but you don't have to rush off on my account, would you like another coffee?

'No, but thanks, seeing you has certainly helped. I was panicking, thinking I needed to respond immediately but you're right, I should take my time. Even if I don't respond until after the release it won't really matter will it? He'll just have to wait.'

'Of course, you're not under any obligation to your father; he's lost his right to any kind of respect from you and I'm sure he must realise that. Take all the time you need, perhaps when you next come we can talk some more about it, but only if it helps. You might even want to put some thoughts on this down on your time line?'

'Yes, I might do that. I'm glad I came, I'd have gone nuts without someone to talk to.'

'I'll be here for another couple of hours today catching up on paperwork, so if you need to ring at any time please do. I'm also here most days and if you ring while I'm with a client leave a message with reception and I'll get back to you when I'm free.'

'Thanks Maggie but hopefully I'll be okay now, I really do feel better.'

Karen left the surgery feeling calmer than when she'd arrived, but was under no illusions that putting the letter out of her mind would be an easy task.

Chapter 23

It was over a month since Jim's funeral and the days had all blurred into each other for Julie, who was barely managing to cope with the circumstances of his death, coupled with a heavy burden of guilt at leaving his parents to make all the arrangements but in the circumstances it had been the only way. Her own parents liaised with Jim's on her behalf, freeing up the time still needed for Simon's recovery. Julie had only just managed to attend the funeral and had found it a most stressful experience even with her father's supportive presence. Emotionally, a deep and dark sadness alternated with a sense of relief and elation, which in turn led to guilt, until Julie could barely make it through each day. At the funeral they had sat at the back of the crematorium, away from the Chambers family, not wanting to cause any embarrassment, and had left quietly after only a brief word with the vicar. Neither party seemed to know what to say but happily there appeared to be no animosity from Jim's parents who had asked if she would keep in touch so that they could see their grandchildren. Julie had agreed although as yet it had only been a written contact, in time she hoped to be able to visit taking Simon and Chloe. Mr and Mrs Chambers had lost their son; she did not wish to see them lose their grandchildren too. They had suffered by Jim's attitude as her parents had, perhaps a relationship could be forged in the future and the children could have two sets of grandparents, as was their right.

For the present, Julie and the children were coasting along, still living with her parents, and with Simon getting better each day. Physically he was doing fine and it had been such a relief to find out that there would be no permanent brain damage, but his emotional recovery would take longer. In his grandfather, Simon had found the male role model that his previous life had lacked and Julie was thrilled to see the bond developing between them. Her mother had taken on the role of homemaker to this newly extended family with relish, spoiling all three of them and feeding them as if they had never eaten before. Julie now had the luxury of time to reacquaint herself with her parents and sister, while still spending most of the children's waking hours with them, making up to Chloe for the time lost while her brother had been in hospital and working hard with Simon to rebuild his confidence and help him come to terms with all that had happened.

Evenings brought the chance to visit her sister and fuss the new baby who was most certainly the centre of attention in their household. Sarah was basking in the joys of being a mother for the second time around and her husband, David, was so obviously proud of their new son, like the proverbial dog with two tails. Rosie was six now and had always been Daddy's little girl, but baby Jake completed their family and they couldn't be happier. Julie was so grateful at having the relationship with her family restored. It was a precious gift which came a close second to Simon's recovery as the best thing that could possibly have happened.

It was a relief not to be burdened with mundane tasks, but she was all too aware that at some point decisions needed to be made about their future as a family, living with her parents indefinitely, although working well, was not a permanent option.

Julie had continued to see Maggie. In the days while Simon was in the coma and Jim had disappeared, she had become a source of strength, and their relationship had crossed the boundaries of counsellor and client, as the two women became friends. Professionally, there had only been two more sessions at the surgery, then friendship took over, and although Maggie was still a great one to talk to, they met for coffee on a different basis. Julie needed friends in her life and Maggie was proving to be an invaluable one.

Julie cradled baby Jake, marvelling at his perfectly formed little hands and tiny features, when Sarah came back into the lounge with two mugs of steaming coffee.

'It's really past his bed time,' she smiled, taking the baby and kissing his soft pink cheek. 'Back in a tick,' she said, taking Jake upstairs.

Sarah was looking great for a new mum, she'd always had style and kept trim and in fashion but the glow of being a new mother added an ethereal beauty that only contentment can bring. Their family home was beautiful too, a large detached house in nearly an acre of gardens. Julie was pleased that her sister was so happy and doing well in her career, knowing how hard she and David had worked to put their home together. Sarah had left school to train for hairdressing, not what their parents had hoped for, but being such a 'people person', she had been disinterested in academic subjects and the thought of working in an office or a bank didn't appeal in the least. Hard work and dedication had paid off and Sarah now ran her own very successful High Street salon which, before Jake was born had been extended to offer other beauty treatments. Maternity leave was welcomed to a point and there were very capable staff running the business, but typically she was keen to go back and although Jake was not yet eight weeks old, plans were already being made to return to work.

'He's an angel, so good, just like Rosie was.' Sarah sat opposite her sister wrapping her hands around the coffee mug.

'Now, little sister, how're things with you?'

'Okay I suppose, but it's still one day at a time…'

'It's bound to be. You'll get there and Simon's looking better every day isn't he?'

'Yes. Physically he's doing well, but it's going to take a long time for him to forget that day… well, forget isn't really the right word is it? He'll never do that, but hopefully he'll be able to come to terms with it. I wish he would talk about it more. I've tried to bring the subject up but he doesn't seem to want to think about Jim or any of the events that happened, let alone talk about them. One thing which is really great is that he's getting on so well with Dad; I'm thrilled about that. I can see what a fool I've been, to have denied them both their grandparents, and Mum and Dad their grandchildren too.'

'Beating yourself up about it won't help,' Sarah said, 'You have to think of the future and enjoy this time you have with them now. There's so much to catch up on and they certainly love having you there. Mum has a new lease of life; she needs to fuss over someone, I suppose I'll take a back seat now.' Sarah teased, 'Talking of the future…' there was a mischievous twinkle in her eyes, 'I've had an idea.'

'Oh no,' Julie grinned, 'Whenever you said that when we were kids, I usually ended up getting into trouble.'

'Ah, we're not kids any more, but we are still sisters…and I have a plan that could help both of us. David agrees, but I want you to seriously consider it and feel free to say yes or no, we're not going to be offended whatever you decide, okay?'

Julie had been sitting comfortably, feeling relaxed and slightly sleepy, but was suddenly alert and interested.

'Sounds intriguing, tell me more.'

'Well, David and I have plans for my return to work. The business is going well, but I need to get back in the driving seat. I do love being at home with Rosie and Jake, but you know me, I can't sit back and be an absentee manager, getting in there, organizing everything and keeping the clients happy is my role. David's been getting estimates for converting the garage and outhouses into a self-contained flat with the intention of getting an au pair or nanny to live-in and look after the children. With all that's happened of late, it occurred to me that you might like to move in there with Simon and Chloe, in return for looking after Jake and taking Rosie to and from school, and there'd be some kind of allowance as well… now don't feel you have to accept, but we'd much prefer to have you rather than a stranger living here.'

Julie had tears in her eyes. 'Oh Sarah, that's such a kind offer…'

'I'm not doing it to be kind,' her sister interrupted, 'It would benefit me every bit as much as you, probably more and it would be great for the children to be together.'

'Oh…' Julie couldn't stop the tears and hugged her sister, completely overwhelmed and unable to find the words to explain what this meant.

'Is that a yes then?' Sarah asked.

'Yes please.'

'Well turn the tap off before you set me going too,' she laughed, 'And have a look at these.'

Bringing out the architect's plans which David had had drawn up, she spread them on the coffee table for them both to look at.

'This will be an open plan living and dining area with patio doors facing the garden,' she explained, 'the kitchen will be at this end with a low half wall separating it from the living space. Upstairs will be two bedrooms and a bathroom, not very big I know, but you can have full use of the garden for the children and you're always welcome here you know that.'

'Not very big!' Julie exclaimed, 'It's fantastic. You obviously didn't see where we've been living before. There's just as much space here, more with the garden, the children will absolutely love it.' She hadn't been so excited about anything for years.

'Are you sure about this? Is David okay with having your sister living on the door step?'

'Yes, honestly, he's much happier about you looking after the children than a stranger and I'd love to have you nearby. I've lost you once, I don't want to lose you again.'

The sisters spent over an hour talking about the future and the possibilities it held, Sarah enthusing about her hopes for the salon and Julie about her children, particularly Simon and the chance of him attending the local school in the new school year, a much better prospect than the one he was due to go to.

Julie couldn't wait to tell her parents about the plans. It seemed so perfect, a wonderful chance to do the sort of work she enjoyed, in a beautiful home with time for her own children as well. Perhaps it wouldn't be forever, the children would grow up of course, but for the immediate future it was ideal.

Denise and Malcolm Spencer sat up late that night, sharing their daughter's excitement, thrilled to hear her making plans for the future and being so optimistic, a future from which they knew this time they would not be excluded.

'It's so good to see you girls together again, you used to be so close. I know Sarah's missed you,' Denise voiced her pleasure.

'I've missed her too Mum,' the excitement suddenly disappeared, replaced by thoughts about the distress she had caused the whole family.

'I'm so sorry for blocking you out, it was just easier to avoid confrontation and give in to Jim rather than face up to his disapproval and temper….'

'It's okay love, we understand,' Malcolm interrupted. 'You did what you thought was best at the time for you and the children, we don't blame you for that, you were a good and loyal wife but it's over now and we can all start again.'

Denise Spencer nodded in agreement as Julie hugged them both, feeling immensely grateful for their love and support. Tomorrow would be the start of preparing for her new life, telling the children was the first priority and she knew they would be delighted. Simon would be able to attend the local comprehensive school; they would visit soon to register for a place. Maybe after that Sarah could give her the 'makeover' she had been promising, a new start and a new look, she couldn't wait to ring Maggie to share the news but it would have to keep until tomorrow, it was far too late tonight but Julie knew sleep would come easier and be more restful now that she had a future to look forward to.

****

It was only four days since Karen Jenkins had last been in Maggie's room, which was quickly becoming a welcome sanctuary, a peaceful haven where she felt she mattered and was valued. These appointments were eagerly looked forward to, even though their counselling relationship was still in the early stages. It was something completely new for Karen, a special time which was becoming increasingly important, a time when there was opportunity to offload any problems and receive support for the decisions she was making. Since being a teenager circumstances had meant that Karen had to take on a role of leadership, being the decision maker, the home-maker and trying her best to be strong for everyone else. How she wished that this kind of support had been available then when she had felt so alone and, at times afraid. She had hoped the past was gone and couldn't hurt her any more but here it was again, reaching out from across the years, like long icy fingers threatening to choke what little security and peace there was in her life, threatening to drag her down to a place she thought she would never have to visit again.

'Would you like to try that Karen?' Maggie's voice brought her back from her past,

'I'm sorry, what was that you said?'

Maggie smiled, she could tell her client was distracted but understood what a difficult time this was for her.

'I was suggesting we make lists. The *'for'* and *'against'* forgiveness lists. If we look at this logically, which seems rather cold I know, it might help you to make some decisions. What do you think?'

Karen was keen; purposely not thinking about her father's letter over the past few days was no more than procrastination. She hadn't even written about it in her time line but knew it would have to be faced soon.

'Yes, that sounds okay.'

'Shall I do the writing?'

'Yes please and then I suppose I'll have to do some thinking?'

'Only as much as you want, let's start with the 'for's' shall we?' Maggie drew a line vertically down the middle of a clean sheet of paper, writing 'For' on one side and 'Against' on the other.

'Gosh, I don't know where to start.' Karen began chewing on the side of her thumb, her face creased with the effort of thinking.

'We could de-personalize it if it helps. Try to think of this dilemma as belonging to someone else, turn it into a hypothetical situation and put yourself on the outside. Right, if your friend came to you with this problem of forgiveness what would you tell her?'

'Probably to come and see you.'

Both women smiled at the joke, Maggie was pleased to see some of her client's spirit and humour coming through even in such a dire situation.

'Thanks for the vote of confidence, but it's you she's asking.'

'Well, I think I'd tell her that she might feel better about forgiving him even though he doesn't deserve it: better about herself I mean. The things he's done are never going to go away are they? But if she forgives him it's an entirely altruistic act, he doesn't deserve forgiveness, so it's an act of grace isn't it?'

'Absolutely, I couldn't have put it better myself. So if I write, *Forgiving makes you feel better about yourself*, will that cover it?'

'Yes, but I'd also say that it would release the guilt feelings she'd be carrying if she didn't forgive him, does that make sense?'

'Sure does to me. I think we should swop chairs Karen, you're doing pretty well at this, anything else on the 'for' side?'

'I suppose she might regret not forgiving him in later years, always wondering what would have happened if she had.'

'Good one, I'll put *Takes away future regrets and what-ifs,* shall I?'

'Yes, and another one, although they're all connected really, is having the knowledge that you've fulfilled your duty, done the 'right thing' as it were, a sense of satisfaction.

'Um hmm,' Maggie scribbled some more.

'And it will avoid bitterness and hatred which fester over time and spoil people's character. It turns inwards and can be self destructive.'

'You've been paying attention, haven't you?'

Karen smiled, it was much easier when you looked at it objectively and it gave her a mental picture of the poor girl who was struggling with this dilemma. She went on, 'There's one which I can't really look at hypothetically as it probably only applies to me, I would gain a parent, my father, and I'm pretty short on family members. The big question is can I do it and will it work?'

The two women moved on to the '*against*' list, much of which was the flip side to what had already been covered. Karen found that de-personalising the problem was so much easier yet was wise enough to know that eventually she did have to make these decisions for herself and be prepared for whatever consequences they may bring.

Chapter 24

Leaving for work, Maggie's hand reached for the front door knob when the telephone rang causing her to momentarily debate whether to answer it or not. Curiosity got the better of her and picking up the receiver, she was surprised to hear Julie's voice.

'Hi how are you?' Julie sounded as animated as Maggie had ever heard her.

'Slow down a bit. Good news is always welcome, but I was on my way out to work. Can we meet up if it's a long story? How about bringing the children for lunch on Saturday, they've never been here and I'd love to see you all again … can you make it twelve? Ben will enjoy having the children, he loves the fuss. They are okay with dogs aren't they? … Fine, see you Saturday then.'

It was a pleasant surprise to hear the excitement in Julie's voice. As a client, hers had been one of the saddest cases Maggie had ever had to deal with and for a while, when her son's life had been in the balance, things had looked like they would become much worse. The extraordinary turn of events with the death of Jim and Simon's recovery were like something from the pages of a novel and it was against this tragic backdrop that the two women had become great friends.

****

The first Saturday in August dawned bright and fair. Being unused to cooking for children and not wanting to resort to chips, Maggie decided on sausage and mash, followed by apple crumble and ice cream which she hoped would go down well with her visitors. After lunch, if the weather held, perhaps a walk out with Ben would be a good idea. It would be a welcome break from the usual Saturday chores of cleaning and shopping and Maggie would enjoy the company of Julie and her children.

The visitors arrived as she was putting the crumble in the oven. Julie's father had given them a lift and they came in apologising for being early.

'It's no problem, but wow, look at you.' Maggie took in her friend's new hairstyle and the clothes and make-up she was wearing. Julie had never looked so good; her hair was cut in a fashionable bob with highlights added to give it depth and colour. The cut really suited the shape of her face and the clothes and make up were stylish and just right for her petite figure.

'You look great.'

Julie smiled, her cheeks colouring slightly making her look like a young girl.

'Make yourselves comfortable while I put the potatoes on to boil,' Maggie grinned.

Ben was delighted to have visitors. He especially liked children; they were always keen to play and had nearly as much energy as he had. Soon he was fetching his ball, wagging not only his tail but the entire back end of his body. Simon was unsure if it was all right to play with the ball in the house and hesitated, so Ben added a few barks to the wagging just to encourage him. Maggie came through from the kitchen. 'Would you like to take Ben in the garden to play? Dinner will be another half hour or so yet.'

'Yes please…Mum?' Simon looked hopefully at Julie.

'Okay,' she answered.

'Me too,' Chloe chimed.

Simon took his sister by the hand as Maggie showed them the way into the little garden.

'It's as much Ben's space as mine, so don't worry about anything, but be warned he does get excited.'

Returning to the lounge, she sat down smiling,

'You really do look good, and I love the new hairstyle.'

'It's Sarah's doing,' Julie confided. 'She's been on at me to let her cut it for ages and I finally gave in, but I'm glad I did.'

'Now, what's all this fantastic news you've got to tell me?' Maggie asked.

That was all the encouragement needed for Julie to launch straight into recounting Sarah's offer of work and a home, leaving nothing out and showing such obvious pleasure at the prospect that Maggie was certain it was an excellent idea. She continued her story as they moved into the kitchen to keep an eye on lunch while they talked. Looking out of the kitchen window Julie was silenced by the sight of her children playing with the dog. Chloe was squealing as she raced for the ball to throw and even Simon was smiling, something of a rarity lately.

'Cat Mummy, cat,' Chloe ran inside shouting.

'No darling, Ben's a dog,' her mother corrected.

'Cat, cat,' the little girl persisted.

'She's right, look.' Maggie pointed to a dark tortoise shell cat sitting high on the garden wall watching the proceedings below with a cat's arrogant stare.

Going into the garden Maggie explained, 'The cat's become quite a regular lately, I think she's taken a liking to Ben and although a little puzzled he seems happy enough to share the garden with her. I don't know her name so I call her Beautiful, which rather suits don't you think?'

'Is she a stray?' Simon asked.

'I don't think so. She wears a collar and seems well cared for and not particularly hungry although she does like to share Ben's food and water. He doesn't really know what to make of that and she's certainly not afraid of him.'

The cat jumped down into the garden as if to prove a point.

'Hello Beautiful,' Chloe said as the cat threaded herself around the little girl's legs, making her giggle with pleasure. A tiny cat, although fully grown, she was mainly black with rich brown streaks through her coat, a lighter brown streak down her nose with a golden 'sock' on her front paw and round yellow-green eyes. As Ben transferred interest from the ball to the cat, Maggie announced that lunch was ready and they went inside to eat.

Simon was quiet during the meal, content to let his little sister be the focus of attention with her girlish chatter. Maggie knew that Julie was anxious for her son, having confided that he wouldn't be drawn into talking about Jim or the events around the time of his death, and although reassuring her friend that it would take time, she too was concerned for the child. By not verbalising his thoughts and feelings he was in some way denying them and disassociating from the reality of it all. It was as if not talking about it would mean that it had never happened. It would certainly be healthier if he could express his feelings, but at only eleven years old, it was difficult to come to terms with the death of a parent, without having to face the appalling circumstances leading up to it.

After lunch, Maggie suggested a walk through the field then on to the park to feed the ducks or have an ice cream at the little café. There were no objections to the plan so, with Simon in charge of Ben, they set off. The route to the park took them through the field where she usually exercised Ben which was also the place where Jim Chambers had confronted her. Having never told Julie of that incident nor of the poisoning afterwards, she probably never would, certainly for the present it was best kept to herself. Reaching the trees, Maggie told Simon he could let the dog off the lead for a run. Ben ran off enthusiastically, knowing the routine and enjoying each minute of it. When they called him after a few minutes, Simon was delighted that the dog came at once.

'Can we have a dog Mum?' his wide eyes turned hopefully to Julie.

'I think that would be a good idea, but not for a while yet. We need to settle at Auntie Sarah's first, then if it's okay with them we'll think about it some more.' The words brought another smile to his face, delighting his mother.

'He can have a dozen dogs if he wants,' Julie thought, but didn't dare say so.

Chloe was tired by the time they reached the park and really 'needed' an ice cream until on the way to the café she spotted the swings and her energy miraculously returned.

'We'll have an ice cream and a little sit down,' Julie compromised, 'and then you can go on the swings.'

Simon found a table outside where they could sit with Ben while the others went in to choose. Their ice creams provided three and a half minutes peace and quiet before Chloe remembered the swings.

'Okay, we'll walk slowly to the swings while we finish these.' Her mother gave in.

'I don't think dogs are allowed in that area so I'll stay here for a while.' Maggie decided.

'Simon?' Julie looked at her son.

'Can I stay for a bit too Mum?'

'If that's okay with Maggie?'

'Of course it is. I don't think Ben would let him go anyway.'

Mother and daughter walked off to the swings, leaving the other two with Ben gazing hopefully at his mistress, his long tongue drooling from the side of his mouth and making a pathetic but irresistible whine. It worked and he got to finish off her ice cream then promptly turned his attention to Simon and a second tasty success. Ben settled contentedly in the shade under the table.

'Mum said your husband's dead.'

Maggie was a little taken aback by the sudden and direct question, or was it a statement?'

'Yes, he is,' she replied simply.

'When?'

'Oh a long time ago now, about fourteen years, before you were born.'

'Do you miss him?'

It was fortunate that she had learned over the years not to be surprised at how candid the young can be.

'Yes, I miss him but it's become easier over time.' The answer was truthful.

'Were you cross with him when he died?'

'Yes, I think perhaps I was, very cross at first. When someone dies it creates all kinds of feelings and emotions in those who are left behind. I was angry with Chris for leaving me, and then I felt guilty because of feeling angry. I was also very sad and confused. It was a difficult time; when people die it can be very difficult for those who knew them.'

Simon was quiet for a few moments, mentally digesting the words.

'I feel a bit like that,' he ventured, 'but I feel guilty because I'm glad my Dad's dead.'

His honesty and articulation astounded Maggie.

'Lots of people have those sort of feelings Simon.' Her voice was quiet, gentle. 'Your Dad did things he shouldn't have done; to your mother, and to you. It's only natural that you feel 'glad' but perhaps it's more a feeling of relief. He caused you and your mum a lot of pain, so now you feel relieved that the cause of this pain has gone away…you don't need to feel guilty, it's okay to feel like that. You were very brave to help your mum as you did and I know she's really proud of you. These feelings will change, but anytime you want to talk, you can come to me, or your mum or grandparents. You have people who love you Simon, they understand and it does sometimes help to talk about it.'

'I don't really like to talk much,' he admitted.

'Then perhaps you could write it all down? If you like writing it's sometimes easier than talking. You could write letters, as if to a friend, or keep a diary and write a little bit each day if you wanted to: just about your feelings and some of the things you think about.'

Simon was looking thoughtful as Maggie continued,

'Or if you don't like writing you might like to try drawing pictures. Some people find that's a good way to express their feelings, going mad with colours or just sketching with a pencil.'

'Would I have to show anyone what I write or draw?' Simon's nose wrinkled, pulling his face into a frown.

'No, not unless you wanted to, the best thing about putting it down on paper is that you can always tear it up if you like, it's up to you.'

After a few more moments of silence, Simon said 'I think I'll write a diary. Shall we go and find Mum and Chloe now?' The subject was dismissed as abruptly as it had begun.

'Wow,' Maggie thought, 'He's quite something.'

****

Saturday morning brought a visitor for Karen Jenkins who was not entirely unexpected. Mike arrived at 9.00 am as Karen was clearing away after breakfast. Hugging him as he entered the flat she was aware that his mood was not good, and the fact that he hadn't brought his family made Karen's pulse race, knowing there was confrontation ahead. Mike folded his six foot three frame onto her small sofa. He always made her flat seem so much smaller than it actually was and even had to duck to pass through the doorway.

'Have you had one of these?' Mike came straight to the point, waving an envelope in front of his sister's face. For some reason Karen experienced a wave of guilt and could feel her face redden with embarrassment, as if she had somehow solicited the letter.

'Yes,' she replied simply, sitting down opposite her brother before her trembling legs gave way.

'So, are you going to reply?'

'I haven't really decided yet.'

'Don't tell me you're actually considering it?' Mike's eyes flashed and his voice was rising in anger,

'Who the hell does he think he is? Did he write this same rubbish to you…? 'I realise how much I love you both, and what I've missed.' What a bloody nerve and he says he's 'made his peace with God'. Are we supposed to be impressed with that? Karen, please tell me you're not going to answer this crap.'

'I honestly don't know what I'm going to do. I've been talking to my counsellor and we've made lists but I'm still not sure.'

'Lists? You must be joking. What does she know about it anyway, it wasn't her mother who was murdered? I hope you're not paying this woman.' Mike's voice had become even louder, Karen was upset and close to tears. There was no talking to him when he was like this; she bit on her bottom lip, looking down to avoid his angry eyes.

'Are you doing this out of some kind of misguided sense of loyalty? He doesn't deserve it you know that! Why should we even give him the time of day after all he's done?'

'I know, and as I said I haven't decided yet.' Karen spoke softly hoping to calm her brother yet expecting an angry tirade. The room however became strangely quiet and raising her eyes, she was shocked by her brother's expression. His face was contorted as if in terrible pain, his mouth was open but with no sound coming out. Moving instinctively to sit beside him, Karen held him as his body began to shake and huge tears started to flow. Mike clung to his sister as she gently rocked him. A loud wail suddenly shattered the silence, a noise of great agony and anguish. The minutes rolled on but the time could have been twelve years ago, the last time Karen had seen her brother cry. She stroked his head, making soothing noises as if to a child while Mike's sobs wracked his whole body. Mike was a child again, a needy child looking to his big sister for comfort.

'This is what he needs,' Karen thought, 'to let it all out.'

'I still see her… Mum. And the blood, so much blood. I hate him

Karen, I really hate him!'

'Shh, it's okay. You don't have to see him again, I understand.'

Mike pulled away from his sister's embrace taking out a handkerchief to wipe his face.

'I'm sorry, I shouldn't take it out on you. I really don't know what I'd do if I saw him again, probably kill him!'

'No you wouldn't, you're not like him in the slightest way, and you don't have to say sorry; I know how difficult this is. If you don't want anything to do with him that's fine, it's your decision and I'll respect that, but I would hope that when I make my decision you'll respect that too. I might not choose to see him, I honestly don't know yet. And just to put your mind at rest, I'm not paying Maggie, I was referred through my doctor and it really helps me, it's been so good to have someone to talk to. You have your family Mike but for me there's no one and there are times when I feel very much alone. The counselling is about me, it's my time and she never tries to tell me what to do, just helps me to explore all the possibilities. You should try it, it would probably help.'

'Don't say you have no one Karen, you've got me, I'm always here for you.'

'I know that, but in this case I knew how you would react and I didn't know if you'd had a similar letter or not so I wasn't going to say anything.'

'Okay, as usual you're the sensible one, I'm sorry I flew off the handle, so show me these lists now will you?'

Karen was surprised that her brother wanted to see the notes she had been making with Maggie but was quite happy to let him. This felt like progress, Mike had so much bottled up anger but having released some of it now seemed able to talk more rationally and for the first time was prepared to look at things from his sister's point of view.

Chapter 25

September came, bringing cooler weather and shorter evenings. It hadn't been a great summer but a reasonably warm one and Maggie had enjoyed the few outings she'd had, some with Sue but increasingly only herself and Ben. Although naturally pleased that her friend had found a partner who made her so happy, Maggie did miss being the first port of call for Sue with exciting news or bits of gossip. Still she hadn't deserted her and would always be there for her, their friendship would remain strong. Sue had suggested a day in York together sometime soon, just the two of them, travelling by train so they could polish off a bottle of wine or two during the course of the day. It had given Maggie something to focus on and look forward to. Sue was great company and there was no holding her back after a couple of glasses of wine.

Gazing out of the window after finishing washing the few breakfast pots, her eyes followed Ben sniffing contentedly around the lawn, always finding some new scent to interest him.

'If he could only learn to push a lawnmower on his way around.' she sighed, looking at the tiny patch of grass which again needed cutting, not her favourite chore. Ben was distracted by their now regular visitor, Beautiful the cat, who had jumped up to her usual perch on the garden wall and was looking arrogantly down at Ben, enjoying the effect her presence was having on him. Maggie looked closer, thinking she could see something tied to the cat's collar. Going outside to investigate she discovered it was a luggage label which appeared to have writing on it. The cat, who had jumped down by then to torment Ben still further, allowed her to untie the label and read it.

To whoever is feeding me.
Please ring my owners, they would
like to talk to you.
285347

Maggie's first instinct was that the cat's owners were displeased at her making their cat so welcome, but curiosity got the better of her and taking the label inside, dialled the number. When a lady answered, Maggie quickly introduced herself and launched into an apologetic speech, 'I've just read the label on your cat's collar and I think it must be me you mean, but I'm not feeding her deliberately, she just sort of helps herself.'

The lady laughed. 'Don't worry, I don't mind you feeding her, in fact it seems to have given her a new lease of life and I'm assuming that you like having Tara visit you?'

'Tara, is that her name? How lovely, it suits her, and yes I do like having her around.'

'Well, she's certainly been much happier since she began calling on you. Tara's always had her sister for company, we've had them for five years, since they were kittens and they've been inseparable. Unfortunately, her sister died a couple of months ago and Tara's been pining ever since but lately she's improved and we wondered if perhaps you had a cat who she's attached herself to?'

'Not a cat,' Maggie replied, 'But I do have a dog and they seem to have formed some sort of bond.'

'Ah that explains it. Well the thing is, we're moving to Devon soon. My husband's retiring and we both have an elderly parent there so it seems natural to move. Now I know this is rather a cheeky thing to ask but, as Tara seems to have taken to you and your dog we wondered if perhaps you'd consider keeping her? I don't think she'd take well to the move, especially now she's found another friend in your dog. I know it's a big thing to be asking you but…' As the lady's words trailed off Maggie made a snap decision.

'I would love to have her. Ben's quite taken to her and she would be company for him while I'm at work. Perhaps you'd like to come round and chat about it some more? I presume you live close by?'

Giving her address to Tara's owner, who was called Evelyn, they fixed a time for later that day when she and her husband could call round to discuss arrangements. And so by chance and with a little help from a luggage label, Maggie inherited a cat called Tara, an incident that brought another pet into her life and heart.

****

Later that evening Maggie rang Julie knowing they would be interested to hear about the new addition to her family and also to find out how Simon was getting along. On the third ring Simon himself answered the phone.

'Hello there, its Maggie here, how are you?' she asked.

'Okay thanks,' came the reply, 'Mum's just taken Chloe up for her bath and Grandma and Granddad are in the garden, shall I get Mum for you?'

'Oh no, don't disturb bath time. It wasn't just your mum I wanted to speak to; I thought you'd all like to hear my news. Remember Beautiful, the cat?'

Recounting the tale, she was rewarded by a couple of little chuckles from Simon, a good sign she thought, asking him again,

'And are you feeling any better Simon?' The reply took a few moments as if he was deciding what to say.

'Yes…I think so. I've been writing a little bit every day. Granddad gave me a notebook with a leather cover and said I could keep it. I've done lots of pages already…Maggie?'

'Yes?'

'Would you like to read what I've written?'

'I would love to Simon, but only if you want me to.'

'Yes, I'd like that, but you won't use any red pen or anything will you?'

'Goodness me no. I'm not bothered about your spelling or how you've written it. It's what you've written that's important and I'm pleased you want to share it with me. To tell you the truth, my spelling is terrible. That's why I do everything on the computer; it checks my spelling for me and makes me look a lot cleverer than I am.

'Uncle David has a computer like that and he says when we're living there I can use it whenever I like.'

'That's great. I'll be able to ask you for help when I get stuck with mine, I'm not very good with technical things.'

'Yeah, any time…we use computers a lot at school and I really like them. The trouble with old people using them is that they're scared to make a mistake, or so my teacher said anyway.'

Maggie smiled to herself, old indeed. She asked Simon to tell his mother and Chloe about Tara and promised to be in touch soon.

'I think he may have turned the corner,' she said softly to herself replacing the phone.

****

It was two months since Karen had first met Maggie. Looking back to the days before her counselling she could see what a mess her life had been. After her mother had died, Karen had become aware of the fragility of life, an awareness which coloured her world and the way she lived it, as if everything which was precious to her could suddenly be snatched away, as it had been for her mother. Counselling sessions had helped her to find out who she really was and why she acted in certain ways. It had been an education, confronting her values and looking at life with fresh eyes. Maggie had skilfully drawn out her personality or 'inner self' as she termed it, gently reflecting Karen's own words and occasionally asking a question which prompted an inner searching in order to understand herself better. Her mother's death in such violent circumstances had influenced her life in a way she could now better understand. One tragic event defined every area of Karen's future. She could now see why she'd avoided romantic relationships for fear of being hurt or let down and how having taken on the role of carer after her mother's death, created a responsibility issue in all aspects of work and family life. There was a new awareness that her life had been trundling along in a rut into which she dragged self imposed expectations which had become stifling and oppressive. Everything Karen did was designed to protect her from further hurt and wasn't really living at all. It was now time to take risks, not outrageous ones, but everyday risks. In an effort to build a social life she had signed up for a painting class at the local college and been bold enough to accept a dinner invitation from James, a colleague at work. Karen had also replied to her father's letter, a tentative step but the desire to open up some channel of communication between them niggled at her. Writing felt safe, a relationship without further commitment at that point in time to meeting face to face, almost like looking out from the spyhole in a door before deciding to open it. Mike wasn't overly happy about this but accepted it as her choice and since the day when he had broken down and sobbed he had resolved to respect his sister's decisions. Their bond seemed stronger than ever, they were talking quite openly now instead of avoiding painful issues.

So here she was waiting to see Maggie for what they had agreed would be their last session which in itself was a little scary.

'Early as usual.' Maggie smiled at her client.

'I thought about being late just to surprise you, but old habits die hard,' Karen grinned. Today there were no pads of paper or coloured pens, only the box of tissues, ever present on the coffee table.

'What would you like to do today?' Maggie asked. Karen took a deep breath and began.

'Seeing as this is our last session, I'd like to complete the time line. I don't think I'll really settle until I've done this.'

Maggie acknowledged this as a brave move with a slight smile but made no comment as Karen took a deep breath and began.

'I need to talk about the day Mum died. It's always there in my mind but its years since I've actually spoken about it. I have actually written it in the time line but speaking the words out loud will hopefully help me to come to terms with it.'

Maggie nodded slowly; her client was certainly taking charge of their last hour together, definitely a good thing.

'It was a bitterly cold Saturday in early February. I usually took Mike to visit Gran on Saturday mornings and that one was no exception. Mum had asked me to bring fish and chips home for lunch and I can remember waiting in the fish shop with Mike, both of us pressed up against the glass fronted counter trying to keep warm. We hurried home, running straight round to the side of the house where the back door was always unlocked. That day it was wide open. I stopped, somehow sensing that something was wrong. Mike laughed, grabbed the fish and chips and ran past me, inside, ready for his dinner. I followed almost immediately, walking into the middle of a nightmare which I will never forget. The kitchen table had been knocked over and behind it Mum was laid on her back in a pool of blood. Her eyes were wide open, her mouth forming a perfect 'o' as if she had been frozen in the middle of a scream. A knife was laid across her stomach covered in blood, but the cuts were to her throat! Mike was screaming and I didn't know what to do, I felt sick. Stupid things crossed my mind, Mum's skirt was twisted up around her thighs and I leaned down to pull it straight, knowing she wouldn't want her legs showing. I couldn't scream like Mike, I couldn't cry either. I felt sick and dizzy but I knew I had to do something so I dragged Mike by his arm out into the garden, still screaming and shivering with shock and cold. I held him close to me and was relieved to see our neighbour at the side of the house, coming to see what was wrong. I don't remember the exact sequence of events after that except that we were taken next door where Mrs Adamson made us hot drinks and sat with us until Gran arrived. The police came at some point and asked questions for what seemed to be an age. All the time I was convinced it was my fault, I shouldn't have left Mum alone, I could have stopped it! It was strange but although no one actually said who had murdered her, I knew it was Dad. It seemed inevitable, yet I still felt the guilt as keenly as if I had been the one to use the knife. I should never have left her alone; if I'd been there it would not have happened!

We weren't allowed to go back in the house even after they had taken Mum away. It wasn't our house any more, it was a crime scene. A woman police officer went in to get clean clothes for us and we went to Gran's. The nightmare dragged on for months, no, years really and that's about it Maggie. You know the rest, I've done enough crying on your shoulder these last few weeks for which I'm very grateful and I do feel stronger for facing it all again.

Now, can I borrow your shredder?'

'Why yes, if you need to.'

Karen pulled a handful of papers from her shoulder bag which Maggie recognised as her time line. The '*For*' and '*Against*' list was also there.

'It's all recorded on the time line but I needed to speak the words out loud so thank you for listening.'

They stood, both moving over to the desk. Maggie switched the shredder on and Karen began feeding it. They chuckled, both having similar thoughts,

'I feel we should be saying a few appropriate words, dust to dust sort of thing!'

When the ceremony was over they sat back down to tie up a few loose ends.

'How are you feeling about the future Karen?' Maggie wanted to ensure that her client would be okay.

'Well, firstly, I'm still corresponding with Dad. I'm not ready to meet him yet, that may not ever happen, but the lines of communication are open and in time who knows? Mike has made his decision, he wants nothing to do with him which Dad half expected but he's still hopeful. I'm feeling so much happier in myself, I seem to have more energy and I'm not the little mouse I once was. I'm starting an art class next month and...' She dragged the last word out, smiling as she teased Maggie.

'Go on then!'

'I've got a date.'

'Wonderful, when, where, who?'

'He's called James and I met him at work. We've chatted a few times but I've always been a little afraid to get involved in any relationship. Anyway, the new improved me has been making an effort, I suppose you could say flirting with him!'

'Well done. I hope it works out for you, you really have come a long way Karen, I'm so pleased for you. You deserve some happiness'

'That's what I thought, so I'm making a conscious effort to look after me as well as everyone else. I think I've managed to shake off the feeling of being responsible for keeping everyone happy and everything running smoothly, spinning plates for twenty four hours a day is hard work. Thank you Maggie, you've been great.'

'It's been a pleasure. You've done all the hard work and now that you're feeling better, take advantage of it and begin to live a little.'

'I'm going to miss you Maggie.'

'Well, you know where to come if you need to see me again, the door's always open, don't feel you have to struggle alone any more will you? And enjoy your date, that's my prescription.'

Chapter 26

Sue insisted on an early start for their trip to York. Maggie never minded getting up early but she had Ben and Tara to see to and as it would be a long day for them, Julie had offered to call in at lunchtime to let them out and feed them, knowing the children would love the opportunity of taking Ben for a walk.

There were plenty of seats on the train, another advantage of being early and they quickly settled down to catch up on each other's news. The journey was only about forty minutes, enough time for a coffee and then they would be there.

York had long been a favourite place for Maggie, having studied for her degree in counselling at one of the colleges there, which had in some way been the start of a new chapter in her life as well as a radical change in career. If the classes finished early enough, she had enjoyed wandering around the old city centre, poking about in antique shops or bookshops. There was one place in particular that she particularly wanted to visit again, a tiny second-hand bookshop with heaps of character. The name itself was evocative of years gone by, '*Jeremiah Vokes, Antiquarian Bookseller.*' Maggie had revelled in the atmosphere of the shop; a low doorway leading into a cool stone room stacked with shelf upon shelf of old books. The smell alone would take her back in time, a damp musty smell of thin yellowing paper. Most of the real history books, including some rare first editions, were on the first floor, reached by a narrow rickety spiral staircase which surely must have contravened health and safety laws, and mainly locked away inside glass fronted cabinets. If you could avoid the low ceiling beams it was fascinating to browse among these ancient tomes of history and Jeremiah Vokes himself was always on hand to pass on some interesting or amusing facts about his beloved books. He was a dapper little man, always smartly turned out with a bow tie fastened neatly at his neck and a variety of brightly coloured waistcoats which added colour to a very black and white shop. Maggie had, in her student days, found some bargain textbooks on counselling from the ground floor of the shop, books which were well above budget if bought new. Another nostalgic visit would be great although heaven only knew what Sue would make of it.

'First stop shops,' Sue declared. 'We'll do the modern ones first and then you can go all oldie worldie on me if you like.'

'Suits me,' Maggie agreed and for the next couple of hours they browsed around M&S and some of the other popular high street chains.

Looking for a coffee shop, Sue proudly declared that she had been unusually restrained in her spending, looking for her friend's approval.

'Yes, you are feeling okay aren't you? I was rather worried when you took six items into the changing room and rejected them all.'

'Cheeky, I can control myself sometimes you know.'

After coffee they set off to the Shambles. Maggie loved the old buildings, now tastefully restored shops many of which retained the character and charm of years gone by. They stopped to drool over the window display of a hand-made chocolate shop. 'Chocolate Heaven' proclaimed the sign above the lintel. Restraint came into play again as they reluctantly moved on.

'Don't you just love the quaint names of all the streets?' Sue asked. 'Low Ousegate, Finkle Street, Coppergate; they're a pleasure to say… beats Main Street and Gasworks Terrace any day.'

Maggie agreed, 'Look, here's another, Lady Peckett's Yard. There are probably some interesting stories behind these names.'

Half way down the Shambles, they came to a small house which Maggie must have passed many times before but couldn't remember noticing. It was a shrine to Saint Margaret of Clitheroe and they ventured inside to see more. No one else was in the tiny house, which was just as well, it was so cramped. They wandered around, reading the various plaques on the wall. From the information they read it appeared that Saint Margaret had been converted to Catholicism in 1574 and became enthusiastic in proclaiming her faith to all who would listen. The poor woman was eventually arrested for proselytizing and tried at court. To protect her family from the consequences of punishment, Margaret had refused to plead, which in itself was a crime in those days. The punishment for such a refusal was 'pressing' whereby the accused was laid on the floor with a small stone at the base of the spine and a door placed on top of them. Weights were applied to the door until they agreed to plead. Margaret did not submit and died after two days of torture.

'Horrendous,' Sue exclaimed, 'How barbaric.'

'Have you read this last bit?' Maggie asked. They read the end of the story, horrified to learn that friends of the saint had cut off her hand to preserve it as a relic and it can still be found in one of York's churches.

'That does it,' Sue shivered, 'We're not visiting any churches today, I've had enough history for now thank you.'

'Humour me for just a little longer…' Maggie cajoled Sue into visiting the antiquarian bookshop she loved so much. Sue was fascinated with the shop itself but proclaimed the books to be dull, whereas breathing in the atmosphere brought memories flooding back to Maggie, but limited the time they spent there for her friend's sake, and they very quickly set off again to find somewhere for lunch.

Turning back onto the Shambles, Maggie almost bumped into a man coming from the opposite direction. They both did one of those embarrassing little side stepping dances, apologizing at the same time, when recognition dawned for them both.

'Peter,' Maggie spoke first, 'What a surprise.'

'Hello there, how good to see you.' His expression showed how true his words were then he suddenly realised he was staring at Maggie with an open mouth.

'Oh... this is my daughter, Rachel, she works here in York and I'm visiting to check up on her.'

'Huh! It's usually me that has to do the checking up Dad, pleased to meet you.' The young woman offered her hand and Maggie found herself looking into smiling blue eyes, the same vivid shade as her father's. Rachel was almost as tall as Peter too, with long blonde hair twisted on top of her head and secured with combs. A striking heart shaped face with dimples when she smiled made her look younger than she actually was.

Sue was then introduced to Peter and Rachel and the four of them stood for a few minutes exchanging tourist talk about the city.

'We were just off to find somewhere for lunch,' Sue said.

'So were we,' Peter replied, 'Why don't you join us? It seems ages since I saw you.'

Sue had noticed how Peter couldn't take his eyes off Maggie and not one to miss an opportunity, jumped in quickly,

'That would be lovely, thank you.'

Maggie actually blushed, much to Sue's delight.

'Oh no, we wouldn't want to intrude, you must see little enough of each other.'

'It's fine by me,' Rachel readily consented. 'I was thinking of taking Dad to a nice new Italian that's recently opened in Fossgate, but maybe a lighter lunch would be better, what's your choice ladies?'

'We were thinking of something light, whatever you decide will be fine.' Sue again took the lead,

'I think the Spurriergate centre would be perfect, there's a wide choice and it's not far,' Rachel said, setting off with the others following.

'It's a Church,' Sue groaned as they turned into a huge ancient Church doorway.

'Used to be,' Rachel informed them. 'It's quite a thriving restaurant now, been up and running for years. You've nothing against Churches have you?'

Maggie laughed, 'She didn't want to do the culture bit today, seems to think there are funny things to be found in Churches.'

'Well not here,' she assured them 'Unless you consider quiche and pasta funny?'

'I'll tell you about it later.' Maggie said feeling an explanation of Sue's reaction was necessary.

They found themselves in a huge vaulted building, almost immediately in a queue that stretched to the door. It was a self-service arrangement so Sue turned to Maggie and Peter saying, 'You two may as well find a table; it's pointless all of us queuing. I'll choose for you, Mags and I'm sure Rachel will know what to get Peter.' It was more of a command than a suggestion, making Maggie's cheeks colour again as she tried to pass a stern telepathic look to her which was lost on Sue who turned away with the smile of a job well done.

'Good idea,' Peter spoke up, 'Perhaps we should try upstairs, it looks a little quieter.'

There was no alternative but to follow him up into the gallery or 'cloisters' as it was called. Here there were only six or seven tables overlooking the main body of the church which was rapidly filling up with hungry customers, obviously a popular eating-place. As they looked over the balcony they saw several family groups, taking advantage of the spacious aisles for pushchairs and children, retired couples, tourists and even a sprinkling of smartly dressed businessmen. The chatter rose high into the ceiling, a happy buzz as tuneful as the hymns that must have been sung in worship here for hundreds of years. The cloister was light and airy with seemingly as much glass as masonry. Taking in the magnificent stained glass windows depicting the birth and crucifixion of Christ, Maggie began to relax as Peter found an empty table for four in the corner beside the balcony.

'Is this okay?' he asked, 'I mean, not just the table, but having lunch with us?'

'Of course, but I didn't want to intrude on your time with Rachel. You must be very proud of her, she's a lovely girl.'

'You're not intruding in the least. I really am pleased to see you again; I didn't expect I ever would, so it's a real treat to bump into you like this. And yes she is a lovely girl but I would say that, wouldn't I?'

Maggie was delighted at how Peter took pains to make her feel so welcome and was somewhat surprised at her own pleasure in seeing him again. Asking how he was getting on she was also encouraged to hear how positive he seemed to be about his life, obviously there had been a real effort to overcome his problems and Maggie was impressed at how he now seemed to be back on track.

'Enough of me, you must get sick of people talking about themselves all the time and I know so little about you, so how about a potted history before the others get here with lunch?'

'I'm not the most interesting of subjects, but if you insist… Maggie Sayer, forty-three years old, nearly forty-four but I'm trying not to think about that. You know I'm a counsellor and have a ditsy friend called Sue. Born in North Yorkshire, only child, parents living in Scotland, I live alone apart from a dog and a newly acquired cat.' Looking into his eyes, she hoped this was sufficient information and the topic could be changed.

'Is that it?' Peter replied, 'I was just settling down to hear a full life story. Tell me how you became a counsellor?'

Uncomfortable talking about herself, she sketched a very brief account of losing Chris and how her whole world had changed, then swiftly moved on in time to talk about training in York and why the city was so special to her. Rachel and Sue then approached with trays of food, providing the perfect excuse to change the subject.

Sue had chosen ham and red onion sandwiches garnished with salad, tea and toffee pecan Danish pastries. As they began their meal,

Maggie explained Sue's reaction to entering a Church and the gruesome ending of Saint Margaret of Clitheroe.

'My year seven's think that story is 'awesome',' Rachel added.

'They love anything gory. We've been doing a project on the Shambles and visited Saint Margaret's museum at the end of last term.'

'Sounds typical,' Sue remarked.

'Bet they drew pictures too.'

'Absolutely, very graphic and colourful,' Rachel agreed.

The conversation changed to more pleasant topics and soon an hour had flown by and it was time to move on.

Walking away after goodbyes were exchanged Sue predictably began the rapid fire questions.

'Well you've kept him quiet haven't you?'

'Sue, he was a client.'

' 'Was' being the operative word. Anyway he told his daughter you'd been his counsellor so it's no secret. What was the problem?'

'Now I know you don't expect me to answer that. He may have told you and Rachel how we met but there's no way I'm telling you any details.'

'Huh. You spoil all my fun. He's certainly keen on you.'

'Don't be silly, he was just being polite.'

'Polite my foot, that man couldn't keep his eyes off you.'

'Honestly, your imagination will get you into big trouble one of these days.'

'Did you give him your phone number?'

'No I did not!'

Sue was absorbed in a magazine on the journey home, giving Maggie a chance to reflect on their day out. Leaning back onto the upholstered seat and closing her eyes, she had to admit that meeting Peter had been a more than welcome diversion. York itself was special, bringing back happy memories of a time in her life when she was undergoing a complete metamorphosis. The options at that point in time had been either to continue in the role of the sad little widow, or make her life count for something. She had chosen the latter. Training for a degree had taught Maggie as much about herself as anything else. The first two levels had been taken locally on a part time basis whilst still working. The actual degree, the practicing qualification, necessitated travelling a couple of days a week to York St. John's College, as well as fitting in various placements. Learning the differing theoretical approaches to counselling proved to be fascinating. Maggie had heard of Sigmund Freud and Carl Jung as well as one or two other notable theorists but had become quite absorbed in reading up on their ideas and reasoning. She grappled with the concepts of Freud's Oedipus and Electra complexes, trying to compromise her own thoughts and beliefs to accommodate his. It was only after the tutor reminded the group that their own opinions were every bit as valid as Freud's, that she could accept her own thoughts as equally cogent and felt more confident in forming and voicing her own opinions.

Soaking up various concepts and debating them in group sessions was fresh and new, and Maggie found the discussions exciting and stimulating. The areas she most struggled with were the self-awareness and self-assessment activities. Of course, Maggie acknowledged that to be an effective counsellor must include knowing her own personality and idiosyncrasies, being comfortable in her own skin as it were, and accepting and being aware of traits she didn't like in her own personality. Some of the activities were to be tackled alone; soul searching questions to answer honestly, even brutally and she coped with these, learning or at least admitting things about herself that surprised and even shocked her. Other self-awareness tasks were to be tackled in pairs or with the full group. Slowly learning to trust her peers, they became a close-knit group sharing intimate details of their lives and thoughts. There was absolute confidentiality within the group that she gradually became comfortable with and reliant upon. Maggie discovered, to her horror, that she held certain prejudices and allowed first impressions to influence her. It was traits like this which needed to be worked upon with the help of fellow students, until eventually feeling she knew more about herself than ever before.

Maggie's reverie was broken as the train pulled into their station and they disembarked for home.

Chapter 27

Peter's visit to Rachel served the purpose of reassuring him that all was well with his daughter but meeting Maggie had made the day even more special. Introducing her to Rachel, an explanation of their connection had seemed in order and he was somewhat surprised when she later asked him if he'd been at all embarrassed meeting her socially.

'Not at all, Maggie's not the kind of lady to make you feel embarrassed about anything. I only saw her a couple of times professionally and found the whole experience a great help in pointing me in the right direction. I suppose in that line of work she's heard it all before, and some.'

Now, thinking about Maggie, Peter knew he wanted to get to know her better. If there had been only the two of them in York, perhaps they would have chatted for longer or he may have found the opportunity to suggest they meet again but there had been no chance to even ask for her phone number in front of Rachel and Sue. Yet, of course, he did know how to get in touch. Maybe…

****

'I had a wonderful weekend,' Sue remarked dreamily on Monday morning.

'Glad you enjoyed my company,' Maggie gave a mischievous smile knowing Sue had enjoyed York but also that the reference would be to Sunday, which had been spent with Alan.

'Oh yes, York was great, but Sunday…guess what? Alan's asked me to move in with him.'

'And by the look on your face that's good news?'

'Of course it's good news. I'm in love. Are you busy tonight, perhaps we could have a chat, if you're free?'

'Of course, come to mine at sevenish, and then you can tell me all the details, but now go and get some work done.'

Within less than five minutes Sue popped her head around the door again.

'Don't tell me… he's proposed marriage now?'

'No, there's a delivery for you.'

Stepping fully into the room, Sue was carrying an enormous bouquet of flowers, an absolutely stunning all white arrangement of spider chrysanthemums, roses, lizianthus and freesias. Bear grass was woven in amongst them, the green defining the white and adding an exotic twist. Maggie stared.

'There's a card, here open it,' Sue thrust the flowers forward. The hand written card said *'Thank you for York and everything else. Perhaps we could pick up where we left off? Peter.'* His telephone number was on the bottom.

'Well, I don't think he means another appointment do you? More like a date if you ask me.'

'But I can't,' she was torn, 'He was a client, it wouldn't be ethical.'

'Don't be ridiculous. That was in the past. Now he's just a rather sexy man who you spent time with on Saturday and has asked to see you again. What's unethical about that? Did you use hypnotism or something?'

'Well I suppose…'

'Maggie Sayer, you're always encouraging others to move on with their lives and take a few risks. Now it's time to do it yourself. Be bold. You'll have to ring to say thank you for the flowers won't you?'

'Yes that's true.'

'And you would like to see him again wouldn't you?'

'Yes again. You're right, it's time I had a bit of fun and he is rather sexy isn't he? Now scat and let me make my phone call in privacy.'

Sue took her huge grin back to the reception desk. She couldn't wait for the evening when there would be chance to grill her friend for all the gen.

Monday's post brought a rather bewildering letter for Maggie. It was from a local solicitor asking her to call at their office and collect a package they were holding for her. It wasn't a firm with whom she'd any previous contact, making the letter even more mysterious. No clues were to be found however many times she read it, so the only sensible thing to do was call at the office as requested, which she decided to do that lunchtime.

Walking through the door later that morning caused her to wonder if it was compulsory for all solicitors to have stuffy, dusty offices. She showed the receptionist the letter and dutifully took a seat to wait for Mr. O. Jenkins, the author of the letter. Whilst mentally rearranging the furniture and adding a few homely touches, one or two plants would give a living feel to the place, Mr. Jenkins appeared and invited Maggie to his office. New blinds wouldn't be amiss in here, she thought, and some fresh flowers perhaps?

'Please have a seat Mrs. Sayer.' Mr. Jenkins motioned to the only empty seat in the room whilst attacking a drawer in his battered old filing cabinet. Finally managing to open the over-stuffed drawer, he pulled out a package then clearing a chair for himself, sat behind the over cluttered desk.

'Mr. Walter Evans, deceased.' He read the words from a note attached to the package.

Maggie sat back in her chair, a lump in her throat at the finality of those four words. She knew that Walter had died, an event which had saddened her greatly, but what on earth was all this about? The solicitor cleared his throat and continued in a very formal manner,

'We are acting as executors of Mr. Evans estate. Several weeks ago he left this package with us with instructions to deliver it personally in the event of his death.' The brown wadded jiffy bag lay between them on the desk.

'Please, take it,' he urged, 'and if you could just sign this for me.'

Leaving the office in a daze, Maggie thought about Walter. He'd been a special client, a fatherly figure of whom she had become very fond. On hearing of his death, her sadness was tinged with a sense of happiness. He had struggled to live without his much-loved wife, Iris, and she hoped that in death they would somehow be reunited and at peace. Back in her own room at the surgery, she sat down and took the package from her bag, carefully opening it to reveal a wad of tissue paper and a letter.

Dear Maggie.

If you are reading this then you'll know I've set off to find Iris. Don't be sad, life was never the same without her and I've been ready to go for a long time now. You were a blessing to me during a difficult time and I thought of you as if you were the daughter we never had. Three boys Iris gave birth to and our only regret was that there was never a little girl. If we'd had a daughter, I'd have been proud if she turned out like you. Enough rambling. What I really want to say is thank you and I'd be honoured if you would accept this little trinket that belonged to my Iris. It's nothing valuable, but she loved it and I hope you will too. I've also included Iris's recipe for scones. You'll be pleased to hear that my cooking skills improved, especially when I put my glasses on. Thank you Maggie, have a good life.

Walter Evans

The tissue paper was wet as Maggie unfolded it, from her own tears, but as Walter had asked, they weren't tears of sadness. An oval pendant fell into her lap and picking it up to turn it in her fingers she was delighted with the green stone, speckled with gold and set in a silver Celtic style twist. It was a timeless piece of jewellery on a fine silver chain, one of the most beautiful pieces she had seen. The value as in all the best gifts was in the thought; Walter had paid her a great compliment which was something she would treasure always. Including the recipe was the icing on the cake, also to be treasured. Maggie would certainly never forget Mr. Walter Evans.

****

The kettle was boiling as Sue tapped on Maggie's front door and walked in. They went through to the kitchen to make coffee and then settled down in the cosy lounge to chat.

'You first,' Sue instructed, 'You've been walking around all day looking like the cat that got the cream, so come on, tell'

'There's not really much to tell. I thanked Peter for the flowers…and he asked me out to dinner.'

'Dinner. Ooh where? When?'

'Tomorrow night at 'The Pheasant' at High Green.'

'Wow, its rather posh there, what're you going to wear?'

'It's only dinner.'

'Only nothing! Just don't go all frumpy and 'smart.' Cute and sexy would be a better look.'

'Are you saying I dress frumpily?'

'No sorry, of course you don't. Just don't be too reserved, encourage him a bit.'

'I hear you but don't worry. I want to encourage him, I really like Peter, but I'm not you. It'll have to be in my own way. And before you ask, I'm not hiding a tape recorder for you in my bag. Now it's your turn to spill the beans. Have you decided yet, are you going to move in with Alan?'

'Hey that tape recorder's a good idea. Seriously though, about Alan. My heart says yes, in fact it says yes yes yes! But I know I should think it through, we haven't known each other that long.'

'That's very sensible of you. What does your mother think?'

'Goodness, I haven't told her yet. I'd be sure to get a lecture about living over the brush and making sure he put a ring on my finger before I let him do any of that 'funny stuff' or he'll never respect me and all that. Actually it's not his respect I want, and it's too late for the ring.'

'So…did you give him an answer then?'

'No, but I did have a good look round to check out the storage space.'

'Sue, you didn't.'

'Of course I did. Storage space is important.' Oh by the way, he's picking me up here at nine. Hope you don't mind but he's on some kind of split shift today and if I don't see him tonight it'll be the weekend before we're both free again.'

'That's fine. I'd like to see him again myself. When's he expecting an answer?'

'When I've decided of course. I don't want to appear too easy.'

The rest of the evening passed quickly in pleasant chatter and laughter until Alan promptly arrived to pick Sue up. He kissed her and greeted Maggie warmly, 'Hey, how're you doing? Haven't seen you for ages.'

'I'm fine thanks Alan, and you?'

'Great. I suppose she's told you what I'm hoping for?' He smiled at Sue as he spoke.

'Yes, I've told her and…I've made my decision.' Sue paused for effect, prolonging the suspense.

'Well?' he looked anxious.

'Yes. As of now you have yourself a live-in girlfriend.'

Alan grinned, then picking her up swung her round in the tiny lounge.

'I think you've just made someone very happy.' Maggie laughed.

'I'll ring the builder straight away,' Alan said

'The builder?' Sue was puzzled.

'What on earth for?'

'Well we'll need an extension to house all your shoes won't we?'

She poked him affectionately in the ribs. Don't worry my love; I'm going to restock the Oxfam shop.'

'Oh good, you're having a throw out before you move?'

'Yes,' Sue chuckled, 'I'm going to throw out all your old stuff to make room for mine.'

****

Despite what she had told Sue, Maggie did take extra care in choosing what to wear for her date the next evening. The very thought of a date at her age seemed silly, but also rather exciting. After trying on half her wardrobe, she settled for the skirt she'd bought last Christmas, a black, flattering fit which flounced just below the knee, teaming it with a soft green jersey top, together they emphasized her curvy figure. Applying perhaps a little more make-up than usual and brushing her short brown curls until they shone, Maggie was ready.

'What do you think boy?' she asked Ben.

Her dog obligingly thumped his tail on the carpet, disturbing the cat who was curled contentedly into his side. Tara got up, giving Maggie a look of disdain before turning around twice and settling back into the dog's warm coat.

'Thanks for the vote of confidence you two.' Her heart leapt as she heard a car pulling up outside.

'Be good,' she whispered to her pets, then to herself, 'And go for it Mags!'

Chapter 28

Simon had completed the first two weeks at his new school and was loving every minute.

'It's brill Mum,' he had told Julie, 'our form tutor's got a wicked sense of humour and has us all in stitches half the time. I've put my name down to try out for the lower school football team, the trials are on Wednesday after school so I'll be a bit late home.'

'That's great Simon.' Julie couldn't be happier with his progress. The new school seemed to be bringing him out of himself and the reports she'd heard about its standards and academic success were impressive. If Simon made the football team, and she was confident he would, it would be an extra bonus.

Things were going well for their little family at the moment having left her parent's house they were now settling into their new home at Sarah's. The builders had done an amazing job with the alterations and everything looked so pristine and fresh.

Julie could hardly believe it was real and not a dream.

'It's no more than you deserve,' her sister insisted, 'You've been through so much, it's time things worked out for you.'

Sarah had returned to work and Julie was looking after baby Jake and Chloe and taking Rosie to school each day. Simon could easily walk the short distance to school alone, something his mother would not have considered where they had previously lived. Chloe had a place in the nursery class at the same school as Rosie each morning, so Julie was out and about for much of the day which presented the opportunity to meet other mothers in the area. Life was at last looking good. There were of course moments when the events of the last few months haunted her. It was still quite raw and Julie would never forget those dark days when it seemed that Simon might die; the children were her life, the centre of her universe, and she couldn't imagine being able to go on without them. Chloe seemed to be the least affected by those terrible weeks. Occasionally she had asked where Daddy was but seemed to accept the fact that he wasn't coming back with almost no emotion. Hardly surprising, the little girl's relationship with her father had been anything but close. Chloe had always seemed afraid of Jim even though Julie was always on hand to come between them, taking Chloe on endless walks or playing with her in the bedroom to avoid confrontation. It had been the same with Simon but being older he had been more aware of what was going on. It seemed to Julie, with hindsight, that Simon had probably understood more than she had given him credit for which placed him in a position that no little boy should ever be in. Still, the signs for the future were good. He was much more open and chatty these days, obviously taken with his new school and Julie felt that his writing and occasional little chats with Maggie were beneficial too. 'Time,' she thought. 'We just need time to get over it.'

****

Julie had invited Maggie to come for tea and see their new home. Their friendship had become important to her. Maggie had been there when Julie had needed her and now in a quiet and unpretentious way she was helping Simon too. It was Wednesday; Rosie was home from school and the two little girls were playing happily in the garden. The French windows were wide open and Chloe shouted out, 'Watch me Mummy' as she came down the slide with Rosie close behind. Julie waved then returned to setting the table. Jake, laid on a quilt underneath his baby gym was knocking the toys above him with his little clenched fist. Julie sighed. The past now seemed like a horrible nightmare, she was truly happy here.

Sarah arrived home early, taking her children off Julie's hands so Chloe came in to see what was for tea. Maggie and Simon arrived together, Maggie straight from work and Simon from his football trials.

'I'm in Mum,' he shouted excitedly, 'I've been picked for the lower school football team.'

'Well done, I knew they wouldn't refuse such talent.'

'Aw,' Simon blushed. 'Can I ring granddad to let him know?'

'Of course you can. Maggie, let me take your jacket then we can do the grand tour before tea?'

'Can't wait. What I've seen already is wonderful, great garden, the children must love it.'

'They do. It's Sarah and David's garden of course but we have full use of it and I don't even have to mow the lawn.' Julie proudly showed Maggie the rest of her new home. It was light, open plan and very simply furnished. The larger of the two bedrooms had been cleverly divided for the children with a partition from the far wall almost to the door. There was a small window in each side of the room, effectively giving them both their own space. Simon's room housed a bed, a built in cupboard and a desk to do his schoolwork. Chloe's area was very pink and 'girlie' with a princess theme.

'Sarah and David have been so kind, I'll never be able to repay them. Mum and Dad too have bought all the new bits of furniture you see. They claim to be making up for lost time, all the birthdays and Christmases they missed.'

'It's terrific Julie, I'm really glad things are working out so well.'

Over tea Maggie told them about Peter, how they had met in York and that they'd had two or three dates since then. Of course she omitted the fact that he'd once been a client, which was history now. Simon sniggered behind his hand.

'What are you laughing at? Think I'm too old to have a boyfriend do you?' Maggie teased him.

'No,' he answered, 'It's just… funny.'

'Well I think it's excellent news.' Julie smiled approval at her friend and the rest of the evening passed light-heartedly as they enjoyed a game of snakes and ladders before Simon went upstairs to do his homework and Maggie helped to bath Chloe and put her to bed.

Maggie always enjoyed the time spent with Julie and the children, her friend could almost be the younger sister she'd always wanted, and her affection for the children was growing too. Seeing how events were working out for them was incredible, they so deserved a good life and a happy future; certainly they were one of the most unassuming families she had ever met. Talk about a silver lining. Still her own life was looking rosy at the moment too; things were certainly looking up, Peter had taken her out to dinner twice and to the cinema together, as well as meeting for a sandwich several times at lunchtime, both seemingly keen to develop their relationship. They'd also had a hilarious evening tenpin bowling with Sue and Alan. Peter and Alan hit it off immediately, both having a similar sense of humour and an interest in playing squash. Games were soon arranged and their time at the gym together was becoming a regular event.

****

Maggie invited Peter for a meal, which would be his first visit of any length to her home. Usually Maggie had been ready to dash out to the car when he came to take her out but she'd decided it was time to cook a meal for him. Now the day had arrived she was a bundle of nerves, wanting the evening to go well yet not confident in her ability to make it so. Cooking to Maggie was certainly not cordon bleu although she was quite capable. Her father had never liked his food 'messed about with' so plain wholesome cooking was what she'd learned as a child and felt comfortable with now. She settled on a traditional roast dinner with roast potatoes and fresh vegetables followed by a lemon meringue pie. As it was Saturday the shopping was the first task of the day followed by a whirlwind cleaning session, leaving time to prepare for the meal in the afternoon. Keeping busy was her ploy to occupy her mind but it wasn't working. A restless, nervous feeling competed with the excitement of anticipating how the evening might work out.

After finishing all the advance preparation she could possibly do and the lemon meringue pie was cooling in the fridge, Maggie took a long hot shower, washing her hair and shaving her legs with care. Drying off, she applied lashings of her favourite body lotion, massaging it well into her skin, particularly her feet. How she detested her feet. The skin was hard and cracked easily and she had lost a toenail years ago when it became ingrown and had to be removed. It looked ugly and consequently she didn't like people to see her feet, envying girls with pretty feet and painted toenails. Brushing her hair vigorously she chided her vanity, what on earth was she expecting from this evening? Yet she still found herself choosing clothes carefully, matching underwear, not too frumpy but not mutton dressed as lamb either.

'This is ridiculous.' she told herself, 'If Peter gets amorous, I might not like it. But if he doesn't I think I'll be hurt. What if he doesn't find me attractive?' Maggie laughed at her own silliness.

Inevitably thoughts of Chris flashed through her mind…but strangely they were not feelings of guilt and the sense of betrayal she might have expected. Yes, this was the beginning of a relationship, the one and only since Chris, but Maggie was embracing the idea with excitement. Peter stirred feelings within her that had long been suppressed and now she had to admit to herself there was a physical attraction and the desire to be with him.

Shortly before he was due to arrive Maggie lit a scented candle in the lounge, telling Ben and Tara, 'Yes I do love you both but there are times when I do not want my house to smell like a zoo and tonight is one of them.' Of course the house didn't smell at all, except for the aroma of roast beef and red wine gravy.

Peter arrived on time bringing gifts of wine and chocolates. When Maggie introduced him to her housemates, Ben ambled over for a fuss and Tara jumped onto the windowsill, stuck her back leg in the air and began to lick her bottom.

'Great start,' Maggie groaned but Peter laughed and accepted her offer of a drink with which she hastily tried to distract him.

The meal was a success. Maggie didn't drop his plate in his lap or spill gravy over the table linen and Peter was very complimentary. Chatting at the table for a while, feeling relaxed in each other's company, Maggie rose to make coffee. Peter's eyes followed each graceful, fluid movement, if she was nervous, it didn't show. The dating game was equally as perplexing for him. Having been with Angela for so many years, it felt awkward embarking on a physical relationship with someone else, yet there was no doubt that he was falling in love with Maggie and if he was reading the signs correctly, she too was experiencing the same emotions. Taking their coffee to the lounge and sitting side by side on the sofa, Maggie was very aware of Peter's physical closeness and a slight tremble rippled throughout her body. It wasn't long before he put his cup down on the coffee table to slide his arm around her shoulders. Leaning against his broad shoulders there was a stirring in her body, a feeling she had thought she would never experience again. Peter's masculine scent excited her; she wanted him to hold her, to touch her, to love her. He seemed as unsure of himself as she was but was certain the attraction was mutual. His hand gently stroked the contours of her cheek and she relaxed, snuggling closer, enjoying the long forgotten sensations sweeping through her body. After a few moments Maggie lifted her head to look into Peter's face. His eyes twinkled as he smiled, moving closer to kiss first her mouth...

****

I feel so much better than this time last year, it's incredible.

Janet wrote in her journal.

It was rather worrying to think of not seeing Maggie each week, but I know she's there if I get really down again and actually I'm feeling quite proud of myself, having done really well lately. Some of the practical things Maggie suggested, like the mood box, are great. I felt like a kid at school again with a project to work on, spending ages covering it with a pretty cotton fabric and decorating the lid with a large cloth flower. It took a few days to fill it with everything I wanted to put in. Firstly there was a CD of Chris de Burgh with some of my favourite songs; I'd forgotten how much I love some of his music. Next it had to be chocolate. Well, Maggie did give me permission to spoil myself. A couple of favourite magazines and a whole bunch of photographs going back to our wedding were next. All the birthday and Christmas cards Paul has sent me over the years are now in there, and I also added a scented candle and a bottle of extravagant bubble bath. When I'm feeling a bit low now the mood box helps to lift my spirits. A long soak in the bath listening to music, then a cup of tea with some chocolate work wonders.

It was a good idea to try a new hobby too so I've decided to take up photography. I must remember to tell Maggie about that next month. It's great because I can go with Paul when he's out researching for an article and take photographs for him to use. Hopefully I'll get better in time, there's not much of a market for images of people's feet.

I really can't believe how far I've come. Corny though it may be, life has taken on a new meaning and I'm so grateful. I'm blessed to have such a wonderful family and each new day is so precious but I'm always conscious of how fragile life and happiness can be, and so I try to make the most of each hour, even each moment. Maggie helped me to see that what happened to me in childhood does not have to define who I am, but how I deal with what happened will define who I go on to be. I'll always be thankful for that. And now, I am going to squeeze this journal into my already overflowing mood box, as I no longer have enough time to write in it every day…my life is too full and busy.

Chapter 29

A wild, windy autumn gave way to a cold, dark winter. Usually Maggie found this to be the longest season of the year, when the days were murky and overcast and the gloomy evenings made her long for spring and the new energy it proffered, but this year would be different. Christmas was to be spent in Scotland with her parents as usual but Peter would be with her, a warming thought which brought back some of the sparkle Christmas had lacked in recent years. Peter too was looking forward to seeing her parents again, having met George and Helen in October on one of their rare journeys south for Maggie's birthday. They had all enjoyed a meal out and her parents took an instant liking to Peter as he had to them. Helen wore an expression of undisguised hopefulness and couldn't stop smiling during their entire visit. Now it was their turn to play the hosts, a role they relished more than ever.

Work for Maggie was busy at this time of year. For many people the stress of the days leading up to Christmas added to their problems whether they were financial or relationship issues. The season of goodwill could be breaking point for many.

Sue was also cheerfully anticipating her first Christmas with Alan, aiming to impress him by cooking a traditional Christmas dinner. The surgery buzzed with the phone never silent as patients ordered prescriptions to see them over the holiday season and tried to fit in appointments with their doctors before they took a well-earned break.

Maggie and Sue managed to meet for lunch on the last day before surgery closed for the holidays.

'We're off first thing in the morning,' Maggie sighed, 'I'm feeling ready for the break and a bit of spoiling from Mum never comes amiss.'

'Lucky you, I'll be slaving away over a hot stove,' Sue wiped her brow trying to look hard done to.

'Your choice, you know Alan would have taken you out for Christmas lunch if you had wanted. He loves to spoil you.'

'I know…but I thought it would be quite romantic to spend our first Christmas together at home with a turkey lunch and all the trimmings. Which reminds me, I must buy some indigestion tablets before the shops shut.'

Laughing at her friend, Maggie marvelled at how well Sue had settled into a new life with Alan. She looked quite radiant these days and although always upbeat, there was something extra which seemed to complete her happiness and was turning her into quite the domestic goddess too. Sue was entertaining similar thoughts.

'It's been an eventful year for both of us hasn't it?' she pondered. 'Things are very different from last Christmas when we were just two lonely old maids.'

'Oh, it wasn't that bad was it?'

'No…but it's more exciting now don't you think?'

****

Peter's car was the obvious choice for their journey, being more spacious and comfortable. Arriving early as arranged, he looked relaxed and as pleased as ever to see Maggie. Loading the car with all the things she was taking, he commented, 'For all we're just a little family of four, we seem to need a fair amount of stuff, especially Tara, she may be the smallest, but she certainly doesn't travel light.'

Maggie glowed, 'a family' Peter had said, she liked that very much. He was right about Tara though, what with the litter tray, travelling box, food, toys and grooming items, she did take up more space than the rest of them.

The journey was uneventful with Maggie enjoying being a passenger and having the opportunity to gaze at the passing countryside, much of which was bleak though seasonal. The sky was a mass of gray cloud, threatening rain, or perhaps snow and the trees were stripped bare, their black branches reaching heavenward, like the gnarled fingers of a witch.

Less than two hours later George and Helen Price were welcoming the couple into their home. The warmth of the atmosphere greeted them immediately they entered the stone built cottage. A recently cut pine tree, which the Prices invariably favoured for the festive season, together with the scent of rich spiced potpourri and freshly made mince pies, evoked memories of childhood winters long ago. Even Peter had that feeling of 'coming home' and was accepted into the family as if he'd always belonged amongst them. The kettle was boiling as they unloaded the car and while Helen made coffee, George helped to carry the cases through to the back of the house. He opened Maggie's bedroom door, putting her case down, and then moved towards the box room next door.

'It's a bit small I know,' he addressed Peter, 'but Helen thought you'd be quite comfortable in here. The bathroom's down the hall there. Right, I'll just go and help with the coffee whilst you two get sorted.'

Maggie turned to Peter, 'Oh Peter, I am sorry. I never thought about the sleeping arrangements. Do you mind having separate rooms while we're here?' Peter had stayed overnight with her on a few occasions since the evening she'd cooked him a meal and they were still enjoying slowly getting to know each other and cherishing their newfound intimacy.

'Its fine,' he smiled reassuringly, kissing the tip of her nose, 'I think it's rather sweet that they haven't assumed anything. Anyway, if loneliness sets in, I know where you are.' He jiggled his eyebrows with a knowing look on his face making her laugh out loud.

Back in the lounge for morning coffee, George was sitting in his armchair with Tara curled up on his knee.

'She's soon made herself at home,' Maggie remarked. Ben of course was in the kitchen, knowing who would spoil him if his mistress wasn't looking.

'Snow's forecast,' George announced, 'hope you've brought the winter woollies.'

'It's okay Dad. I warned him so we're well prepared.'

As if on cue it snowed on Christmas Eve, then again on Christmas morning. The surrounding countryside looked stunning covered in a crisp, pure white. Ben darted around like a puppy on their walks out, while Tara preferred staying indoors to keep an eye on the fire.

It was the Price family tradition to have Christmas dinner before any present opening. This had the benefit of giving them a more relaxing morning and something other to do than sleep after their meal. Mother and daughter worked together to prepare a delicious turkey lunch, with sufficient to last for a month if they became snowed in. George and Peter went to the local pub to get out from under the cooks' feet. Helen couldn't help but notice how happy Maggie seemed to be.

'I don't think I need to ask if it's serious do I? You're positively glowing.' She smiled at the sound of her daughter humming carols.

'It's wonderful, I never thought I'd feel so happy again Mum, it must be love.'

'Oh it's love all right, and for Peter too,' she observed with a knowing look and a twinkle in her eye.

Lunch was almost ready as the men arrived home, George chattering in full flow on his favourite subject, informing Peter of the differences in soil in this area to back home. Maggie smiled. She had changed into a new red skirt and a cream silk top, looking flushed from the warmth of the kitchen and the happiness in her heart.

'Excellent as usual my love,' George pronounced as he sat down to a heavily laden table, each dish prepared especially with him in mind. It could have been a scene from a glossy magazine, the traditional turkey dinner with all the trimmings and every available seasonal vegetable, the large open fire consuming thick logs and turning them to ash, with a dog and a cat sprawled the full length of the hearth and a tree resplendent in the corner with a cornucopia of parcels stacked beneath.

They ate enthusiastically, Maggie determined to choose only a little of everything but with so much choice she still ended up eating far too much. Peter couldn't praise Helen enough and insisted on he and Maggie doing the washing up, while Helen had a well deserved break. As they washed and dried the dishes, a feeling of contentment settled on Maggie, which wasn't just from the delicious meal they'd shared. Working in compatible silence for a while, each had their own thoughts, until suddenly a crash shattered the peace as Peter dropped a large serving dish.

'Oh no….. I'm so sorry. I hope it's not a valuable family heirloom.'

Maggie tried to keep a straight face, 'Well actually, it did belong to my great grandmother and Mum's particularly fond of it….'

Peter's face fell, 'I'm really sorry, I don't know what happened, it just slipped. I seem to be so clumsy these days.' Only then did he noticed the twinkle in her eyes and the smile she was trying to suppress.

'You minx, you're teasing me aren't you?'

'I couldn't resist, you're such an easy target. It's one of Asda's basic range, so don't lose any sleep over it.'

The afternoon was spent opening presents, the expected and some surprises. Maggie looked at the boxes of chocolates piling up beside her, normally unable to resist opening them, today she didn't think it was possible to eat again for a week. When all the parcels were opened

Helen announced, 'We didn't really know what to get you both, so we've arranged a day out for us all tomorrow, our treat, and we've booked somewhere posh for lunch so wear something special dear.'

'Not more food Mum. And you've given us some fantastic presents; you don't need to do anything else.'

'It sounds a marvellous idea,' Peter joined in, 'But I hope you'll allow me to take my car, so you can relax and enjoy the day yourselves.'

Maggie was delighted at this offer and rather surprised that her father agreed so readily, he usually enjoyed the role of chauffeur, but it would be more comfortable in Peter's car for them all.

After Helen and George retired to bed later that night, the younger couple sat in front of the fire, reliving the day.

'Seriously Peter, I hope all this family stuff and tradition hasn't been too much for you?'

'Far from it, it's been an absolute joy. I had a rather distorted view of Christmas last year from the bottom of a bottle. It's been a privilege to share with your family, they're such amazing people. Now I know why I like you so much.'

'Well, tomorrow's a bit of a surprise. We usually just recover from the excesses on Boxing Day. I don't know what's prompted this.'

Peter put his arms around her shoulders and pulled her close, 'I'm sure it'll be fun whatever's in store. Now… how soundly do your parents sleep?'

****

Boxing Day was bright and sunny if rather cold so they wrapped up well for their walk with Ben after declining anything more than orange juice for breakfast. Maggie's parents were giving nothing away about the day's plans, but she dressed as her mother had suggested, glad to have brought a suitable outfit, and Peter too seemed to have made a special effort. The women sat in the back seat so George could navigate. A good covering of snow made the hills look spectacular with the sun reflecting from them giving the appearance of clean, white freshness everywhere.

'At least I get a break from the garden when it's covered with snow; everyone's looks the same so it's a good excuse to be lazy.'

'Dad, your garden's always immaculate. You should see it in summer Peter.'

'If that's an invitation, I'm in.' he replied.

They seemed to be taking the route back to England.

'We thought you'd like a look at the touristy areas around the borders.' Helen remarked casually as they were approaching Gretna.

'Are Gretna and Gretna Green one and the same place?' Peter asked.

'Just about,' George told him, 'Why don't you pull in over there and we'll take a look around.

Maggie had been here on a few occasions with her mother to a large retail outlet on the outskirts of the little town and she was surprised to see that it was open and buzzing with shoppers. Thankfully they headed in the other direction, avoiding the tourists swarming about with cameras. A piper was playing and they paused to watch a young couple who had just been married and were laughing cheerfully as they posed for photographs beside an anvil.

'I think it must be coffee time now,' George suggested so they made their way inside the Gretna Green Hotel in search of refreshment.

'Rather romantic don't you think?' Peter whispered to Maggie.

'Yes, but I'm amazed it's so busy. I hope we're going somewhere a little quieter for lunch.'

Comfortable seats in a quiet alcove were soon located and coffee ordered. Maggie gazed around at the sumptuous decor of the hotel, able to see what attracted young couples, the luxury and romance just oozed from every corner. A young woman at the other side of the room caught her attention. Turning to her parents she remarked on the woman's resemblance to Sue.

'Wait a minute, it is Sue!' Shock and confusion showed in her face but Peter smiled knowingly leading her over to her ecstatic friend.

'Maggie,' she wailed, 'were you in on this too?'

'In on what? What on earth are you doing here?' On seeing Alan she began to put things together.

'We're getting married,' Sue squealed. 'He's had it arranged for ages but didn't tell me until this morning. It's like eloping, it's so exciting, and he's even booked the bridal suite, although I think they're all bridal suites here!'

George and Helen joined them and Peter began introducing them to Alan.

'You've all been in on this haven't you?' Maggie laughed.

'You mean you didn't know?' Sue couldn't believe it and she was incredulous too; it was such a tremendous surprise and she was so glad to be there to share their day. The so-called 'dinner out' was the wedding breakfast, but there was little time to talk, the registrar was waiting for them.

Maggie had so many questions to ask Peter, but they would have to wait. Life seemed so good at this moment, it was almost frightening. Squeezing Peter's hand she listened to Sue and Alan make their vows with tears in her eyes but the ceremony was over all too quickly and they gathered outside for photographs. The bitter cold soon brought them back inside for a meal. Between courses, Maggie at last had the chance to talk to Sue uninterrupted.

'Did you not suspect anything?' she asked.

'No, truly I had no idea. Alan must have been so busy. The two couples over there are his friends from training college and their girlfriends; I'll introduce you later. I think you know most of the others. Alan very sensibly didn't tell my mother until Christmas Eve and she's livid that she couldn't buy the whole 'mother of the bride' outfit, but I'm glad she didn't get the chance, I couldn't have done with all of her fussing.'

'So you're really okay with this whole thing? You don't mind not planning your own big do?'

'Oh Maggie, this is so much more spontaneous and romantic, it's amazing! Alan's thought of everything. He took me shopping for a so-called 'party dress' that was to be for the police ball in the New Year. I didn't suspect a thing. He only told me last night and by then everything was taken care of, even down to this lovely posy of roses, he's such a romantic… and really, could you honestly see me in a huge wedding dress looking like I should be covering a toilet roll or something? No, this is my dream, it couldn't be more perfect.' The look on her face endorsed her words and Maggie was thrilled for her. Having seen how happy Sue was, Maggie could relax and enjoy the rest of the celebrations which admittedly were amazing.

The official photographs had been taken earlier, but after the meal most of the guests went outside with Sue and Alan to take some more informal shots. There was a distinct chill in the air by then but it could do nothing to dampen the party spirit.

Peter put his arm protectively around Maggie and she leaned into his warm body.

'Maggie,' Sue shouted, but before there was time to answer, Sue had thrown the roses directly at her. Catching them before realising what they were, she felt her face begin to glow. Peter turned, smiling, and softly kissed her cheek.

Chapter 30

The drive home was quiet and uneventful, except in Maggie's head where thoughts buzzed around making her feel dizzy. The exuberance she felt almost made her nervous, everything in the garden was truly lovely, but could it last? Her parents had certainly taken to Peter as he had to them and her mother was so obviously excited about the relationship, perhaps even as much as she herself. Thoughts of Sue swam through her mind as well. Her friend had seemed so delighted and so much in love with Alan but Maggie had to admit to a degree of jealousy, a niggling fear that Sue's time would be so taken up with Alan and her new life as a married woman that their friendship would take second place. But of course, this was how it should be and Peter was in her life now. Her eyes were closed as these thoughts interweaved in her mind and Peter seemed content to let her doze while he concentrated on the driving. At Scotch Corner they stopped for a drink. Neither of them wanted a meal so they shared a toasted tea-cake.

'What on earth are you going to do with all that food your mother has sent back with us?' he asked.

'Well, she did make it clear that half of it is for you.'

'It could come in handy if we get snowed in, there's enough to last for weeks.'

Peter needed a walk to stretch his legs; she thought he was looking tired, but then so was she; it had been a hectic few days.

It was mid afternoon when they reached Maggie's home and while Peter unpacked the car, she stored her mother's goodies away in the kitchen. There was that slight uncertainty in her mind as to whether Peter would be staying the night. The physical side of their relationship was still very tentative and she still held on to a little shyness, which he thought quite endearing and now she wondered how to approach the subject, not wanting to show an expectation, but not wanting him to leave either. Peter solved the dilemma for her, 'I'm absolutely bushed,' he said. 'If you don't mind I'll head off home now, get sorted and have an early night. The spirit is willing, but....' he smiled, not needing to finish the saying. Maggie looked into his face; he did look weary, the journey had taken its toll but he did have the energy for a hug and a gentle kiss and as he left, told her that he loved her.

****

It was unusual for Maggie to feel lonely, but that was her primary emotion that evening. After taking Ben out for a walk she found herself some cheese and biscuits in the kitchen, finishing it with one of her mother's mince pies. She was a little disappointed that Peter hadn't stayed, but his declaration of love was comforting, the words had felt like a little knot of warmth underneath her ribs and of course she would be seeing him the next day. They both had a few more days off work and had planned to visit Peter's eldest daughter, Jane, whom she had yet to meet. There were a couple of appointments which he needed to keep in the morning, but after that he'd promised to come round to help her eat the left-overs. Perhaps the fact that Sue was still away added to Maggie's rather sombre mood; she would have enjoyed a good old natter with her friend and now there was so much to talk about, it would take them ages to catch up. Eventually she decided that an early night was a good idea for her as well and surprisingly she fell asleep almost as soon as snuggling down under the duvet.

Maggie slept soundly until the phone rang at eight-thirty. She must have sounded half asleep as her mother's voice said, 'Goodness, I didn't wake you did I? I thought I'd catch you before you left for work.'

'I've got the rest of the week off Mum; I thought I'd told you.'

'Sorry dear, you probably did. I was really checking to see that you arrived home all right and to tell you what a wonderful time your Dad and I had. We think Peter's lovely.'

'I'm the one who should be sorry Mum; I should have rung last night. The journey was fine and I'm glad you like Peter, he's really something isn't he?'

'Yes, he is, and you have full parental approval.'

'Approval for what exactly?'

'Anything you like dear!' was the swift reply.

There was no turning over for another half hour, Ben and Tara had expectations, so Maggie got out of bed and headed for the shower.

Peter arrived at eleven, looking much fresher than the previous day and bringing Maggie a huge bunch of chrysanthemums, enough to fill two vases.

'Oh Peter, they're gorgeous, thank you. Does this mean I have to make you a coffee now?' she grinned.

'No, we'll wait until lunchtime shall we? Come and sit down, I want to talk to you.'

He looked quite serious and for a moment she felt a flash of something inside her, panic, or excitement, she couldn't tell. It always amazed her how many thoughts can flash through the human brain in such a short time frame. In less than thirty seconds, she visualised Peter proposing, or ending their relationship and was surprised at the strength of the desire for it to be the former and not the latter.

'My appointment this morning was with Dr. James,' he began. Strangely her immediate thought was that Peter had visited the surgery in connection with her, illogical though that seemed.

'He wants me to go for some tests and I felt I should tell you.'

'What kind of tests, what's he looking for?' A sudden panic was rising within her.

'He's not sure, something neurological he thinks. I've been getting a lot of headaches lately and feeling quite tired, so he's sending me for a body MRI scan and a brain scan too.' Peter took hold of her hand. 'It's likely to be nothing; I haven't been so fit for years, what with going to the gym and everything these days. I've been a bit clumsy of late and had a bit of dizziness. Probably some sort of virus.'

Maggie was stunned. Peter smiled trying to make light of it, but she had been around doctors and surgeries long enough to know that Dr. James suspected more than a virus. Thoughts of Chris came flooding into her head and an involuntary moan escaped from somewhere deep inside.

'Hey, come on. It's probably just old age catching up with me; don't go all maudlin on me.'

With a sudden determination Maggie switched her mood, blanking out a myriad thoughts and feelings. Forcing a smile, she gave him a hug.

'I'm sure you're right. Now, what did you have in mind for today?'

'A lazy day here with you? A bit of 'us time' you call it don't you? And if we could escape from the animals, upstairs maybe for an hour or so, all the better.' Peter's arms went around her, it felt like being wrapped in a warm blanket. They went upstairs and he very gently made love to her. Maggie clung to him as if she would never let go, experiencing such bitter sweet emotions and wishing the hour would never pass.

****

Jane lived in a small, picturesque market town about forty minutes drive from Peter. Much of her time was taken up with baby Emma, who had reached the age of one and the stage of wanting to be picked up by no one other than her Mum. Secretly Jane loved this clinginess; it made her feel needed and provided the excuse to spend time with Emma without feeling guilty about neglecting other duties. Not that her life was hectic. Brian, her husband, was an easy-going, affable man and they had agreed on Jane taking a five year career break to raise Emma and hopefully any other siblings that may follow. They were not in the least a materialistic family and gratefully enjoyed their lifestyle with no desire for upward mobility as regarded careers; Brian had a secure job which he loved and they managed well but most importantly, they were happy.

The only blot on the landscape lately for Jane had been concerning her father. Both Jane and her sister had been devastated when their parents split up; it was totally unexpected, hurling both girls through the full spectrum of emotions, feeling guilty and irrationally blaming themselves. Watching her father sink into depression was a painful experience for Jane, one in which she felt powerless to help, especially with Emma demanding so much of her time. Jane was of course delighted to see the change in her father, anticipating this visit with pleasure, especially as Maggie would be with him. Rachel had already met her and the sisters had worked out that it was probably the meeting in York which had sparked the relationship. During their frequent phone conversations, Maggie and their dad was currently the favourite topic of conversation and now Jane was about to meet her in person.

Maggie's anticipation of spending the day with Peter was slightly marred by a nervous anticipation of meeting Jane. When she and Sue met Rachel in York, it was on another level entirely, Peter was barely more than an acquaintance then and it had been a chance meeting. Today, however was a planned visit and Maggie's nervousness emanated from the feeling, which she couldn't shake off, of being on approval, her status had now changed to that of being Peter's girlfriend, an entirely different relationship.

There had been an exciting, almost delicious feeling of late that this time in her life was the beginning of a new chapter, but yesterday's revelations cruelly changed that feeling into the kind of turmoil she had hoped never to experience again.

Peter arrived in a determinedly cheerful mood. He had in fact, been trying so hard to be upbeat and chirpy since the visit to his doctor that Maggie was convinced she could see the strain etched on his face. However, she went along with the mood, after all, why anticipate a bad diagnosis before the tests had even been completed?

'Are you going to tell Jane about your scans?' she ventured when they had set off on their journey.

'Whatever for? It's probably something and nothing. I didn't tell you to make you worry you know, I just want to share every part of my life with you. I'm sure it'll be fine.'

The subject was closed for the time being. Perhaps he was right and it would be nothing. Maggie did have a tendency to think that happiness was for others, not her and she had been grateful for finding a measure of contentment after Chris died, making it difficult to accept that this new found happiness would last.

Maggie had a feeling of déjà vu when Jane came out to welcome them, finding herself looking into the same blue eyes as Peters and Rachel's. The fair hair too was the same shade as her sister's but cut short into a practical bob. Jane greeted them enthusiastically. Emma, balanced on her mother's hip, feigned shyness hiding her face, even from her grandfather. A welcome coffee was soon brought and father and daughter began to catch up on recent events.

'How was Christmas at your mother's Jane?'

'Really good. This little one took centre stage of course, she's been absolutely ruined. Rachel dotes on her, as does Mum of course. How were your festivities up in Scotland?'

'Oh, it was more than just Christmas, there was a wedding too.' Peter laughed as Jane's jaw dropped in surprise.

'No silly, not us! Maggie, you tell Jane all about it while I get those presents out of the car.'

Jane was a captive audience for the story, loving a good romantic tale as much as anyone and responding with appropriate 'oohs' and 'aahs' in all the right places. Peter soon returned and gifts were exchanged, Emma once more being the focus of attention, the excitement of the parcels dispelling her shyness. The atmosphere throughout the day was relaxed and Maggie felt completely at ease and truly welcome, understanding now why Peter was so proud of his family.

Chapter 31

The New Year brought new challenges. Maggie's client list was increasing, so much so that she'd taken on more hours at the surgery. Sue had returned from honeymoon and the friends eventually found the time to catch up with each other's news. The one thing Maggie did hold back from Sue was her concern over Peter's health, knowing the reason for her silence was partly denial. Of course she justified this in her own mind, trying to convince herself that it was reasonable to assume there was no problem until it actually presented itself and she wasn't going down the route of 'crossing bridges' like so many of her clients did. Peter too played the situation down. While remaining in good humour, which she could tell was not always how he felt, he would not talk about his feeling which Maggie understood was an attempt to protect her. If this was his way of coping, then it was okay for the present. Besides, she didn't want to be his counsellor; she wanted to be his lover.

An appointment came through with remarkable speed, for the scans and a follow-up appointment with a neurological consultant two days later for the results. Maggie appeared more nervous than Peter, who maintained his virus theory, even if it was just for her sake.

****

Peter laid on the hard surface wearing a hospital gown. Although the room was bright and warm it had a cold sterile feel about it, and he felt very much alone. The radiologist explained what would happen and what to expect, then scurried off behind a screen where he talked through a microphone. A grinding noise signalled the start of the scan and Peter closed his eyes as his body was moved slowly through a tunnel, in time to a series of clicking, grinding noises, followed by stillness. Occasionally the disembodied voice gave instructions.

'Hold your breath please, for as long as you can. Turn your head to the left; now the right.' It was all quite painless, but rather surreal. He had a sensation of floating, of being in a dream, knowing that this was the easy bit; the results were what really terrified him.

Peter spent the next two nights at Maggie's. The time passed more quickly when they were together and he knew that it was as much on her mind as on his own. Peter vacillated on whether or not to ask her to go with him to the specialist. Part of him wanted her to be there and he also trusted her to absorb more medical details than he would himself. On the other hand, asking her to accompany him gave the appointment greater import than he had wanted it to have. Finally, the problem solved itself; Maggie offered to go. Naturally he refused, brushing it off as a routine, insignificant appointment, but as he'd hoped, she persisted and the offer was accepted without it being turned into a major event.

With time arranged off work, Peter and Maggie entered the hospital on a cold wet late January morning. They were prompt, but prepared to wait, as always seemed necessary for such appointments. Eventually, Peter's name was called.

The neurologist, Mr Hassen, was a slightly built middle aged man in a pin striped suit. A friendly, open face and wide smile revealed a gold front tooth as he greeted the pair with a handshake, which, from him seemed quite appropriate. The results of the MRI scans were on a disc which the neurologist had already uploaded onto the computer. He began by asking Peter how he was feeling. Peter replied honestly, that for the last few weeks he'd been feeling tired, which was no surprise as the holiday period and work had both been busy times.

'Well, I'm afraid that the MRI has shown up some scar tissue, which is partly what we were expecting.' The doctor scrutinised the screen as he spoke.

'What kind of scar tissue, I don't understand?' Peter queried.

'The scan results suggest Multiple Sclerosis. I'm sorry Mr. Lloyd, but there's no easy way of putting it.'

Peter's face blanched. Maggie looked at him with concern. She had come across MS before and knew there were different types and degrees. Reaching out to hold Peter's hand, she faced the doctor.

'MS is treatable though isn't it?'

'To a point yes; but it's one of those perplexing conditions which has never been entirely pinned down. We assume it's an autoimmunity disease, but research is far from complete. The immune system is the body's defender if you like, a highly organised and regulated system. If an aggressor invades the body, a virus perhaps, the immune system attacks the invader and then withdraws.'

Peter was looking quite blank, hearing the words, but finding it hard to digest their meaning. Maggie listened with a concerned expression on her face. None of this was entirely new to her, but she wanted to understand as much as possible for Peter's sake. Mr. Hassen continued, 'Obviously there needs to be communication between the immune system and the brain. With MS, we suspect that a foreign agent alters the immune system so it perceives myelin as an intruder and attacks it. Myelin is a dielectric, an insulating material which is essential for proper functioning of the nervous system. While some of the myelin repairs itself after such an assault, some of the nerves are stripped of their myelin and scarring occurs. That's what we found from the MRI. I hope that's a little clearer Mr. Lloyd?'

'Umm, yes, partly. It sounds very technical, but what I really want to know is how it's going to affect me. What's in store for the future?'

'The type of MS we're seeing here is the most common type, the Relapsing-Remitting, or RR. This is how up to eighty percent of sufferers begin. As the name suggests, there is a series of attacks, followed by a period of remission, where most or all of the symptoms disappear. This could be for a matter of weeks, months or even years. Each time there is an assault, a little more of the nervous system is damaged. To answer your question about the future is very difficult. As attacks occur, disability of physical functions will also occur, perhaps only temporarily, but each time leaving the system a little weaker. About fifty percent of sufferers will go on to develop Secondary Progressive MS, but usually it can take a decade for this to happen. There are cases of MS that are mild, and often undetected, until symptoms are viewed retrospectively. Each individual is different, and, it has to be said, research and medication is advancing all the time.'

Peter's mind was spinning. The doctor went on to mention symptoms such as depression, limb weakness, muscle spasm, visual impairment. It was simply too much to take in which Mr. Hassen must have realised.

'I think we've covered enough today Peter.'

Maggie noted the use of his Christian name and felt the compassion which accompanied it.

'Perhaps you'd like to make an appointment with your GP to talk these things over, and I'd like to see you again in six weeks. Was there anything else you'd like to ask today?'

Peter was silent. Maggie spoke for him,

'Thank you Mr. Hassen, you've explained it very well. I'm sure we'll have more questions next time, but for now, I think that's all.' She turned to Peter, who nodded managing a tight smile, and then they left the consulting room.

Peter remained silent during the journey home. Maggie expected him to come in for a coffee, but he muttered something about needing to get back to work, which she knew wasn't the case. It was understandable that he needed time to think and absorb everything Mr. Hassen had said, but she felt hurt that he wanted to be alone rather than with her, thinking they were closer than that. All she could do was to give him his space and ring later to see how he was.

****

Maggie didn't have a client until mid afternoon. Needing to talk to someone, she called Sue and asked if they could meet for lunch. They decided on a sandwich in Maggie's office, which afforded more privacy than a cafe would at lunch time.

'Well?' Sue began expectantly, 'Have you got good news to share, or what?'

'Cut to the chase Sue won't you?' she replied knowing that Sue was expecting an engagement to be announced any day.

'I'm afraid it's not the good news you're expecting... quite the opposite in fact.'

Sue's face took on a concerned expression, not always the joker people took her for, she sensed her friend's sadness. Maggie spoke rapidly, not able to bother with pleasantries.

'Peter's been diagnosed with MS.' She had to swallow quickly to keep her rising emotions in check. Sue pulled the chair closer to put her arm around her friend. Maggie rested her head on her shoulder and began to cry softly. Drawing away after a few minutes, she reached for a tissue.

'So, do you want to tell me about it?' Sue's voice was soft and attentive.

Maggie launched into a repeat of what the neurologist had told them almost parrot fashion, calm now but with a sadness in her eyes that almost broke Sue's resolve to be strong. When she'd finished, Sue asked how Peter had taken the news.

'That's part of the problem. He wanted to be alone, which I have to respect, but it hurts that he won't share his feelings with me.'

'He will in time, it's been a shock, it's just his way of dealing with it, he is a man, and you know they don't do talking very easily.' Sue's attempt to lighten the atmosphere brought an effort of a half smile to Maggie's face, which suddenly turned into anxiety, quickly asking,

'You won't tell anyone will you? Perhaps I shouldn't have told you, Peter's daughters don't even know yet.'

'I could take offence that you even have to ask me that. Of course I won't say anything, but this is about you, and you need to talk even if Peter doesn't.'

'Sorry, I didn't mean that you couldn't be trusted.....I'm so mixed up at the moment, I'm not surprised he needed to be alone, I wouldn't be much help.'

'You will in time. Excuse me taking on your role here, but does this change your relationship in any way? I mean, you've been through such a lot in the past, everyone would understand if this was something you couldn't cope with.'

Maggie was obviously stunned.

'Of course it doesn't change anything, not for me anyway. I know how I feel about Peter and love him more than I ever thought possible. When Chris died, I thought there could never be anyone else. Peter can't replace him, but I love him with the same intensity. I'm not foolish enough to think this won't affect our relationship, but as far as I'm concerned, we're a couple and I want that to continue.'

'Good. You do the fighting talk so well, and I'm right behind you girl. I don't know much about MS, but can you remember in that American TV series, 'West Wing' I think it was, the president had MS, and he managed to run the USA. With you beside him, Peter will sail through this.'

'You're good for me Sue, thanks. I only hope he'll feel the same...'

****

Peter was devastated. Visions of a wheelchair coming towards him like some iron monster waiting to entrap him flashed into his mind, with a future of dependency and no control of his body, but dependant on whom? Not Jane and Rachel, they had their own lives to lead; and certainly not Maggie. Peter loved her with his whole being, and was on the verge of asking her to marry him, but everything had changed now. How could he saddle her with an invalid who needed looking after? She'd suffered enough in her life and he had wanted to be the one doing the caring. There was nothing else for it; he would have to break off their relationship. It would be painful, but for Maggie's sake it was the only way forward. He would cope as long as he could, and then take each day as it came.

Maggie telephoned Peter later that evening, trying to sound positive, 'Hi, how are you feeling?'

'A little tired to be truthful, and you?'

'I'm good, concerned about you of course.....want to come round and we can talk? It's not easy on the phone.'

Peter agreed, but without any hint of his usual enthusiasm. Maggie prowled around her little house anxiously until he arrived, then greeted him with a hug, which was barely reciprocated. An uncomfortable silence hung between them, as if they were meeting for the first time, comparative strangers. Peter took the initiative.

'Maggie, I've done nothing but think about this MS thing all day... and I've made a few decisions.'

'Already?' The serious look on his face frightened her.

'Yes and I really think we should stop seeing each other.......It'll be best all round.'

'No. Is that really what you want?'

'It's for the best Maggie.' His eyes were clouded as he spoke.

'But I love you Peter, I need you.'

'You don't need me hanging around your neck like a millstone.'

'You're not a millstone. We don't know how this disease will affect you; it's too early to make decisions like that.'

‘Please, trust me on this, it’s for the best.’ His voice was breaking, he didn’t trust himself to go on. He rose from the chair and silently moved towards the door.

‘Peter...’ Maggie’s voice was barely a whisper as she watched the man she loved walk out of her home. The door closed quietly and after a few long moments she heard the car engine start up as Peter began to put just a few miles, but a huge wedge, between them.

Chapter 32

Maggie slept fitfully, waking early to find her duvet in a heap on the floor and Ben with his chin on the mattress looking at his mistress with big shining brown eyes. Not wanting to get up she pulled the duvet back on the bed and buried her face into its soft warmth. Ben jumped up beside her; something he rarely did, and nudged his way under the cover, seeming to sense her pain. Closing her eyes she wrapped her arms around Ben finding comfort in his faithfulness. The tears wouldn't come having cried throughout the night and now she was exhausted. It was Saturday, no work to lose herself in, no clients to see but was that a good thing? Maggie lay under the duvet, unaware of the time, nor caring either. It was only when Ben began to whine that she thought about her pet's needs and forced herself to get up to let them out into the garden.

Resisting the temptation to go back to bed, she put the kettle on to boil and fed a slice of bread into the toaster, all the while telling herself to be strong, hadn't she suffered before and come through it? Shouldn't she be looking at things positively, overcoming the negatives? Yes, she knew all the little tools to employ to cope during dark times, but lacked the energy. It was so much easier to help other people overcome their problems, for herself she didn't even know where to begin.

The phone rang and Maggie almost pounced on it, hoping it would be Peter telling her he'd changed his mind.

'Hi Mags.' Sue's voice, usually so welcome, disappointed her.

'Oh. Hello.' The dismay reflected in her tone.

'Well hey, don't be so pleased to hear from me will you?'

'Sorry, I just thought it might be Peter.'

'Okay, apology accepted, I can see how I'd be a disappointment now. Look, I've a day to myself today, Alan's working so I wondered if you fancied meeting for a coffee in town?'

'Thanks Sue, but I'm not ready yet. I thought I'd hang around the house today, a bit of pottering, lazy day, you know.'

'You're not moping about this MS thing are you Maggie? Because if you are and you want me to come round, I can.'

'No, I'll be fine, just not very good company today, another time maybe?'

Maggie felt bad for not telling Sue what had transpired last night, never usually keeping secrets from her friend. Perhaps it was the hope that Peter would get in touch and everything would be fine so she wouldn't need to burden Sue or anyone else with her problems. Sitting staring at the phone she had an overwhelming desire to ring Peter, to beg and plead yet she knew that wasn't the way to go. He must make his own decisions and needed the time to do so.

The weekend seemed to drag on forever. Maggie did what was necessary, feeding Ben and Tara whilst the effort to care for herself was too much. A couple of bowls of cereal passed for meals and she nibbled on an apple to keep hunger at bay. Saturday was spent in her pyjamas, flicking through channels on the television to see if anything captured her interest. It didn't. She knew she was doing everything wrong, but she hadn't the energy or desire to make any kind of effort.

After another restless night Maggie made an effort to pull herself together. Showering and washing her hair, she ate a quick breakfast before taking Ben on a long walk; her poor dog had only been as far as the garden the previous day. A crisp cold breeze was refreshing but not as invigorating as it would usually be. When the road was behind them, Ben was let off his lead and scooted happily into the trees, sniffing in all the usual places. Maggie's mind still reeled with thoughts of Peter, longing to comfort him and be comforted by him, but knowing the decision must be his. Maggie believed very strongly that each individual has the right to make their own choices in life and throughout her working life she'd respected each client's decision, even if she personally felt it to be wrong. The very essence of her training was based on the fundamental belief that it was only the person concerned who had the ability and the right to make their own decisions. Her thoughts drifted to Julie Chambers. In their early sessions, Maggie's heart had ached for Julie, wondering why on earth she stayed with a man like Jim, a heartless bully who didn't deserve such a wonderful family. It had been difficult to resist persuading Julie to leave her husband, knowing such decisions belonged entirely to the client and it would be wrong to attempt to influence her. In Julie's case, fate had taken things out of her hands.

Maggie was overwhelmed by sadness. For years she had contentedly walked her dog, thrown herself wholeheartedly into work and taken pleasure in friends and family but now it wasn't enough. Peter had come into her life bringing a taste of how much sweeter and more fulfilling her future could be, yet all too quickly happiness had once again been snatched away. Despondently calling for Ben she put him on his lead and headed for home. The need to talk to someone was overwhelming, not her parents; they would be too emotionally involved and would most probably insist on coming down and wrapping her in cotton wool. Sue was the one, with her solid down to earth common sense. She had shunned her the day before but now needed her comforting presence. Maggie picked up the phone and dialled the number before even taking off her coat.

'Don't worry about Alan,' Sue reassured arriving half an hour later, 'He's glued to the computer screen looking for some new hiking gear, he'll not even miss me until his stomach growls. Virtual shopping, huh, it can't beat the real thing.' She plonked down on the sofa next to her friend and looked at the sadness in Maggie's eyes.

'What is it Mags? It's more than just this MS thing isn't it? You were so positive when we spoke on Friday, what's happened?'

'Peter doesn't want to see me anymore,' she blurted out, 'he's ended it!'

'Oh Maggie no, surely not! He's probably just confused and upset, he'll be trying to protect you, I'm sure he doesn't mean it.'

'But he was so determined. I invited him round on Friday evening to talk about it but when he came he'd already made the decision.' She looked tired and bereft. Sue ached for her friend but could do little except be there.

'It's early days yet,' Sue tried to console her. 'He needs time to really get his head around this whole thing then I'm sure he'll be back. I've seen the way he looks at you, Peter loves you every bit as much as you love him. Give it time, he'll see sense.'

Sue insisted that Maggie returned home with her for lunch and wouldn't take no for an answer. When they arrived Alan gave them both an enthusiastic welcome, picking up from his wife's expression that something was wrong and instinctively knowing to tread carefully. Maggie hadn't much of an appetite but ate the meal for Sue's sake, glad of the company but feeling herself to be a very poor companion. After lunch and coffee she made her excuses and left for home, glad to have brought her own car so as not to rely on her friends for a lift. After taking Ben for an extra long walk she tried to watch a DVD she'd been given for Christmas but after the first fifteen minutes, realised that she hadn't a clue what it was all about so turning it off she set up her ironing board to at least do something useful. The rest of the afternoon and evening dragged until Maggie eventually decided on an early night to try and catch up on the sleep missed the previous night; she didn't want to be half asleep at work the next morning.

Thankfully sleep did come until the alarm woke her at seven o'clock. If she had dreamed at all she couldn't remember, and at least she felt physically refreshed even if still raw and hurting inside.

Monday passed in a bit of a haze, as did Tuesday and Wednesday. Maggie had to concentrate particularly hard to give clients her full attention, feeling dreadfully guilty when she couldn't focus as well as usual. Sue, as ever, was a brick, keeping cheerful and finding the least little excuse to pop into her friend's office to check up on her. The evenings were the worst when the time seemed to drag. Every time the phone rang her heart flipped and then there was the disappointment of it being only Sue or her mother. Maggie still had not told her parents and it was becoming difficult to deflect her mother's questions without being totally dishonest. Why she couldn't bring herself to tell them she didn't know, perhaps she was still hoping that Peter would change his mind. What she did know was that it had to be his decision, not hers.

By the following Friday Maggie was shattered. It had been the longest week she could remember since Chris had died and the pain was every bit as acute. Having no clients on the afternoon she intended to go straight home, but Sue had other plans.

'You can come out with me for a coffee or come back to my house, but I'm not leaving you alone to wallow,' Sue announced.

'Please Sue, I really am tired.'

'I can see that, but we need to talk, I can't take much more of your long face.'

'Okay, but come to mine will you?' Maggie relented, not offended by her friends words, she was sick of her long face too.

When they were settled with a coffee, Sue began.

'Now I know it's none of my business, but I'm going to stick my nose in anyway. I think you should go round to see Peter and get this silly situation sorted out. It's obvious that you love him and I know for a fact that he loves you too, so what's the problem?'

'It's not as easy as that, you know it isn't. Peter has made a decision and I'll have to respect that. My whole life is devoted to empowering people to make their own decisions. I can't just barge in and tell Peter what to do.'

'Well, if you don't I will,' Sue spoke firmly and was obviously serious.

'You can't do that. I know you mean well, but that would be entirely the wrong course of action.'

'So what is the right course of action?' Sue asked. Maggie was silent for a moment before replying.

'There isn't one. I have to accept his decision.'

'Wrong answer,' Sue countered. 'There is always a solution and I think you're making this much more complicated than it really is. Okay, so you believe that each person has the right and the ability to make their own choices in life, I've heard it all before and normally I would agree with you. If however, you saw someone who had chosen to walk across a level crossing as a train approached would you stand by and say, 'it's his decision, there's nothing I can do''

'That's not a fair analogy Sue.'

'Why not? Here are two people, who incidentally I am very fond of, who are madly in love and one of them has misguidedly decided that it would be better for the other if they threw away their chance of happiness, when in fact that decision is only causing pain to both of them. I think it would be in order to challenge that decision and if you won't do it, I will.'

Maggie looked at her friend in amazement, and then she slowly smiled, 'You know, I think you should be doing my job. All right, you win, I'll go and see Peter, I suppose I've nothing to lose but my pride.'

'When? I want to know when you're going, because if you don't do it soon you'll change your mind, I know you.'

'I'll go tonight, will that suit?'

'Yes, and then you'll go home and ring me with all the details.' Sue grinned.

At seven o'clock that Friday evening, Maggie was standing outside Peter's flat feeling like a nervous schoolgirl. Thoughts of every possible scenario had plagued her all evening, the 'what ifs' that she so often warned clients about. When Peter opened the door he was obviously surprised to see her and for a split second Maggie wanted to turn and run but her happiness was worth one more try. Peter recovered his composure, quietly standing to one side to let her enter.

The flat was a mess, in fact on closer inspection Peter was a mess. He looked tired and older somehow. Maggie had the terrible feeling that perhaps he'd resorted to drinking again, then was annoyed with herself for even thinking such a thing.

'How are you Peter?'

'I've been better, and you?'

'Me too. We need to talk.'

'There's nothing to talk about Maggie, I can't...'

'Please, tell me honestly, is your illness just an excuse to disentangle yourself from me. If so, then I'd rather you simply came out and told me. Don't use the MS as a way to dump me because you've lost interest.'

'Maggie,' Peter was horrified. 'I love you, that's why I can't do this to you. You've lost one husband; I can't put you through that again.'

'And I don't get a say in it?'

'But surely......I could be an incontinent vegetable.....you don't deserve that.'

'Now you're looking too far ahead. The prognosis isn't a given thing. You could die of old age before you reach anything like that stage. I don't want you to be chivalrous; I want you to be my husband.'

'What?'

Maggie was flushed, with anger, embarrassment and pride. Had she really just proposed to him?

'What did you say?' he asked again.

She took a few deep breaths, time to think before speaking again.

'I think you heard me Peter, I asked if you would marry me. I ask because I love you and can't bear to live without you. I'll take the rough with the smooth, whatever happens. Since we've been together I've been so happy.......but I know that happiness is like a moth, you think you've snatched it in your hand and it's yours, but when you look, it's turned to dust. You're my happiness Peter. I ask you because I love you and if you love me too, then please say yes.'

Tears were spilling down Peter's face. He reached out and stroked her hair.

'My darling Maggie, if you're sure, if you'll really have me, then yes, I'll be honoured to marry you.'

A few hours later Maggie remembered her promise to Sue to ring when she got home. It was too late for phone calls by then, her friend would have to wait, but if she knew Sue, she would have already pieced things together and would know that there was no way Maggie would have the time, nor the inclination, to ring until the morning.

The End